Dear Little Black Dress Reader,

Thanks for picking up this Little Black Dress book, one of the great new titles from our series of fun, page-turning romance novels. Lucky you — you're about to have a fantastic romantic read that we know you won't be able to put down!

Why don't you make your Little Black Dress experience even better by logging on to

www.littleblackdressbooks.com

where you can:

- ♥ Enter our **monthly competitions** to win **gorgeous** prizes
- ♥ Get **hot-off-the-press** news about our latest titles
- ♥ Read **exclusive** preview chapters both from your **favourite** authors and from brilliant new writing talent
- ♥ Buy **up-and-coming** books online
- ♥ Sign up for an essential slice of romance via our **fortnightly email** newsletter

We love nothing more than to curl up and indulge in an addictive romance, and so we're delighted to welcome you into the Little Black Dress club!

With love from,

The *little black dress* team

Five interesting things about Kate Lace:

1. When I left school I joined the army instead of going to university – there were 500 men to every woman when I joined up – yesss.

2. While I was there I discovered that there were more sports than hockey and lacrosse and learnt to glide, rock climb, pot hole, sail and ski. I also discovered that I wasn't much good at any of them but I had a lot of fun.

3. I met my husband in the army. We've been married for donkey's years. (I was a child bride.)

4. Since I got married I have moved house 17 times. We now live in our own house and have done for quite a while so we know what is growing in the garden. Also, our children can remember what their address is.

5. I captained the Romantic Novelists' Association team on University Challenge the Professionals in 2005. We got to the grand finals so I got to meet Jeremy Paxman three times.

Also by Kate Lace

The Chalet Girl

The Movie Girl

Kate Lace

little
black
dress

First published in 2007
by LITTLE BLACK DRESS
An imprint of HEADLINE PUBLISHING GROUP

First published in paperback in 2008
by LITTLE BLACK DRESS
An imprint of HEADLINE PUBLISHING GROUP

A LITTLE BLACK DRESS paperback

1

ISBN 978 0 7553 3833 7

Typeset in Transit511BT by Avon DataSet Ltd,
Bidford-on-Avon, Warwickshire

Printed and bound in Great Britain by
Clays Ltd, St Ives plc

Headline's policy is to use papers that are natural, renewable and recyclable
products and made from wood grown in sustainable forests. The logging and
manufacturing processes are expected to conform to the environmental
regulations of the country of origin.

HEADLINE PUBLISHING GROUP
An Hachette Livre UK Company
338 Euston Road
London NW1 3BH

www.littleblackdressbooks.com
www.headline.co.uk

This book is for my mum, June Lace.
Thanks for the great name!

'They *are* jo
      mid-toenai
angle, as she sta
brunette curls
frown puckered
the toes of he
managed to lo
waggled up an
forward in the ta
screen the faux
rectify itself.
   'What have t
a sigh. Gemma'
plate resting on
slice of toast and
   'That bonnet
least.'
   Zoë glanced
considering it's
   Gemma nar
mean . . . Oh, r

'So what's the problem?' Zoë shut her magazine and put on a semblance of paying attention.

'This series is set in the Napoleonic Wars so 1840 is far too late. It's like doing a series set during the Second World War with women wearing mini-skirts and wet-look boots.'

'If you say so, Gem. But you are the only person in the country who would know or care.' She reopened her magazine.

Gemma shut up. Zoë was right. In the great scheme of things it was nothing, but it irritated her no end that whoever did the costumes on this production couldn't be arsed to get it right.

Zoë finished her toast, licked her buttery fingers, then wiped them dry on her jeans, before turning the page to the next story.

'You going to help in the shop tomorrow?' she asked, not lifting her eyes from the page.

'Jean said she wanted me in. Besides, I've nothing else to do.' Gemma sounded completely hacked off.

'You'll get another job soon.'

Gemma snorted. As far as she was concerned the whole movie and TV industry sucked. Crewing up for new programmes and films seemed to be done entirely on the old-boy network. Buggerlugs Productions – or whoever – asked you to work on the next costume drama because you had worked on the last one. But how could you get a foot in the door in the first place if that was the way it was always done?

Getting a foot in the costume-designing door had been Gemma's driving ambition ever since she could remember. As one of four daughters in a family where money was on the tight side, she grew up watching her mother run up basic cotton skirts and dresses for her offspring. Consequently, Gemma had been dressing her dolls with the leftover scraps of fabric ever since she had first managed to thread a needle for herself. At first, her dolls had just simple skirts with elasticated waists to wear but, as Gemma's skills increased, she began to try to make them look like the screen heroines she saw on the box when she watched the old movies shown on Sunday afternoons. Before long her dolls had pelisses and fichus, bustles and cloaks and Gemma knew more than was natural for an eleven year old about pin tucks and Honiton lace. She didn't just dress her dolls, she also began to design clothes for herself. Her sisters had all gone through a similar phase of making their own clothes – although they'd never been keen on dolls – but the novelty of cutting out, tacking and sewing had soon palled and they'd preferred to use their evenings and weekends to earn money to spend in Miss Selfridge or Top Shop. Gemma, however, could never understand the draw of shuffling through dozens of identical outfits to find the one to fit you, knowing that you would be bound to see someone in 'your' dress sooner or later. Why not, she argued, make something for yourself that was exclusive? Her older sisters had smiled indulgently (and perhaps a little patronisingly) at her and said she'd understand about fashion when she was older. But Gemma, who studied pattern books and magazines far more assiduously than her siblings, was well aware that fashion didn't necessarily mean being a clone of every other teenager in Southampton.

It was taken for granted that she would study textiles at GCSE and A level, but it surprised all her family when she got a place at a fashion college. Her family didn't do higher education. Her sisters had all gone straight out to work as soon as they left school, just like their parents and grandparents had. That was what the Browns did, her father, who worked in the docks, had said, but Gemma was adamant about going. Secretly, he was proud of her, of course, though for the life of him he couldn't work out why she had to go to a swanky London college to learn how to make frocks. Couldn't she do that already?

Since leaving fashion college, Gemma had stayed in London because she thought that was where she had the best chance of making it into films or TV. Besides, she and Zoë, her best mate since day one of college, had a flat that was affordable and many of her fellow graduates were also staying put. Over the previous three years on her trips home from college she had decided, rather sadly, she now had far more in common with her fashion student friends than she did with her sisters, whose height of ambition was to settle down and have kids. Of course Gemma wanted to settle down and have kids of her own one day too. Well . . . maybe. But not yet. Not for ages.

She had landed a couple of jobs designing costumes for kids' programmes and had done the styling for a series of mobile phone ads and a video for some sort of corporate training programme. Other than that, she'd been living pretty much hand to mouth, demonstrating sewing machines several days a week in a specialist haberdashery. It was all right for Zoë, she was assistant manager in the same shop – which was why Gemma had managed to wangle a part-time job there too – and Zoë loved what she did, absolutely adored it, although Gemma couldn't see the draw of advising the old biddies who frequented it about crochet cottons and tatting shuttles. However, unlike Gemma, Zoë liked retail: she loved interacting with people, she got a thrill out of ordering new stock, and she got a buzz out of arranging the skeins of silks and hanks of wool. Besides, Zoë did not have her heart set on a career in films. Gemma sighed at the hopelessness of her ambition.

'Something will come up. Honest.'

Gemma sighed again. Yeah, maybe, but she'd been out of college almost a year and had precious little on her CV. And being the sewing-machine demonstrator in Sew Wonderful wasn't going to cut much ice in the media job market.

Gemma finished her toenails and admired the result. Then another costume howler caught her eye and she zapped off the TV in disgust.

'I was watching that,' protested Zoë. 'It's got Jono Knighton in it. I don't care how crap the costumes are or how shitty the storyline is, I just want to gaze at him.'

Gemma had to concede she had a point and zapped it back on. The drama might be a pile of pants but he was lush. She gazed, too. Blond floppy fringe, blue eyes, wonderful cheekbones and a smiley, kissable mouth. And the way he strode about, dominating the scene in the film. There was no mistaking who was the star of that production. Utterly gorgeous . . . and talented.

'Here, have you seen this?' Zoë, multitasking – reading, watching and ogling – turned her magazine towards Gemma so that she could see the pictures she was referring to. 'This is their house. Get a load of that!' The house in question belonged to the Knightons.

Gemma dragged her eyes off Jono and took the magazine off her.

'Fab-u-lous,' she agreed. 'Goodness, what style. Fancy living in a place like that!' In the pictures Jono and his wife, American actress Rowan Day, looked every inch the happily married showbiz couple they were. Gemma ignored blonde, svelte and beautiful Rowan and slavered over Jono. He was just as hunky in the photographs as he was on TV. Yup, complete babe-magnet and utterly fanciable but not quite gorgeous enough to keep her glued to the rubbish costume drama. Even Jono didn't have quite enough phwoar-appeal to stop the crap costumes from bugging her. Besides, he was a married man so, realistically, there was no point in lusting after him at all. If he could get a woman like that willowy American sex-bomb, there was no chance for a petite brunette like her. Or a curvy brunette like Zoë. She tossed the remote and the magazine over to her flatmate.

'Well, I'm not going to watch this tosh, even with Jono in it. The costumes are winding me up,' she said. 'I'm going to bed.' And walking on her heels so as not to smudge her newly painted toes, she hobbled into her bedroom.

She sat on her bed and checked her nails were dry, then took off her dressing gown and selected some bed-time reading from the shelf by her bed. *Regency Uniforms and Headdress* hardly qualified as chick lit, but it ticked all Gemma's boxes. As she snuggled under the covers and opened the book at the section on shakos, busbies and bearskins, she wondered if she would ever make the breakthrough into big, glossy costume dramas. Someone completely incompetent obviously had, if the film she had just been watching was anything to go by, so if there was a God, she, with all her knowledge, skill and expertise, should be able to as well.

The next day, Gemma walked with Zoë the mile or so from their dilapidated King's Cross flat, which they had now lived in together for nearly three years, to the shop in Camden. The flat was pretty grim and the area not the best but, as students, it had been all they could afford and it had the advantage of being handy for the Tube and central London. As Zoë had pointed out, when they'd first viewed it, they only wanted somewhere to sleep. Three years on, they did rather more than that in the flat but they'd got used to it and had stopped seeing the flat's faults.

Rather than walk along the busy, crowded pavements, they took the pretty route along the Regent's Canal, which was looking fantastic in the late April sunshine. It was a slightly longer route but it was much more pleasant than sticking to the grubby, noisy main road. As they walked they chatted with the comfortable ease of lifelong friends despite the fact that they'd only known each other for a shade under four years. When they'd met on the first day of freshers' week they'd clicked instantly and since then, from boyfriend trouble to nights out on the lash, they'd been there for each other.

They climbed up from the canal and along the road to the shop. On the outside, it looked old fashioned: the paintwork was a smoky green, and the windows on either side of the door were slightly bowed with age and Georgian in style. It reminded Gemma of the shop that Bagpuss lived in – even more so when you examined the eclectic muddle of sewing requisites that made up their window display.

Zoë unlocked the door and swung it open. The old-fashioned bell that hung on a spring at the back of it jangled loudly. Zoë picked up the post and then ran through to the back of the shop to deal with the alarm system before it went off. The alarm was about the only modern thing in the shop – well, that, the electronic till, and some seriously professional sewing machines. Gemma shut the door and switched on the lights, which flickered on down the length of the shop, illuminating as they did the rainbow-coloured racks of ribbons and braids, the silks and tapestry wools, the crochet cottons and sewing threads, bolts of fabric, displays of buttons made of every material and in every conceivable colour, needles for sewing and knitting, crochet hooks, dress and knitting patterns, interlining, zips, snips, hooks and fasteners and anything else you could possibly require if you wanted to work with textiles. Along one side was a long, wide table for measuring out the bolts of cloth and which also doubled as the shop's counter. The place was a dressmaker's heaven.

'Coffee?' called Zoë from the door to the staffroom.

'Please.' Gemma lugged one of the sewing machines off the shelf near the window and put it on the worktable, then, taking several reels of cotton from a drawer, she began to thread it up. It was a complicated job – this was a state-of-the-art overlocker – but Gemma's nimble fingers whizzed the threads around the hooks, spools and wheels. She was halfway through getting it sorted when the phone rang. Gemma walked across the floor to answer it.

'Hello, Sew Wonderful.'

'Hi. Is that Gem? It's Jean here.' Jean was the owner and manager of the shop. 'I'm going to be late in. Some pillock has just T-boned my car and I'm waiting for a tow truck.' She sounded completely pissed off.

'God, I'm sorry. You all right? You're not hurt?'

'I'm fine, thank you – and, sadly, so is the pillock. Although he may not be when I have finished with him.

He was driving a BMW, which obviously stands for Big Male Wanker.' Gemma could always tell when Jean was really angry: her language went from very ladylike to something her father would have found profane in Southampton Docks. Judging by the noises in the background, the Big Male Wanker didn't appreciate her description. 'Anyway, the upshot is that I won't be in for at least an hour, maybe longer. You and Zoë will have to hold the fort.'

'No probs, Jean. I'll tell Zo.'

'Thank you, my dear. See you later.'

Gemma went into the staffroom to break the news to Zoë. She was getting the float ready for the day's trading whilst making the coffees.

'You'll just have to serve customers instead of working the machine. Not to worry, it's unlikely we'll be overrun with women wanting to buy overlockers. Take this.' She handed Gemma a dozen bags of coins for the till and a handful of notes. 'I'm supposed to do the banking run in a minute but I don't want to leave you alone in the shop.'

Gemma glanced through the staffroom door, back into the shop to make sure it was still empty. It was. That was the thing about haberdashers: unlike newsagents and grocers, people were rarely moved to dash in for an urgent zip or dress pattern on their way to work. They hardly ever got busy till after ten – sometimes later.

'If you went now, you'd be back before the rush. And you'd probably miss the queues in the bank,' she said.

Zoë considered the logic of this. 'You're right.' She grabbed the paying-in book and her coat, stuffed the canvas bag with the previous day's takings in her pocket, then legged it. Gemma clutched the bags of coins to her chest, picked up her cup of coffee, and made her way back to the counter. She wasn't supposed to have her coffee with her while she served, but who was going to know? She filled the till and then, as she sipped her illicit coffee, she cast about for something to occupy her time till either Zoë returned or a customer walked in.

She caught sight of a trade magazine and began to flip the pages, marvelling at some of the beadwork on the more upmarket dress materials that were advertised in its pages, when the door jangled. A striking woman, who bore a passing resemblance to Sharon Osbourne, swept into the shop. She was attractive but not beautiful, although she had good dress sense and nice hair and nails. She was probably the wrong side of fifty, Gemma reflected, although she knew how to make the most of herself. But she had a hard look about her. Probably something to do with all that varnish and lacquer. Gemma hid her mug under the counter and shut the magazine. She smiled at the customer, who barely acknowledged her as she marched over to the rack of braids, ribbons and piping.

Gemma toyed with the idea of going over to offer advice but decided against it. The old bat could fend for herself if she couldn't even be bothered to be civil.

'Is this all you've got?' The woman's imperious voice matched her appearance and deportment and she gestured to the selection of trimmings dismissively.

'Yes. Is there something in particular you are looking for?'

'I want a flat gold braid, about two centimetres in width.'

'Can I ask what for?' Gemma needed to know because it mattered if it was purely for decorative purposes or if it was likely to adorn something that might need cleaning or machine washing. Customers didn't like to find that the gold lace they had chosen was going to need a lifetime of specialist care. Much better, in most instances, that the customer chose a cheaper, synthetic, more hardwearing option than the fabulous and sumptuous trimming that had caught their eye in the first place.

The customer sighed heavily. Gemma forced her mouth to keep smiling. Obviously, this woman was of the opinion that all shop girls were complete morons who were barely capable of getting their knuckles off the ground. Huh!

'Frogging.' She said it with a raised eyebrow that signalled *and you won't know what that means, will you, my girl?*

Gemma smiled even more sweetly. 'Is it for a military uniform?' The result was perfect. The woman looked as if she had swallowed a wasp. Gemma had to restrain herself from punching the air. Yesss.

'Erm, yes.'

'Any particular period?'

She looked even more discomfited. 'Regency.'

Gemma thought for a moment. She didn't want to sound too glib. 'Well, there were a lot of different regiments around then. Did you have a particular one in mind?' She could see she had this woman completely wrong-footed. Gemma almost felt sorry for her: she was looking extremely uncomfortable and embarrassed.

'Cavalry.'

'Oh.' Gemma tried to look helpful and caring. 'Like the Twentieth Dragoons?' she asked innocently.

The woman swallowed and said, rather tightly, 'Yes, precisely.'

Gemma made a mental bet that she hadn't a clue what

the uniforms of any of the cavalry looked like and thought that any old gold braid would do as long as it wasn't too elaborate or wide.

The door pinged open and Zoë came back into the shop.

'All right there, Gemma?' she asked as she took off her coat and headed through to the back to hang it up.

'Just fine. This lady wants to buy braid for a Regency cavalry jacket.'

'Well, Gemma's the one to help you there,' said Zoë, breezing past them. 'World's living expert, she is.' She carried on to the staffroom, leaving Gemma feeling deeply smug and the customer looking even more uncomfortable.

'I see.' Sniff. 'And, if you don't mind me asking, how . . . ?' She raised her eyebrows in part question, part amazement.

Obviously, anyone of Gemma's age couldn't possibly want to take an interest in history. Double-duh! She held her hands by her sides to help resist the urge to smack. 'My dissertation at fashion college was on eighteenth- and nineteenth-century military and naval uniforms. Fascinating subject, don't you think?' Gemma stretched her lips over her teeth. It was the best she could manage by way of a smile.

'Er, yes.'

She obviously knew nothing at all about it, thought Gemma gleefully. But she was moved by curiosity to find out why someone with little or no knowledge on the subject wanted to make a replica uniform. Of course, there was one reason that sprang to mind instantly, but Gemma didn't even want to think about going down that path. Besides, if her suspicion was right, what good would it do her? Yet another wardrobe incompetent, with a job in the theatre or TV that they didn't deserve, making costumes that were anachronistic or just plain wrong, while she, Gemma, who would get it perfect, was stuck here in a shop . . .

No, sod it; she *did* want to go down that path. Who was she kidding? She was squirming with curiosity. She was desperate to know the truth behind this woman's request because there was just a chance . . . a slight possibility . . . She felt her heart-rate step up.

She breathed deeply to make sure her voice was steady. 'So can I ask what this uniform is for?'

'A costume drama for the cinema. A film about the Peninsular War.'

Gemma's heart began to beat even faster. 'Who's making it?' she asked, trying desperately to sound casual.

'Butterfly Films.'

Gemma had heard of them. Actually, anyone with any interest whatsoever in films and TV had heard of them. They had swept the board at the previous year's Baftas for their adaptation of *Mansfield Park*. Like Merchant Ivory, they had carved a very special place for themselves making costume dramas. Except, Gemma thought, that while the *drama* side of their speciality was fine, the *costume* side left a lot to be desired. And if this woman was their costume designer . . . No, she couldn't be. Surely, if you were about to embark on something as big as this, you would have mugged up on everything about the era in question? Perhaps she was just a gofer.

Gemma couldn't control herself any more. A bubble grew inside her – a bubble that was filled with a desire for knowledge. It grew and burst. Gemma wondered if the pop was audible. She asked, 'So have they finished crewing up?'

'Why?' The woman shot a cold glance at Gemma accompanied by a sniff. Hadn't she ever heard of hankies? Gemma wondered, though she knew it wasn't that kind of sniff. It was the sort of short, sharp nasal intake that made Gemma think of her last head teacher bollocking an unruly class before handing out detentions. Concentrated disapproval all expressed in one, tiny inrush of air.

'It's what I trained to do – costume. It's the sort of thing I'd love to get involved in.' Out of the corner of her eye she saw Zoë creep closer to eavesdrop on the conversation.

'Really.' Sniff. The woman sounded completely disbelieving and uninterested.

Shit, thought Gemma. She should have been more subtle. Too eager, too needy, blown it.

'Have you done much?'

A glimmer of hope flickered into life. Gemma could hardly breathe. Perhaps I haven't blown it after all, she thought. Sniffy-woman wouldn't ask if she were planning to deliver a kiss-off. Gemma detailed her modest CV to date.

'Not exactly impressive.' The disdain dripped.

'She's only been out of college a year,' said Zoë. 'Give her a break.'

Gemma felt her whole body sag with despair. Well, if sounding too needy hadn't been a no-no then having a friend getting irate on her behalf was probably going to kill any chance dead. The little flame of hope that had been burning snuffed itself out, lemming-like, in an act of suicidal despair.

The woman turned round and gave Zoë a steely stare which should have killed on the spot. Zoë, to her credit, just stared back. For several seconds the pair duelled with locked eyes like two stags in the rut. The costume lady lowered her gaze first. Blimey, thought Gemma, she had underestimated Zoë completely. Then she realised this might be a bad thing. Damn. The old biddy had lost face. Not good. It was probably the final straw. Oh, well. She sighed inwardly. She would still have the job here in the shop. Who wanted a poxy job in the movies anyway? It would probably be crap, not a bit like her imagination had cracked it up to be.

'Do you have a card?' An icy voice brought Gemma out of her self-pity.

'A w-w-what?' stammered Gemma.

'A card? Your address? So I can get in contact with you?'

'No, sorry. Hang on. Just a mo. I'll write it down . . .' God, she was sounding like a moron, burbling and almost incoherent. Gemma dodged back behind the counter, hauled a length of receipt paper out of the till, and wrote her name, address and mobile number on it. 'Here.'

The woman took it and sniffed again. Then she reached in her handbag and extracted a small piece of card. 'Give me a ring. I'd like to see your portfolio.' There was a pause. 'You do have one, don't you?'

Gemma nodded vigorously. 'Yes, yes. When?'

'Ring me and we'll arrange a date.' She swept out.

'She didn't buy her braid,' said Gemma, stunned.

'Who cares?' said Zoë, skipping up and down on the spot like a two year old needing a wee. 'Who cares! This could be your big break.'

Gemma felt quite weak as it all began to sink in. 'Yes, it could, couldn't it? How long do I give it before I phone her?' The bell over the door had hardly fallen silent.

'You don't want to sound too needy.'

'But I am, I am.'

'Yes, obviously, but it wouldn't do for her to know quite how desperate you are. Wait till tomorrow.'

'Tomorrow?' Gemma squeaked.

'All right, this afternoon.'

Gemma looked at her watch. 'But that's hours.'

'And promise me one thing,' said Zoë, suddenly serious. 'When you talk to her, don't rubbish the designs you've seen on TV recently. The people that worked on the shows may be mates of hers. The designs may even have been hers, for all you know. You really don't want to annoy her by sounding all superior. If you work for her, you're going to be her assistant, an underling – don't forget that.'

Gemma nodded. Zoë was right. She often was.

It was almost lunchtime when Jean made it into the shop, ticking like a clock with indignation.

'Why are young men, who shouldn't be allowed out without a responsible adult, allowed to drive motors that powerful? . . . Really!'

Zoë brewed her a soothing cup of tea and made sympathetic noises while Gemma almost burst with her news.

Finally, Jean said, 'You look pleased with yourself. Have you finally got a job?'

'Not really,' said Gemma. 'Well, maybe. I don't know.' Then she gabbled out the saga of the woman and the braid.

Jean looked at the watch. 'Best you make that phone call, then. And when she's done that, Zoë, you had better go for lunch. I shan't bother with a break today. I had a sandwich while I was waiting to get the car taken to the garage. Two hours for that truck to arrive. I ask you!'

Gemma skipped into the staffroom. She sat for a minute to compose herself. She reminded herself of Zoë's advice about being overly critical of costume disasters on the screen and reminded herself not to sound too desperate. She glanced at the card to remind herself of the woman's name and to check the number, then she took a deep breath and dialled.

'Arabella Minton.'

'Oh, hi. Umm, we met this morning. At Sew Wonderful.' She paused, waiting for Arabella to say something positive. Silence. 'Anyway,' she blundered on, 'you said to phone you. You gave me your card.' Still nothing. 'To arrange a date for me to show you my portfolio ... So when would be convenient?' She shut up. There was nothing else she could say without sounding like she needed care in the community.

'I see. Will you be free next week?'

Gemma nearly made the flippant retort that she was only out on day-release at the moment, and that next week she'd be banged up again – but she restrained herself.

Instead, she said, 'I work in the shop part-time, but I am sure I can get time off for an interview.'

'It won't be an interview.' Sniff.

For a ghastly moment, Gemma thought the sniff meant she had upset the bag again, but then she remembered that everything she'd said in the shop had been punctuated by a disapproving-sounding sniff and yet she had still given her a card.

'Well, whatever you would like to call it,' said Gemma soothingly.

It worked. 'I may be able to offer you something. Subject to approval from the production office. Of course,' sniff, 'it is totally dependent on the quality of your portfolio.'

'Oh, yes. I completely understand that.'

'Can you make next Monday?'

Gemma didn't even bother to check her diary. She knew Jean would let her go whether she was rostered to work in the shop or not. 'Yes. Where do you want me to meet you, and what time?'

Arabella gave her the address of Butterfly Films and told her to be there at 'eleven sharp'. After she put the phone down Gemma sat on the chair, hugging herself and thinking that her insides must feel like champagne in a bottle just after the cork had been removed. She thought she was about to fizz over with happiness and excitement. When she told Zoë, she jumped about almost as excited as Gemma although, when they had calmed down sufficiently to regain coherence, they decided not to buy the champagne just yet; it was a bit premature when she hadn't even got the gig.

'Got to keep a sense of perspective, Gem,' said Zoë. 'It's a long shot, after all. You might not get it.'

But I'm going to, Gemma said to herself. I am going to get this job, I know it.

Gemma sat on the edge of a chair in an office that was utterly chaotic. The light came in through a long line of skylights in the roof. Gemma thought it might be cold to work here in the winter but what would she not give to find out? She looked about her. All over the walls were half-finished sketches with swatches of fabric pinned to them. There were books and drawings scattered all over the desk. At one end was a long work table with a coat or jacket partially cut out. The rest of the fabric, with the pattern pinned to it, was in danger of sliding on to the floor, which was already littered with scraps of tissue and cotton and material. Gemma itched to give the place a good spring clean and to sort it out. How could anyone work in such a mess?

She tried not to stare at Arabella's face as she leafed through her portfolio of designs and sketches of late eighteenth- to early nineteenth-century clothes.

'Can you cut patterns?' she shot at Gemma suddenly.

Gemma was so distracted by the state of the room that she almost had to think about her answer. 'Yes. Yes, I can.'

'Good. We probably won't need you to make anything – we have professional makers. It's the designing that's important.' More leafing, staring at her drawings. 'Why did you choose this period?'

'I was fascinated by the uniforms. It's like people went into battle dressed in their Sunday best. And I just think the whole era is so romantic. So I decided I wanted to learn more about it.'

Arabella nodded. 'Well, you seem to know your stuff.' She pulled a large sketchbook off the desk next to her. 'What do you think of these? They're turn of the eighteenth and nineteenth centuries. They're for the next production.' She raised her eyebrows challengingly at Gemma. 'The film set in the Peninsular War?'

'Yes, I remember.'

'The storyline is fictional. Remember *The Pride and the Passion*?' Gemma nodded. Great film. She'd fallen in love with Cary Grant when she'd seen it one wet Sunday afternoon a few years back. Of course, she'd realised later that he was about a century older than her – that was the problem with old movies. She remembered it had also starred Sophia Loren, who had been luscious and who had given her hope that you didn't have to be a blonde to be stunning. 'We're making something similar.'

It sounded good to Gemma. Lots of uniforms, which

would allow her to shine. The female cast wouldn't get much in the way of glamour, though. If she remembered correctly, Sophia Loren had been dressed as a gypsy – plenty of chance to show off her cleavage, but not a lot of costume changes or elegance. Still, with a cleavage like that . . .

'So will there be any female characters in it?'

Arabella nodded. 'I haven't seen the scripts yet, but quite a few, I think. Camp followers and the like.'

'Whores *de combat*,' mused Gemma, remembering an old joke.

Arabella gave her a look of annoyance and ignored the comment.

Gemma opened the sketchbook and began to peruse. 'Umm . . .' She wasn't sure quite what to say. *No good* was almost tactful but not quite. *Crap*, which was what she really thought, was bound to be a mistake. 'Well, um, they're um . . . very colourful.' She smiled weakly.

Arabella rewarded her with a carbon-copy of the stare that should have felled Zoë in the shop. 'Very colourful?' Her eyes narrowed and she sniffed. Shit, she looked dangerous.

'Well, what I mean is, I expect there are lots of limitations to what you can do when you are working with cameras.' Arabella looked slightly mollified. 'And of course I imagine you only get a very restricted budget.'

'This is true. But we don't compromise on historical accuracy, despite all that.'

Oh, don't you, thought Gemma. If these uniforms were supposed to be of the very early 1800s she was a teapot. The sketches she was looking at were of uniforms from the Victorian era.

'Well,' Gemma said, deciding to risk everything, 'if

these are designs for a Regency drama, I would say that this style was a tad late.'

'Oh, would you.' The tone was icy again.

Gemma nodded. Bugger, bugger, bugger. Why couldn't she just lie and say, 'Oh yes, lovely, perfectly right for the time'? Because she'd been brought up not to fib, that was why. She sighed, hope fading.

'Right, well, I think I have seen all I need to. I'll be in touch,' said Arabella.

Gemma stood up and took her portfolio back. This was obviously the *don't-call-us-we'll-call-you* brush-off. 'Thank you,' she said, fighting down her disappointment. She'd been so close and then she'd wrecked it. As she left the office, she tied the ribbons on the top of her portfolio and then walked down the metal outside stairs into the yard.

The studios had once been an old brewery but now the big rooms, where the hops and malted barley had been turned into beer, had been converted into rehearsal rooms, prop stores and sound stages. All about her people were bustling about – guys with reels of cables, people in costume, efficient-looking twenty-somethings with officious-looking millboards. Gemma so longed to be a part of this she almost ached.

She'd known this was her world ever since her father had hauled the family up to Manchester to see an aged uncle. The weather had been dreadful, the uncle's house small, and her mother, in a fit of exasperation, had booked for her and the girls to go on a tour of Granada Studios while her father and uncle reminisced about old times and generally chewed the fat. The feeling she had now was just like the feeling she'd had that day when she'd stood on the set of *Corrie* and sat in the Speaker's Chair in

Granada's very own House of Commons and then had seen the wardrobe department: racks and racks of dresses and costumes from every period you could care to mention. It was then she'd decided that she wanted to work in films, to make such wonderful clothes for her screen idols to wear, and she had been aiming for that goal ever since.

But, not this time, she told herself. She'd managed to miss her big chance and she felt completely gutted. A man she recognised walked past. She was just about to say 'hi' when she realised that she knew him from a soap and not from real life. The feeling of loss and disappointment cut even deeper. Oh, the fun of working with celebrities and actors and films and . . . with a big sigh she went back to reception and handed in her visitor's pass. Then, wondering how she was going to tell Zoë and Jean that she had blown her big chance, she made her way back to the Tube station and Camden.

'Never mind,' said Jean. 'She sounds a cow by all accounts. You are probably better off not working for the likes of her.'

'But I don't care if she *is* a cow,' wailed Gemma. 'When I was there it was so exciting and alive and I felt as though I could fit right in.' She stopped. She could feel her eyes pricking. She blinked a couple of times, hoping that the tears would recede rather than spill. She sighed, brought herself under control. 'I can't believe I fucked up. Especially when you told me not to be critical of other people's work. But it was so wrong. It would have been criminal not to say so.' Zoë might not have agreed with her but she didn't say 'I told you so', for which Gemma was pathetically grateful. She deserved to hear it, but it might have been all that was required to push her over the edge and into a sob-fest.

She mooched around the shop for the rest of the day, carrying out her duties, demonstrating a couple of sewing machines, and even selling one to a customer, but she looked and felt like a wet weekend. When Jean closed the shop, she took a twenty out of the till and gave it to Zoë.

'Go and buy the girl a drink. Get her to cheer up. If she's like this tomorrow, tell her to stay at home. With a face like that I swear she'll drive customers away.'

Zoë didn't need telling twice and dragged Gemma off to the nearest wine bar.

'I don't feel like drinking,' protested Gemma.

'Look, neither do I—'

Gemma snorted.

'I am just obeying orders,' said Zoë piously as she caught a barman's attention and ordered a bottle of Soave. She handed over the cash, grabbed the bottle, glasses, change and Gemma, and pushed her way through the press of customers hollering for booze, to a vacant table at the back. She poured two generous slugs out and picked up her glass.

'To better times,' she said.

'Yeah, right.' Gemma toyed with her glass, twirling the stem between her fingers.

'Looking at it won't cheer you up,' said Zoë, knocking back a big slurp.

'No.' Gemma sighed again.

Zoë was beginning to lose patience. 'Now just look here a minute,' she began, but she didn't get any further as Gemma's mobile rang.

Gemma picked it out of her handbag and looked at the number, then shrugged and answered it a touch warily as she didn't recognise it.

'Yes?' she said cautiously. 'Gemma Brown here.'

Zoë sipped her wine and watched her friend's face, her natural feminine curiosity causing her to wonder who was calling her. As she looked, Gemma's face went from sullen to smiley faster than a Formula 1 car could go from nought to sixty. Zoë made sign language to indicate she wanted to know what the cause of this transformation was. It was obviously something good as Gemma was now wriggling like a kid on Christmas morning. All Zoë could gather was that Gemma was agreeing with everything the caller was saying. A succession of 'yeses' didn't enlighten her at all to the nature of the call. By the time Gemma rang off she was almost beside herself.

'Cheers,' said Gemma raising her glass, grinning like the proverbial cat from Cheshire. 'To better times.'

Zoë narrowed her eyes. 'You've changed your tune and, if you would rather drink that wine than wear it, Gemma Brown, I suggest you tell me who that caller was.'

Gemma smiled enigmatically and took another sip. 'That would be a waste of wine though.'

'And two minutes ago you didn't want to have anything to do with alcohol at all.'

'So a girl can change her mind.'

'You'll have to change your clothes as well, if you don't look sharp.' Zoë drew her arm back, half-full glass aimed at her friend.

'Well, if you must know, that was Arabella Minton.'

'Who?'

'Snotty braid-lady.'

'You mean . . . ? Shit!'

'I do. I start a week on Monday. Assistant costume designer.'

A split second later all the heads in the crowded, noisy

wine bar turned in the direction of a piercing, ear-splitting shriek that shrilled from a table at the back of the room. Then people who were within viewing distance could see two grown women jumping up and down on the spot and hugging each other across a table. The wine bottle went flying, sending wine cascading on to the floor, but they didn't care. They continued to hug and shriek.

J ono Knighton was sitting on a chair in the corner of the
studio waiting to go on the set of *Sophie's Sofa*. Where
he was, beside the audience seating but hidden from
them by a curtain, he was almost in complete darkness
compared to the brilliant lights shining on the set, which
was designed to look like an up-market drawing room,
something you might find in a minor stately home:
regency stripe wallpaper, a big comfy sofa, a fake sash
window on the rear wall that appeared to look out over
parkland . . . A set that, if the viewing figures were to be
believed, six million people tuned in to look at every
weekday teatime. Well, they tuned in to look at the set *and*
the lovely Sophie Green and her A-list guests. Right now
Sophie was interviewing a kid who had just won some sort
of music competition and was tipped to be the next Yehudi
Menuhin. Jono would swap places with the prodigy
during the commercial break. Then it would be his turn to
get the Sophie treatment.

It was generally agreed by most celebrities that nailing
a place on Sophie Green's sofa meant you had made it. She
and Parky ruled the British TV chat-show circuit and

agents busted their collective guts to get their clients on to one or other programme, preferably both. To get both was the ultimate seal of celeb status and Jono was lined up for Parky later on in the week. His agent, Max, had nearly wet himself with excitement when he had broken the news to Jono.

'You owe me for this, Jono,' Max had said, almost jumping up and down with glee, his jowls shaking in sympathy as Jono had pumped his hand in thanks.

Jono had smiled and pointed out that he would get his fifteen per cent of the appearance fee, which would pay back quite a lot of any debt involved. Then he'd asked, 'But what about Rowan?'

Max dismissed the idea with a wave of his pudgy fingers. 'We'll pitch for her when she's got something to sell. It's you the public want right now. You're the hot property at the moment.'

Which was true but it wouldn't make it any easier for his wife. Only a couple of years ago, if Max had got him this sort of publicity opportunity, the chat-show host would have insisted that Rowan ought to be invited along too. Jono and Rowan had been like Posh and Becks – you couldn't have one without the other. It had only been recently that Rowan had changed and her popularity had waned. Jono shut his eyes and thought about the old Rowan.

Rowan hadn't always been a hot-shot star. When he'd first seen her, when he'd first fallen for her because, quite simply, she'd been the most beautiful creature he'd ever clapped eyes on, what with her incredibly slim figure, fantastically ash-blond hair and pale grey eyes, her career hadn't been going well. It had juddered to a halt in the States, having barely taken off and so she'd decided to try her luck in London.

They shared Max as an agent and their paths had crossed at various parties and at the houses of acting friends. They were both young, good looking and shared a passion for the stage, and she, like Jono, had managed to get the occasional bit-parts in movies and had picked up minor roles on the London stage, but nothing mega. And as they began to spend more and more time in each other's company, Rowan had avowed that she felt as much for Jono as he did for her and their names had begun to be linked with increasing frequency. Not, at that stage, by the public but certainly by others in the business.

Then they had been cast together in *Anthony and Cleopatra* at the Globe and everything changed. The critics had gone wild, but not as wild as the audiences had. The sexual tension on the stage had been electric and everyone said they were the new Richard Burton and Elizabeth Taylor. Suddenly they couldn't move for paparazzi and press who had finally woken up to Rowan's fabulous beauty. Better still, offers for parts had flooded in. In the midst of all the frenzy they married. Yet more exposure, more publicity and Rowan had thrived on it. Jono, less so. He'd never got off on that sort of adulation. He'd always wanted to be an actor but the drive hadn't been stardom – he just loved acting. But for Rowan it was different. To become a star was her *raison d'être*. And now she was one, boy, did she behave like it – or she certainly had over the last couple of years.

It seemed to Jono that Rowan must have read every biog about every badly behaved, drugged-up, drunken Hollywood star who had ever lived and taken those books to heart as if they were 'how to' manuals. Of course it hadn't helped that work, once again, was slow coming Rowan's way. She no longer received as many scripts as she had a year previously, and the ones she did get sent were often second rate. The fact that the press were saying that Jono's most recent film, the one about to go on general release, might earn him an Oscar nomination had made her moody and depressed. Her last picture had been panned by the critics and the audience figures showed that the judgement was universal. Jono was getting all the limelight while she was disappearing off the public's radar.

Of course, she had had some publicity recently but not of the right sort. All that stuff about 'all publicity is good publicity' was bollocks when you'd had the sort that she had had in the previous few weeks. First, there had been some unflattering pictures that made her look fat. Then there had been the very public accusations from her ex-stylist about her temper tantrums that hadn't helped matters. The final nail in the coffin had been a picture of her falling out of a taxi outside The Dorchester. No one had believed her when she'd protested that she'd just caught her heel in the hem of her dress . . . Pissed was what the tabloids had said and pissed was what the public believed. Well, they would, wouldn't they?

Not that the scale of her drinking was public knowledge yet but it was going to come out sooner or later if any more pics like that got published. The wonderful, vivacious, beautiful, talented actress that he'd fallen for was becoming an egocentric, brittle, insecure drunk who was a nightmare to live with. She was now irrational and temperamental and although part of Jono still loved her, she seemed to be hell-bent on alienating him. He was worried for her health, both mental and physical, and he was terrified that if he left her – which, though once unimaginable, was becoming daily more tempting – she would spiral into a vortex of self-destruction. He knew that he was her only safety net, the only thing between her and skid row. Rowan's father was an unknown and her mother had died just after she'd come across to England. As far as Jono knew, she had no other living relatives, no one else to help him or to share the responsibility.

Life with Rowan was becoming a living hell but his vows had included worse, sickness and poorer, and just because two of the three were now a constant in his life it didn't mean he could give up on her. But there were days when he wished he wasn't half so principled, days he wanted to bang her into some rehab programme somewhere so that he could get on with his own life. To be free of the millstone that she had become. How much longer, he sometimes asked himself, should he put his own happiness on hold because Rowan couldn't or wouldn't see what she was doing to the pair of them? If she wanted to destroy her own career, then so be it, but he knew there was a real danger that his own career and happiness might get caught up in the carnage too.

Now he was about to appear on Sophie's and Parky's shows and he knew that Rowan was angry and upset that she wasn't invited too. But, as Max said, it would be madness to turn the chance down – people just didn't. So, despite the fact that it made sense, and despite the fact that the film studio was very happy that he was going on to publicise his latest film, he couldn't help feeling that this was the sort of thing that might make his wife's fragile ego even more brittle.

He gave a little sigh. There was certainly one thing to be said about living with Rowan: life wasn't boring. But a tiny bit of him yearned for ordinary and peaceful. Normal – that would be nice. He wondered what it would be like.

A swift nudge in the ribs brought him back to the present.

'The floor manager wants you to stand by,' said Max.

Jono stood up and moved to the edge of the set. He could hear the studio audience rustle with excitement as they realised who the next guest was. He didn't turn towards them or acknowledge them in any way. He had the impression that the floor manager was barely keeping a lid on them as it was. If he smiled or waved at them the chances were they might erupt. He didn't think that would go down well and even though he knew his worth, he wasn't going to irritate the production team by doing something crass. He might be on the way up right now but, in the future, when perhaps things might not be so good, he wanted people he'd worked with to remember him with affection, not as some jumped-up, egocentric prick.

'And we'll be right back after the break when we'll have a real treat for you,' said Sophie, beaming at a camera. The red light on top of it flicked off, as did her smile. Instantly, the kid was bundled off the sofa and Jono felt a hand take his arm. The audience hollered and clapped and whistled as he was led forward.

'Watch out for the cables,' said a voice in his ear over the racket as he was led to the sofa through the gloom of the studio. Treading warily, Jono walked on to the set and into a wall of heat and light. He could see Sophie giving one of the production team hell if her facial expression was anything to go by. As he approached her expression changed and her smile was switched back on. It had almost as much wattage as the lights dangling from the rigs. One of the crew managed to quieten the audience and Jono turned his attention to his host.

'Mr Knighton, I am *so* utterly thrilled to meet you.' She gushed and simpered and held out her hand, which Jono took briefly as he sat down. She might be the darling of the daytime audiences but there was something about her – a falseness – that grated. A make-up girl appeared from somewhere to the side of the set, a bag of brushes, paints and powders slung around her waist. Even as he opened his mouth to make some polite reply, she got to work dusting his forehead and chin, then she combed back his blond fringe. He waited until she was finished and had moved across to apply some more lip-gloss to Sophie before he lied smoothly about how delighted he was to meet her. 'And it's Jono, please.' Sophie smiled coquettishly – at least, Jono reckoned, that was how she thought she smiled. Whatever it was, it didn't float his boat.

'Stand by!' cried the floor manager. The make-up girl vanished; Sophie sat up straight and gazed at the camera in front of her as there was a count-down from five. The floor manager signalled they were on air.

'Welcome back,' said Sophie. 'Well, I promised you ladies out there a real treat this afternoon and I was not exaggerating. *GQ* magazine and *Vanity Fair* have both dubbed him Britain's answer to Brad Pitt. *Sun* readers voted him the man they would most like to date and *Red*'s readers have decided he has the sexiest bum of all time. And when you look at the competition he was up against – it makes it a devastatingly sexy one.' Sophie lowered her voice to a whisper and looked coy, which Jono found nauseating, as she added, 'And having seen it in the flesh,' *giggle*, 'so to speak, I can vouch for it. Ladies and gentlemen, please welcome Jono Knighton.' The studio audience went wild and the camera panned to him. Jono smiled and nodded and tried to look pleased but inside he was worried what effect this adulation would have on Rowan. He was certain she was watching. She rarely did anything else these days but watch the TV. And he prayed the camera didn't have Sophie's hand in shot, which was resting on the inside of his thigh.

He moved slightly in the hope he might dislodge it but her grip only tightened a fraction. He wondered if he was going to be able to control his gag reflex for the ten minutes he was scheduled to spend in simpering Sophie's company. Up close and personal – and she seemed hell bent on getting very up close and personal indeed, if her body language was anything to go by – she was scarily predatory. Jono thought it was like a fluffy, cutesy, Disney cartoon lioness suddenly morphing into the real thing – one that hadn't had a square meal in a week, and which was practically eyeing up supper with its napkin tucked in and a knife and fork at the ready. Man-eater didn't even come close.

'So Jono' – she leaned forward so he could see right down the front of her top – 'what's it like to be the hottest box-office draw for a decade? The film industry is calling you a destination star. That' – she switched her gaze to the camera – 'means that people like us go to a film just because it has Jono in it.'

'Well, it's jolly flattering. I mean, a comment like that is terrific for a chap's ego.' For nearly two years now, since Jono's star had really been in the ascendant, he'd perfected his public persona: that of slightly absent-minded, middle-class, thoroughly nice chap. Someone who found the kind of things that were happening to him a little bit perplexing, and the success all a bit of a shock – and as for the adulation and the fans . . . It worked like a charm: middle-aged women wanted to mother him because he looked young and vulnerable, twenty-somethings wanted to bed him because he was good-looking, men found him non-threatening because obviously he was a complete wuss, and teenage girls could indulge in harmless fantasies about him because their mothers thought he was 'safe' for all of the other reasons. Even the press liked him. The act even seemed to con Sophie, judging by the way she was drooling. He added now, for good measure – he didn't want to look completely stupid – 'It doesn't do the old career much harm, either.'

'I should think not,' she simpered. 'I should imagine you get offered more scripts than you can shake a stick at.'

'I am very lucky that some fantastic material comes my way. Of course, the downside is that it's sometimes tricky to choose what to do next.'

'Does the fact that you're married to Rowan Day influence your decisions at all? I mean, do you go for scripts that have a part for her, too?'

Jono studied Sophie briefly. He might wish to appear like he was a likeable bumbler, a bit of a public school buffoon, but he was no slouch mentally. Swiftly, he tried to work out where this line of questioning might be leading. Any mention of Rowan always got him on his guard.

'Well,' he said smoothly, 'of course it's always a bit of a lark to work on something with Rowan. It makes the romantic scenes more fun' – he dropped Sophie just a hint of a wink, which he knew the camera would pick up – '. . . if you get my drift.' The audience roared with smutty laughter. 'But that apart, we're still terribly in love and I hate being separated from her for a moment more than I have to be. Obviously, the more she and I can work together, the happier we are.' He stared at Sophie.

Outwardly, he looked as if he was just waiting for the next question, but inwardly he was challenging her to read anything into his last answer. And anyway, there was a chance of a part for Rowan (but not him) in an American series being made by Magnum Opus, but he wasn't going to bitch up Rowan's chances by even hinting at it. Until it was in the bag and the ink on the contract dry, his lips were sealed on that subject.

'It's just that I've heard', said Sophie, 'that you told one studio that you wouldn't make the film unless they wrote in a part for Rowan.'

Shit, thought Jono. Where the fuck had the bitch got that from? He smiled and laughed loudly. 'Goodness, fancy believing I had clout like that. Crikey, if I thought I had, I might just try it on. What a fab wheeze!'

The audience rocked with laughter. The moment was defused and Sophie looked at her notes for the next line of questioning.

'Your next film is due out shortly. Was it fun to make?'

Rowan was sitting on the edge of her pale cream sofa, her hands clenched around the edges of a white cushion, staring fixedly at the plasma screen on the opposite wall. What right had that bitch Sophie Green to imply that she, Rowan Day, couldn't get a part unless Jono put a word in? Of course she could get parts. She was just going through a bad patch. Lots of actresses did. Her luck was bound to turn around soon. She stared morosely at her drink. Even she knew that she shouldn't be relying on luck and there had been a time – only a few years back – when she'd had wonderful parts lined up back to back. Then suddenly they'd dried up.

She took a slug of her whisky. It wasn't fair that Jono

was still getting loads of parts and she wasn't. Jono said it was all her fault; that she shouldn't have slapped that director in front of the rest of the cast and crew and that was when all her troubles had started. But he was a lousy director; he didn't understand the problems she'd been having with the part, and he'd been impossible. And it hadn't been a hard slap. She was sure no one else remembered what she'd done. Besides, she hadn't lost her temper with a director since.

She looked back at the screen on the wall. The camera angle changed a fraction and she saw where Sophie's hand was placed. With a shriek of rage she threw the cushion at the screen. Her aim was lousy and, despite the size of the vast screen, it hit the wall to one side. Angry and frustrated, she took another slug of her drink, then she slumped back on the sofa and began to cry as she watched the interview continue. Everyone loved Jono and no one wanted her. She let her self-pity wash through her along with more whisky.

Gemma, not required at the shop, was spending her day off getting her ironing pile down to proportions that meant it didn't require her to hire sherpas to bring garments down from its lofty peak. She was also watching *Sophie's Sofa*. Very little ironing was actually being done at this precise moment because she was transfixed by the sheer beauty of the man on the show. The blouse she'd been ironing lay ignored, draped over the board, and the iron gave out little intermittent, exasperated puffs of steam as she leaned on both elbows and stared and stared. Now she wasn't being irritated by dud costumes she could concentrate on his fantastic bone structure and his wonderful blue eyes. Surely, she thought, he had to be wearing tinted contacts. No one could have eyes quite such a fantastic shade naturally?

Lucky old Rowan, she thought, as she gazed at him. If *she* were married to Jono, she wouldn't give a fart about a career. She wouldn't want parts written for her in Jono's films, she'd just want to spend all her time making his life wonderful. Not that Rowan appeared to be doing much of that if the gossip in the glossy mags was to be believed. There had been that dreadful picture of her in the gutter by some smart London hotel just last month. Furthermore, there were rumours all over the place about Rowan's unstable temperament, to say nothing of the fairly regular stories that she was a complete control freak who made ridiculous demands on all who had anything to do with her. Though, surely, she wasn't the only film star in history to behave like that, and, besides, perhaps she wasn't as bad as the papers made out; even Gemma knew you couldn't believe half of what you read in the press.

Sophie finished her questions and thanked Jono effusively. He leaned forward and kissed her in a luvvy sort of way on both cheeks. Gemma was green with envy. Lucky old Soph, she thought. Gemma put her hand to her cheek as she tried to imagine what it would feel like to be so honoured. She was still in a fantasy world of her own when Zoë came home from the shop half an hour later.

4

About ten days later, Gemma climbed the outside stairs to the costume designers' office feeling nervous and happy in equal measure. She opened the door and looked at the mess and chaos with a feeling of proprietorial affection rather than horrified amazement. If this was how her new place of work functioned then she would fit in with it. She heard steps clumping up the metal steps behind her. She turned. A sour-faced blonde barely glanced at her before she pushed past and into the office. Gemma followed her.

'Hi,' she said. 'I'm Gemma Brown.' She held out her hand. The sour-faced blonde looked at it as if Gemma was offering her a rotting fish, not a handshake.

'I know,' she snapped. Then added with a sneer, 'I'm Tina.' She ignored the hand and turned her back on Gemma. She hung up her jacket, dumped her bag in the bottom drawer of a filing cabinet, and plugged in the kettle. She was obviously an old hand, and judging by her attitude, far from pleased at having a new assistant.

Gemma felt quite shaken. This wasn't the response she'd been expecting. Maybe a fatted calf being dished up would have been overkill (well, it certainly would have been for the calf), but a pleasant 'hello and welcome' wasn't too much to ask, was it? Apparently it was. She raised her eyebrows briefly and blinked as she tried to regain her composure and wondered whether Tina was angry at having her as an assistant or just at having an assistant in general. There was the possibility that Tina was a little challenged in the social skills department but if that were the case, how on earth had she ever landed a job – especially such a terrific one?

No doubt, thought Gemma, she would find out all about Tina over the coming weeks and months. It was unlikely that the wardrobe department was so huge that they would not be working pretty closely together – which, considering how vile Tina had just been – wasn't a particularly comforting thought. She made up her mind to do as little as possible to cause offence and upset things further. She put her handbag on the counter that ran round most of the room and sat down. There were questions she would have liked to have asked, but she decided it was best not to just yet. She decided not even to ask if she might have a cup of tea too, although it would have been no trouble for old sour-puss to have dropped a second tea bag into another mug while she was making her own. Gemma sighed, feeling totally unwelcome. Perhaps it would get better as the day wore on, but judging by the way Tina kept her back to her that was unlikely.

By the time Arabella arrived five minutes later, the atmosphere was so cold it was probably reversing global warming. She glanced at the two girls. 'I trust you have introduced yourselves. We're a small team, so it is as well if we all become friends.'

Gemma thought she heard a snort. Tina obviously had different views on the subject.

Arabella regarded them and then just said 'good' before putting her bag down and pulling out a chair to sit on. Even she, with her thickly varnished exterior as protection, must have detected that not all was sweetness and light.

'Right,' she said, smiling at Gemma, 'I'll show you around the studio later on, and introduce you to the other crew members. I think a number of posts have yet to be filled and some of the crew will be transferring from other Butterfly productions as they wrap.' She smiled her bright, hard smile again. Gemma wondered whether, if she did that too often, her hard exterior would crack and craze like an old oil painting. 'Right now, however,' Arabella continued, 'we need to get some basic admin jobs done. I am told we will be getting the first draft of the script through today, which should give us an idea of the number of characters we will be dealing with. I am also told that the casting process will be getting underway this week.'

Tina stopped looking completely sullen and paid attention to Arabella.

'Any idea who they plan to get for the leads?' she asked.

'Well,' said Arabella, a conspiratorial note in her voice, 'I have heard a rumour . . .'

'And?' said Tina.

'Well, of course it is unsubstantiated, but the whisper is that they want Jono Knighton and Rowan Day.'

Gemma was so startled that she nearly fell over. She just managed not to let out a squeak of excitement.

Tina, however, seemed more sceptical. 'Rowan? It'd be all wrong for her. No, I can't see it. I don't think she could do the accent.'

'Well, Renée Zellweger pulled off Bridget Jones,' said Gemma, forgetting her earlier vow not to upset Tina.

Tina shot her a look. 'It's not the same thing at all. It wouldn't be fair on Rowan to make her try to pull it off.'

Gemma, nettled, shrugged and shut up. She could have mentioned Gwyneth Paltrow in *Shakespeare In Love* and all her other English roles too, but decided that would alienate Tina even more – not a wise move at this stage of the proceedings. Although, for the life of her, she couldn't work out why the girl seemed to hate her so much already. She was the new girl on the block, and until she had established herself, got her feet under the table and gained Arabella's total confidence, she was going to do nothing to muck up her chances, and if that meant sucking up to the poisonous Tina, then suck up she would. But despite Tina's attitude, which was putting a bit of a dampner on the day, Gemma felt a thrill of excitement. Fancy working with Jono and Rowan! How fabulous would that be? And how jealous would Zoë be!

'So,' continued Arabella, 'I want you, Gemma, to tidy up this office and get the decks cleared ready for our new project, and Tina, I'd like you to go across to the production office and see if the script is ready. If it is, I'd like you to go through it and do the character costume breakdown.' She smiled at her two assistants.

'Okay, everybody?' Gemma was fine about the arrangements, although it appeared that Tina was far from happy. Why, Gemma was at a loss to understand: working out how many characters there would be in the film in total and what they would be wearing at any given time on the screen was hugely responsible and not a job that should be given to someone new to the whole process. Obviously, Tina, as the more senior, had to do this tricky job while she was only allowed to do menial stuff, but judging by the way she flounced out of the office, Tina didn't share Gemma's opinion.

Arabella pulled a sketchbook out of a pile of paper on the counter. 'Right, the mess in here' – she made a circular gesture with her hand to indicate she meant absolutely everything – 'all relates to previous productions. We're starting from scratch with this next one. Chuck anything that doesn't look as if it has any use. Save what you think should be salvaged.' Gemma gulped – and how on earth was she supposed to make the distinction? Was this some sort of test? If she got it wrong, would it be 'Hello, P45'? She was about to open her mouth and ask questions when Arabella gushed on. 'When you've sorted the worst of the mess out, I'd like you to look at these. They are Tina's initial designs for uniforms.' She sniffed. 'I'd like you to go through them and see what else we are going to need. Oh, and while you are at it, check them for accuracy.' Another sniff.

Gemma was shocked. 'But, I'm not sure it's my place.'

'You're the expert.'

'But it doesn't seem fair on Tina. I can't correct her stuff.'

'Why on earth not? You're my assistant not hers.'

Gemma was even more confused. 'Yes, I mean, I know you're the costume designer, but if Tina is your chief assistant, aren't I just the, well . . .' Gemma wasn't quite sure whether office-tidier and sweeper-upper were proper job titles.

Arabella sniffed and looked mildly irritated. 'Yes, I am the costume designer and you are assistant costume designer and Tina is wardrobe assistant.'

'I think you've got us the wrong way round,' said Gemma helpfully.

'No, I haven't.' Arabella enunciated the words in a scarily definite way.

Gemma swallowed. 'You mean, Tina is ... I am senior ... ?' Blimey. Her worries about cocking up the tidying-up job had now been completely usurped by the implications of her position.

'Precisely. I sent Tina to get the script because she knows where to go. And I tasked her to work out how many of the cast we are dressing because I want you to get on with the job of designing – with my help, of course.'

'Of course,' echoed Gemma, thrown by it all. Well, that could explain everything. No wonder Tina hated her guts. She had been demoted and Gemma had taken her place. Shit. This was not a recipe for a happy team. Gemma glanced at the door to make sure Tina wasn't about to reappear. 'Were those her sketches you showed me the other week?'

Arabella nodded. 'She can be slack. She doesn't do her research properly. I need someone I can rely on utterly. This is a huge production. Millions are being spent on it. It's being scheduled to hit the cinemas in the winter next year so as to maximise the chance of nominations for all the major awards. *All* the major awards,' she repeated with an almost religious fervency. Clearly, thought Gemma, awards were important to the Studio. Well, she supposed they would be important; they could make a difference to box-office profits, that was for sure. 'I am determined that the costumes for this production are going to become a watchword for historical accuracy.' Arabella had a passionate gleam in her eye. It was almost as intimidating as her steely stare. 'It is essential, *absolutely essential*, they are correct in every detail. Do you understand me?'

'Okay,' said Gemma, nodding and smiling nervously. 'Yes, I understand.' Then she had a lightbulb moment – a scary lightbulb moment that made her feel even more uncomfortable. Maybe Arabella wanted a Bafta or even an Oscar for herself. Butterfly Films might have swept the board at the Baftas with *Mansfield Park* but, she remembered, it hadn't taken the award for best costume; that had gone to a series about the Pre-Raphaelites. And that might have rankled with Arabella. She wouldn't want to lose out again and Gemma would need to make sure she didn't. It seemed that Tina had been demoted because she had fucked up. Gemma got the impression that if she wanted to stay in films she had to make sure the Bafta was coming Arabella's way.

'I've been in this business a long time, Gemma,' she confided, 'and I've worked on some great productions and some that have gone straight to DVD, but this is my big chance. This is my pension plan, if it works, so I have to put everything I have into it.' She sniffed, but this time it didn't sound disapproving, it sounded worried.

Suddenly Arabella didn't seem quite so scary. Gemma realised that their positions weren't so very different. They both were dependent on the quality of this production for their future security and maybe it was just as hard to keep your place on a production company's crew as to get it initially.

Arabella muttered something about a meeting, told Gemma to carry on, and then left. Gemma made a start on the tidying. She would have liked a guide as to where to put stuff away or how they liked things organised, but with nothing being forthcoming she decided to use her initiative. The sketchbooks she piled in one corner. She cleared everything off the corkboards and put the pins in a jar. The half-made jacket that obviously hadn't been touched since her interview, she folded up and put in a carrier bag that was lying around. If neither Arabella nor Tina claimed it she would bin it. She found a dustpan and brush and swept up all the trimmings and scraps, the cottons she wound up neatly on their reels and placed in order in a drawer, and by the time Tina returned from the production office about an hour later the office had been transformed.

Tina looked at the much tidier space and made no comment at all. But Gemma had decided that it was going to be a cold day in hell before Tina forgave her for usurping her. Gemma thought about taking her to task for being unfair, but what was the point? If Tina was going to be unreasonable, Gemma having a go at her was hardly likely to make the situation better.

Without saying a word, Tina dumped a couple of fat scripts on the counter, made herself a cup of tea, and then got busy reading one of them making notes and lists as she went. Gemma pointedly made tea for herself and carried on sorting, stacking and tidying. The atmosphere in the office stayed resolutely poisonous.

When Gemma started sketching out designs it got even worse. At least Arabella was back by then, so Tina simmered unpleasantly in the corner and wasn't able to make unpleasant comments or stick her feet out when Gemma passed, as she had done earlier on. Gemma began to wonder if she was going to be able to cope with this job with Tina being so vile but reminded herself that if she gave up she would regret her lack of backbone for ever.

It got no better as the week wore on. But, despite Tina

doing her best to poison the atmosphere, Gemma loved her job. Every time she went down the outside steps from their attic office at the studio, she encountered someone or something to remind her just what it was about the film industry that had her in its thrall. She would pass a face that she was utterly familiar with from one of her favourite soaps, or would see equally familiar bits of set being carted around the place, or would find herself handling costumes from past productions. One day, standing in the queue at the canteen, she realised she was behind two of the stars of a soap she followed. On screen these two women were permanently at daggers drawn so it came as a bit of a shock to overhear them discussing what they were planning to do that weekend and swapping notes about the progress of their respective grandchildren. Of course, in her heart, she knew these people were all actors, but it still surprised her when she saw their real selves not their screen persona. It was utterly exciting and Gemma had to make a real effort not to gawp and stare. She was sure that one day she might become blasé about it all but it was going to take a long time. And if she got this excited just passing stars in corridors and on the stairs, what was she going to be like when she had to dress them?

All of these things made working with Toxic Tina bearable and made her bless the day Arabella had walked into Sew Wonderful.

'I flatly refuse to have the name Martha,' said Rowan, looking at Jono and Max angrily. 'It's dreadful.'

'Not at all,' said Max. 'It's biblical.'

'So's Judas,' hissed Rowan.

'Darling,' said Jono soothingly. 'Darling, I am sure if it's possible, Butterfly will see what they can do. I expect it can be changed if you insist.'

'Do you think so, honey? It's just that Martha is so old-fashioned.'

Jono held his tongue and resisted telling her that as it was a period drama 'contemporary' was not going to be a word that would be associated with it. He sighed quietly. 'I understand how you feel,' he said.

'Anyway, this war . . . Who're the Brits fighting?'

'The French.'

'But you said the action is all in Spain.'

'Well, yes. You see, after Napoleon—'

'Forget it,' said Rowan. 'The last thing I want right now is a goddam history lesson.'

'I just thought—'

'Well, don't.' Her pale grey eyes narrowed and she

snapped her fingers at Max. 'I'll tell you what I do want, though.' Jono knew what was coming and resisted the urge to look at his watch. 'I may not want the goddam history but I do want a goddam drink. Max?'

Max, showing a surprising turn of speed for someone of his dimensions, almost ran across to the bar in the corner of the Knightons' sumptuous sitting room.

'Whisky?' he asked Rowan.

'On the rocks,' she confirmed.

'Anything in it?'

'More Scotch.'

Max slugged the Scotch into a glass over several ice cubes. Rowan sashayed elegantly over to him and took it out of his fingers, blowing him a kiss as she did so. Jono was, once again, struck by how fabulously beautiful she was. She looked so fragile and waif-like and, despite the things she did to her body, her skin was still flawless. If he didn't know what she could be like these days, he could fall in love with her all over again. But she was like those tiny Amazonian frogs – beautiful to look at but sheer poison. If only . . .

'One for you, Jono?' asked Max.

Jono shook his head. He had a feeling it would be prudent for him to remain sober. 'But help yourself, Max.'

'Too early for me.'

Jono rolled his eyes. Max and his big mouth! He braced himself and waited for the explosion.

'And how early is that, Max?' asked Rowan in a dangerously quiet voice.

'Well, not *early,* exactly,' Max blustered. 'What I meant was that I've got my car here and . . .' He looked at Jono for help.

'Max is going on to a boozy do at the Groucho,' lied

Jono smoothly. 'If he has a drink now he'll have to leave his car in town – or risk driving over the limit – and you know how he hates to do that.' Jono laughed, hoping it didn't sound forced. 'Actually, *I'd* hate him to do that. I think I've paid for most of that Lamborghini. I couldn't bear the idea of having to earn enough for Max to be able to afford another one. I'll be working till I'm eighty.'

Rowan's shoulders relaxed and she began to resemble a cobra about to strike just a little less. She took a gulp of her drink as she contemplated the two men and worked out whether she believed them or not. 'Whatever,' she said, and took another swig.

Jono sighed and Max grabbed his briefcase, ready to make a quick getaway. If Jono had a go at Rowan about her drinking it often got ugly. He didn't want to witness another of their scenes.

'So shall I tell Butterfly to send the contracts?' he asked hopefully.

'Yes,' said Jono firmly, before Rowan could cause more trouble. 'Get them biked over to you and if they're okay, bring them round tomorrow for us to sign.'

Rowan finished her drink and wandered back over to the bar to fill her glass up again. 'Martha,' she said. 'Ha!'

'It's official,' said Arabella. 'Jono and Rowan are playing Captain Turner and Martha.'

Tina brightened and then shook her head. 'It's not right for Rowan,' she muttered, although she was obviously pleased to be working with Ms Day.

Gemma had to physically stop herself from doing handsprings or turning cartwheels. Wait till she told Zoë. Zoë would be so green.

A thought struck her. My God! Fancy having to help him with his costume. She shook with so much excitement she had to lean against a filing cabinet for support. Arabella was saying something. Gemma made herself pay attention and stop swooning over Jono.

'Of course, we'll hire most of the costumes the extras will need. And the same goes for the minor roles. However, the principals will have theirs designed especially for them. I've heard Rowan can be quite particular, so we must make sure we listen to what she wants. I am sure her ideas will be perfectly valid.'

Gemma was quite surprised. Was Rowan, from America, going to know about English fashions in 1810? Were her ideas going to be valid? And listened to? Blimey O'Reilly, she thought. This was not the way forward if Arabella wanted an industry award. But, she remembered her vow to keep schtum so she said nothing and wondered just how much leeway Rowan was actually going to get.

'So,' continued Arabella. 'Tina, I want you to get on the phone to the costume suppliers, Angels, and to talk to them. You've got the schedule for when they plan to shoot the big crowd scenes, haven't you?' Tina nodded. 'Make enquiries with them about the availability of uniforms for the early eighteen hundreds for those shooting dates. And remember to factor in shipping times.' Tina went off to speak to the theatrical costumiers. 'And Gemma, I want you to get on to the agents of the other actors and get their clients' details; their photos, measurements and so on. Go and see Mary in the production office. She's got the numbers. When you get hold of them, tell them to get them to us as soon as possible. As soon as we've got them we need to go through Tina's breakdown, check that the list is correct, and start designing their main costumes.

Obviously, for the men this will mean their uniforms.' Gemma nodded. 'By the way,' Arabella shot at her, 'you have read the script, haven't you?'

Gemma nodded. It seemed to her to be a remake of *The Magnificent Seven* crossed with *Zulu*. The storyline entailed a band of British soldiers defending a Spanish village from marauding Napoleonic troops in search of food, but outnumbered by dozens to one like Michael Caine and his gang at *Rorke's Drift*. The love interest – which had been startlingly absent in both *Zulu* and *The Magnificent Seven* – was to be provided by the lovely Rowan Day playing Martha, Captain Turner's fiancée, who had trailed after the British Army disguised as a lowly camp follower because she couldn't bear the thought of him being away from her for so many months. Yes, highly likely, Gemma had thought, as she read through it. Just the sort of thing a well-bred Georgian miss would do – bugger off to foreign parts, unchaperoned, with no means of financial support or knowledge of the language, and in the company of several thousand brutal, licentious soldiers and several hundred camp followers. She thought that even a twentieth-century ladette on a gap year might find it a tad daunting. However, she'd gritted her teeth and told herself about the willing suspension of disbelief and all that crap and carried on reading: no sooner is Martha holed up in the village with the troops, surrounded by the Napoleonic forces outside, baying for blood, than her identity is discovered and she and her fiancé are reunited. He is wounded and it is only her skill at nursing – and where had she learned how to do that? – and her love that pulls him through. Cue epic battle where plucky Brits trounce Johnny Foreigner, followed by ride into the sunset and credits. *Eugh*. However, with

Rowan and Jono heading the credits it was almost a racing certainty that it would be a box-office smash.

Gemma sent up a little prayer that Arabella wouldn't ask her what she had thought of it. Hers not to reason why, hers but to sew and dye . . .

'Did you like it?' asked Arabella.

'I'm sure it'll be a hit,' said Gemma. Which was probably true.

'Good. Now I want you to start sketching out designs for Jono.' She pulled one of the sketchbooks out from the pile in the corner. 'These are a few of my ideas so far. You might like to use them as a basis.' She flipped it open to show a page of infantry uniforms.

Before she could stop herself, Gemma blurted out, 'I thought this was the Peninsular War. This regiment didn't fight out there.'

Arabella fixed her with her hardest, titanium-steel glare. 'Are you sure?'

Gemma swallowed and nodded.

Arabella snapped the book shut with a sniff. 'Check. Then get on with those designs – although, if you're right, you won't be able to use these.' She slid the sketchbook back on to the counter. 'I'll arrange for the maker to accompany you and me to the Knightons' house to measure them and to discuss their costumes.' She swept out of the room and clattered down the metal stairs. Not even Arabella could make the descent of those stairs seem elegant.

Gemma got out her own sketchbook and sat at the big counter. She tried to work, but the thought that she would soon be meeting Jono Knighton in the flesh excited her so much that it was almost impossible to concentrate. Suddenly, she just had to give in to the urge to have a little dance around the office. She sobered up and sat down quickly enough though, when Tina walked in. The last thing she wanted was to give Tina any more reason to hate her.

Gemma's jaw dropped when she saw the house on Kingston Hill. It was one thing seeing it in pictures in Zoë's magazine, but it was quite different seeing the real thing. She and Arabella and a mousy little woman, whom Arabella introduced as Pat Bain and who didn't appear to be able to speak more than one word at a time, had driven out of London in a car provided by the studio, which Gemma had thought swanky enough when they'd stepped into it. Now they were turning off the main road between Wimbledon and Kingston into this huge, sweeping, gravel drive at the end of which was a vast mansion, and the car didn't seem quite so swanky after all. Barely adequate, in fact. In front of the house were a shiny red Lamborghini, a large Discovery and a little powder-blue sports car that Gemma instantly coveted. Not that she didn't covet the house behind as well: a huge, perfectly proportioned wisteria-covered Georgian mansion, in soft-pink brick.

'You wouldn't get change out of about twenty million, would you?' said Arabella. 'And if it overlooks Richmond Park, which I would bet good money it does, I reckon you could probably add on another five.'

Gemma was too stunned to answer. She wished Zoë was with her to share the experience.

A short, fat, balding man opened the door, introduced himself as Max, and took their coats. He was so busy telling them how *wonderful* Rowan and Jono thought the script was and how *excited* they were about their parts, and how *thrilled* they were to be working with Butterfly, that he didn't think to ask their names. Gemma realised who he was from what he was saying and was rather surprised. She had expected someone representing such high-powered clients to look more go-getting. This bloke looked as if he wouldn't be able to negotiate a one-way system let alone a complex contract.

'Come in, come in. Jono's waiting for you in the snug. Rowan's getting dressed and will be coming down in a minute.'

Gemma glanced at her watch. Max seemed to imply that Rowan was only just about getting out of bed. Crikey. It was nearly eleven. Still, she supposed that if you were as wealthy as she was, you could do as you damned well pleased. Lucky old Rowan, thought Gemma with a hint of envy; looks, money, stellar career, Jono, this house, a decent lie-in every day . . . What more could a girl want?

A rustle above her head caused Gemma to look up. Descending the sweeping staircase that she recognised from the photographs in the magazine was Rowan, wearing a wonderful peach satin dressing gown. So much for 'getting dressed'. Perhaps Max should have said 'putting something on'. However, as dressing gowns went it was pretty spectacular. It was the sort of thing Katharine Hepburn had worn in the *Philadelphia Story* – very forties, very film star. The sort of dressing gown that probably cost more than the entire contents of Gemma's wardrobe. It was the sort of dressing gown that you didn't put on when you got out of the bath and were about to slap on a face mask. This was a dressing gown to make an appearance in, which Rowan was definitely doing – as were her endless legs, revealed by the split up the front, and her cleavage, exposed by the plunging neckline. In fact, there was very little of Rowan Day that wasn't making an appearance. *Wow!* thought Gemma, clocking the unbelievably pale hair that cascaded over her shoulders like a length of silk, and the peach fabric, which shimmered and rippled over her body and the stairs behind her, and which emphasised the soft, glowing tones of her skin and her wonderful, luminous beauty. She was so tall and so slim, and what a complexion she had! It just wasn't fair. Which was, she reckoned, exactly what Rowan wanted them to think.

Rowan reached the bottom of the stairs and paused for a second, just to make sure that her entrance had achieved the full effect. Judging by the look on Max's face – and considering he must have seen her make numerous entrances – it had.

'Hello,' she drawled, her hand resting lightly on the newel post. 'How lovely to meet you.' She paused, waiting for the introductions to be made.

Max leapt forward. 'Rowan,' he said, 'this is—' A flicker of panic crossed his face. He didn't have a clue what their names were.

Arabella stepped forward. 'Arabella Minton. And this is my assistant, Gemma Brown. And this is the maker who will be measuring you for your costumes, Pat Bain. We're delighted to meet you, Miss Day. A real honour for us all.'

No disapproving sniffs or steely looks for Rowan, noted Gemma, but lots of charm. Well, it was Rowan Day, superstar, she was talking to, not some underling.

Rowan, still standing on the bottom step, extended her hand. Gemma suppressed the urge to giggle. She might be as rich as Croesus and a film star, but royalty she was not. Gemma had a feeling that had she knelt, avowed undying allegiance to her and kissed her hand, Rowan would have regarded it as only as much as she deserved.

Gemma shook the proffered hand with enthusiasm and vigour. Judging from the expression on Rowan's face, she was more used to something much more limp-wristed. Gemma's urge to giggle got worse.

Pat silently stretched out her hand in turn but Rowan had had enough and returned her own to her side.

'Please, follow me,' she said as she stepped down to their level and led the way towards the back of the house.

Gemma, Arabella, Pat and Max pattered after her as she swept through fabulous rooms, throwing doors open as she went. Gemma tried not to rubber-neck too much. She wanted to appear blasé and sophisticated but she knew her eyes were out like organ stops.

Rowan stopped and her entourage skidded to a halt behind her. She threw open a final door with a flourish and paused dramatically. Gemma longed to laugh – her performance was verging on the farcical.

'Jono, darling,' she cooed, 'the costume people from the studio are here.' She stepped aside and Gemma felt the smile freeze on her face as she clapped eyes on Jono Knighton. Blimey! There he was. In the flesh. Her heart did a little series of flic-flaks in her chest. She had never seen anyone quite so gorgeous in her life. And even though she knew exactly what he looked like from pictures and films she wasn't prepared for the presence of the man. He had charisma and star quality and magnetism in bucketloads and Gemma was smitten at first sight. She knew it was hopeless, she knew he probably wouldn't even notice her, but she was completely besotted.

6

J ono watched Rowan make her usual entrance. He had once wondered why she couldn't just walk into a room like most human beings but then her larger-than-life personality had been one of the things that had first attracted him to her. He supposed that she could no more just slip into a room unnoticed than he could eat his own head. And her flamboyance and presence were part of the essence of Rowan – that and her outstanding beauty. With her blond hair and her pale grey eyes, which had a bizarre luminescence that the cameras just loved, she was almost beyond beautiful. Ethereal was a word that journalists regularly applied to her. Well, he thought, she might *look* ethereal, but underneath that fabulous exterior was a hard woman. Although, these days, she was brittle rather than hard, and she covered her vulnerability with rudeness.

He watched as Rowan stepped aside with a flourish, as though she were some sort of conjuror's assistant and a spectacular trick was about to be revealed. But instead of a trick, all he saw was his agent (definitely not spectacular, but he did quite often pull off magic with contracts), two middle-aged women – one rather well-turned out and one a wispy little mouse – then, around the door, peeped a young girl who was desperately trying not to laugh at Rowan by the look of her. And why not? Rowan had gone over the top, yet again, and apparently it hadn't impressed the girl. If Rowan thought she was playing the part of a magician, then this girl seemed to think she was more Tommy Cooper than David Blaine. Jono suppressed a grin too. How refreshing.

The girl looked across the room and their eyes met. Her expression changed in an instant. She straightened her face and assumed a studiously serious air. Jono had to suck his cheeks in even harder. He saw her eyebrows twitch up a fraction, as though she were challenging him to admit he was thinking what she was, too. He looked away. If he didn't he was going to corpse.

'Max has brought Butterfly's wardrobe department to visit us,' Rowan said. 'This is Arabella, this is Pat, the maker and' – she turned and gestured at Gemma to step forward – 'this is – sorry, sweetie . . .' She looked at Gemma, who was still staring at Jono and who failed to respond instantly. 'Name, honey?' she snapped.

'Gemma,' Gemma said, blushing.

Jono could see how uncomfortable Rowan was making them. Time to put these guys at ease.

'Hello,' he boomed in his best hail-fellow-well-met voice. 'Terrific of you people to trek over here just for us. We jolly well appreciate it, don't we, Rowan?' Rowan looked as if she couldn't be appreciating anything less. Jono wished that, just once in a while, she'd unbend a little when there wasn't something in it for her. She'd be just fine and dandy with the press providing she was expecting to be photographed or interviewed. She was great with the fans – as long as they didn't hassle her – and she could be good with other actors. 'You never know with whom you're going to share the limelight, sweetie,' she'd once said. But the industry underlings? The set designers and the continuity girls and the like? Forget it.

Jono had tried to explain to her that these people wielded quite a lot of power and were all involved in how she appeared in front of the camera – from the gaffers to the make-up girls – and if she pissed them off there were endless subtle ways they could get back at her. Light her less sympathetically, make her up less beautifully, style her hair less flatteringly. And then there was the industry rumour machine that all these underlings fed into and off. They all had their cliques and technical association, they met at the endless movie shenanigans and they exchanged gossip. And what did they gossip about? The stars. And stars that had a reputation for being bastards to work with soon found that people stopped wanting to work with them altogether. So word had certainly got round about Rowan being very difficult on set. Couple that with the business of the slapped director, and it wasn't hard to figure out why she wasn't getting the work these days.

Jono stepped forward, hand outstretched, and shook first Arabella's hand, then Pat's, and then Gemma's. Arabella said something banal about it being such an honour to meet him but when he shook Gemma's hand she just looked so happy he found himself grinning back.

She looked like fun. Probably no hang-ups with her. So stunningly normal – well, normal compared to the sort of people he mostly seemed to come into contact with these days. Just . . . really pleasant, and nice, and, well – if he were honest – pretty. Not beautiful, like Rowan, just girl-next-door pretty. He saw Rowan looking daggers and dropped Gemma's hand. He transferred his grin to Arabella, and tried to make it look like a general, welcoming grin. Rowan's face relaxed slightly.

'So, tell us what you need from us, and what you want us to do?' he gabbled to cover up his interest in Gemma. 'We are yours to command, aren't we, Rowan, dearest?' Judging by the look in her eyes, Rowan didn't entirely agree, but she had to be measured if she wanted halfway decent costumes – even she realised that. 'But first, how about some coffee?'

'I'm sure these guys are in far too much of a hurry to want to wait for coffee,' said Rowan.

'You're right, of course, darling. Max, go and organise some coffee would you, then we can drink it while we work.'

Rowan's luminous eyes went all squinty. She looked like a Siamese cat about to attack. 'If you think that's a good idea,' she said, making it obvious that she didn't.

Jono ignored her. 'Good, that's settled.' Max pottered out of the room in search of coffee and Rowan threw herself on to a sofa in the snug and held her head at an angle designed to catch the light from the window and to show her features at their most favourable advantage. In the golden spring light that streamed through the big Georgian sash window, she reminded Jono of the sort of reclining figure that you found in an oil painting – all pose and only two-dimensions.

Gemma walked over to the window and looked out, the sunlight catching her too and burnishing her brunette curls into a halo round her head. There was nothing artificial about her, he realised. Sure, she was probably wearing make-up, all the women he knew did – well, apart from Pat apparently, who just seemed to crave invisibility – but she hadn't been styled and groomed, nipped and tucked like Rowan and most of the other women he'd met in recent years. He cast a sideways glance at Arabella. And there was another one who had succumbed. He reckoned at the very least her hair colour was enhanced and he'd bet his bottom dollar that her smooth forehead wasn't the result of a worry-free life but a few little injections every couple of months. It was simply impossible to believe that a woman of – what, fifty-five, he guessed – didn't have any wrinkles at all on her forehead.

'Right,' said Jono, 'what's your schedule? I mean, how much of your day are we going to take up?'

'Not too much, I hope,' said Arabella smoothly. 'I am conscious of how valuable your time is.'

'You'd better believe it, honey,' snapped Rowan from the sofa. 'So get on with it.'

Jono sighed inwardly. It wouldn't cost Rowan anything just to try to be nice to these people. After all, they were here for her benefit. She hadn't always been like this. When she'd been starting out she'd been excited to co-operate and be polite, but somewhere along the line the stardom and adulation had turned her head. It had been a gradual process and Jono hadn't noticed the meta-morphosis until her spoilt behaviour had become so entrenched that she threw her weight around as standard.

Arabella, however, didn't seem to be offended. Maybe she was used to this sort of rudeness from the people she dealt with. Jono felt sorry for her if that was the case.

'Well, we could measure you separately. Pat and Gemma could make a start with Mr Knighton while you and I discuss the costumes for Martha. Then we can measure you while Gemma shows Mr Knighton her ideas for his uniforms. Would that suit?' she added brightly.

'Whatever,' said Rowan.

Jono felt the need to make up for his wife's lack of manners. 'Sounds a splendid plan. As long as it suits you, Arabella. I mean, you're the expert in all this, aren't you?'

'Good,' said Rowan. 'In that case, your assistant and the maker can get busy in here. You and I will go to my bedroom, where we'll be more private.'

Max entered with the coffee and put the tray on the table. They took a break while he passed it around, offered milk, sugar and homemade biscuits, then disappeared muttering stuff about phone calls to make.

Jono noticed that Gemma tucked into the shortbread with relish. Rowan, of course, refused it. How refreshing to see someone who didn't give a damn about all that calorie-counting crap.

He watched as Gemma returned to the window. He didn't blame her, it was a fabulous view. It was one of the reasons he loved this house. That, and the pool in the basement – oh and the beautiful garden. Rowan loved it because it was big and expensive; bigger and more expensive than most of their other movie-star friends' houses. And that counted for a lot in Rowan's book.

'Lovely, isn't it?'

He saw Gemma start. He hadn't meant to make her jump. Poor girl, he thought. It was probably all a bit intimidating for her.

'Yes. You're very lucky to live here.'

Rowan's voice scythed across the room. '*Luck* had nothing to do with it.'

Christ, couldn't Rowan be civil, just for once in her life? Jono thought.

Gemma spun round to answer Rowan. She looked confused and embarrassed. 'No, no. I didn't mean you don't deserve this. I meant that I think you're lucky because I would love to live somewhere with a view like this.'

Rowan gave her a hard stare and put her cup down. She appeared placated. Perhaps she was going to be nice to the girl after all.

'So where do you live, Gemma?' she asked.

'In a flat near King's Cross station.'

'Where the hookers hang out,' said Rowan. Her implication was obvious.

Typical, thought Jono. Typical. He turned away in annoyance. She could be so utterly bloody sometimes. Where had the beautiful, witty and talented woman that he'd married gone? When had she morphed into this rude, unstable and often drunk bitch? She was still beautiful, that was for sure, but her character was now warped and dark. Every day it was getting harder to love her and there were occasions when he wondered if he still did. He supposed he must still have some feelings for her as he worried about what she was doing to herself. She seemed unable to stop herself from doing things that were damaging her, and if only she could quit her habit of lashing out at those around her. Jono sighed inwardly. She wouldn't listen to his advice. It was as if she didn't want help. She accused him of being a patronising bastard and of not understanding her. And now, on top of everything else, her drinking had become a joke. Despite the fact that she was obsessed with her outward looks, she didn't seem to give a damn about her inner health.

He smiled at Gemma, to try to reassure her that Rowan's remark wasn't meant as it had sounded. He could hardly upbraid his wife in front of studio employees. He hoped Gemma understood. He'd have to make it up to the girl somehow; he'd be nice to her when Rowan left to discuss her costumes.

He took his hat off to Gemma when she answered coolly, 'Well, it's not the best part of London to live in, that's for sure, but it's central and handy for the Tube and for work.'

'Obviously.'

Gemma smiled at her tormentor quite graciously – as if she was flattered by the fact that such a star had condescended to talk to her. Had she not understood the jibe Rowan had just made? wondered Jono. Or had she deliberately risen above it? Good for her if she'd done the latter – it made her classier than Rowan.

While Rowan lounged on the sofa and sipped her coffee – her earlier observation that they were too busy to make time for it now forgotten – Jono returned his attention to Gemma. She was the complete opposite of Rowan, as far as he could judge. While Rowan was tall, slender, blonde and American, this girl was petite, curvy, brunette and English. And she seemed to have a lively sense of humour. Gemma turned round and caught him staring. She coloured.

'How do you see the character of Martha?' asked Arabella to fill the silence.

'Anyone called Martha is going to be a complete hillbilly,' said Rowan. 'Martha? I ask you.'

'It was a popular name at the time,' said Arabella.

'Huh. That's as maybe, but I'm not buying it. It sucks.'

Arabella looked a little flustered. 'Maybe that's something—'

'Maybe,' interrupted Rowan icily, 'that's something you can pass on to the director when you see him.'

'Yes. Right. Meanwhile, about the character herself—'

'Let's leave these guys here to get on with the measuring,' said Rowan abruptly, standing up. 'I suppose you've got some swatches and designs to show me?'

Arabella hastily put her coffee on the table and got to her feet too. 'Of course.' She quickly gathered her things together and raced out of the room in Rowan's wake.

Pat began to fiddle with her tape measure. She seemed to want to get on with her allotted task. Jono got to his feet too.

'And what about me? I imagine I'll have to have the uniform appropriate to my rank and regiment. I don't really have any views about colours or cut or anything. Just make it so I look the part. Oh, and don't make the breeches too tight if I have to do any riding.' He grinned. 'I know from experience the havoc skintight trews can play when you're on the back of some nag.'

'I'll make a note,' said Gemma. 'Right,' she said, putting down her own cup. 'How do you want to play this, Pat?'

'I'll measure and you can write down the figures,' she said in a voice scarcely above a whisper.

'Okey-dokey,' said Gemma. She reached into her bag and brought out a notebook and pen.

'Right, then we'd better crack on,' said Jono. 'Time is money and all that.'

'Well . . .' She grinned. 'I'm paid a lot less than you per hour, so if you look at how many pence an hour we waste in terms of my time, it's negligible – but for you . . . Oooh,' she glanced at her watch. 'There goes another thou.'

Jono couldn't help but be amused. And he was pleased that Gemma didn't seem to have been nettled into submission by Rowan's rudeness earlier. Spirit and a sense of humour. Great. He grinned at Gemma. 'Do you want me with my clothes on or off?'

'Off. Obviously. However, that's a question for Pat, so you'd better ask her.'

Jono couldn't remember the last time he'd had a girl flirt with him as harmlessly as this. His smile got even broader.

'Pat?'

'You don't have to undress,' Pat whispered as she unwound her tape measure. 'Now then,' she added almost inaudibly, 'if you could just stand still while we get going.'

Jono fell silent as they set to work: Pat measured his neck, shoulders, arms, back, elbow to wrist, elbow to shoulder, chest, waist, and every conceivable square inch. As she reeled off the numbers, Gemma carefully wrote them down. While she concentrated on her work, Jono was able to watch her unobserved.

He really liked this girl. She was the sort of person he'd love to have a drink with one day – just a couple of glasses in an out-of-the-way pub, to have a laugh and a joke and a good time. No strings, no complications . . . Ah, but what was the point in even thinking about it. He never seemed to socialise with people he really liked these days. Generally, he had to be nice to people he would normally cross the street to avoid. If he were still single, if he weren't so sodding famous, if he didn't get recognised everywhere he went, he would have loved to have asked Gemma out. But, obviously, it was a non-starter. Pat finished measuring and wound up her tape measure.

'Could you show me where Rowan has gone?' she breathed. She coloured and jiggled. Obviously, having to speak when not being spoken to was a bit of an ordeal for the poor woman.

'Of course,' said Jono and led the way out of the room.

When he returned, Gemma was, once again, staring out the window at the view across Richmond Park. She was so taken up with the beauty of the scene in all its spring glory that she wasn't aware of his return until he spoke, just behind her.

'I'm told you're the one who knows all about uniforms.'

Gemma jumped and spun round. 'I beg your pardon?'

'Uniforms. You know all about them.'

'A bit,' she said.

'That's not what I heard.'

'How?' She was perplexed.

'Oh, Max had to ring the studio about something and while he was on the phone I got him to ask about what the plans were for my costume. They said not to worry; they'd got a girl on the case who knew her stuff. Described you as a walking encylopaedia of knowledge on the subject. Now, I don't want to seem judgemental but, try as I might, I can't see anyone describing Arabella as "a girl".'

He could see her trying to look disapproving but the laughter won out.

'I suppose I am a bit younger than her.'

Jono's eyebrows hit his hairline. 'I think you're either being very sweet to Arabella or doing yourself down.'

She smiled shyly at him again. 'Maybe. But she's the one with all the experience and I'm the newby.'

'But you're the one with the knowledge about uniforms.'

'Yeah. Sad, isn't it? Comes of not getting out enough.'

'I find that hard to believe. You must have men queuing round the block to date you.'

Gemma frowned at him. 'Well, not that it's any business of yours, but I don't,' she said coolly.

Jono regretted his last glib remark. He'd overstepped the mark. This relationship was 'professional' and he'd just strayed into 'personal'. He decided to change tack. 'So, if you know all about uniforms, maybe I could come over to Butterfly and you could show me pictures of the options.' He hadn't really meant to invite himself over to the studio but he'd enjoyed her company so much it would be cool to work with her some more.

Gemma shrugged. 'Don't you trust me to design something for you that will be just right?'

'No, no. Not at all. It's just . . .' It was just what? That he liked her? He wanted to see her again? Obviously, he couldn't tell her that. She'd think he was mad – or weird. But she looked like such fun and, dear God, he needed some fun in his life.

'Well, then.' She paused and stared at him as if she was trying to work him out. 'Anyway, I've brought some sketches with me, so you needn't worry about schlepping across London. I wouldn't want to waste any more of your valuable time,' she finished lightly.

Jono nodded. 'Oh, right. Let's have a look at them, then,' he said, feeling strangely disappointed that an excuse to see her again hadn't borne fruit.

7

Jono was still staring at her. Gemma returned his gaze and was aware of an unbelievable chemistry. Her heart rate was going ballistic and her skin was coming out in goosebumps. She hoped to God Jono wasn't aware of the effect he was having on her. If he was, it might complicate things.

She took a deep breath and cleared her throat. Time to behave like a professional, not some starstruck fan. 'Right,' she said carefully, hoping her voice sounded normal. 'Let's look at those sketches.'

Jono nodded. 'Yup. You're right. We must get on.'

Gemma grabbed her portfolio from where she'd propped it against a chair. 'Here,' she said, as she untied the ribbons at the top. She opened it out but it was too big to handle comfortably. She rested it on the seat of the sofa. 'I don't know what you think of this lot.'

Jono came and stood beside her. They were almost touching. Gemma was incredibly conscious of his proximity. She flicked over the page to show him several sketches that she'd made.

'I like these. Fabulous,' said Jono.

'Well, you can't wear all of them. You have to pick one. That's how regimental uniforms work. You'll wear the same kit all the time – pretty much.'

'And what else might I have to wear?'

'Nightshirts, that sort of stuff.'

'I like that idea. A nightshirt could be rather sexy.'

Gemma wasn't going to be drawn on this so all she said was, 'Not necessarily.'

Jono knelt down to get a closer look at the drawings. Gemma, feeling uncomfortable towering over him, knelt beside him.

'What on earth are you up to?' said Arabella walking into the room. Rowan and Pat were close behind her.

Gemma scrambled to her feet, her face crimson. 'Sorry,' she murmured.

'Have you finished?' asked Arabella, closing a notebook she was carrying and stashing it in her handbag.

'Yes,' said Gemma. She noticed Rowan was giving her a long look from across the room. Gemma got the impression she hadn't liked the closeness of her husband to her at all. Gemma felt quite guilty, although the whole thing had been entirely innocent.

'Right, well, if that's everything,' said Rowan, wafting around the room and snuggling up next to Jono, claiming possession, 'you guys can go.' It was more of an order than a suggestion.

'Yes, thank you,' said Arabella. 'We'll be in touch about a fitting when the toiles arrive.'

Rowan let go of Jono and drifted out of the room. 'Whatever,' she said over her shoulder as she left.

'More coffee, anyone?' asked Jono, obviously embarrassed at his wife's off-hand and cavalier behaviour.

'We must be going,' said Arabella, firmly.

Shame, thought Gemma. She could have spent hours in Jono Knighton's company – and not just because he was a superstar. She really, really liked him. He was funny and – well, ordinary. Not the least bit up himself. Not like Rowan. And he seemed to like her. Nah, she told herself. He was just being polite.

'I'll see you out, then,' said Jono.

They made their way back through various rooms to the front door. He opened it for them and held out his hand. 'Thank you very much for coming all this way. Rowan and I really appreciate it.' Arabella took his hand and he leaned forward and kissed her lightly on both cheeks, before turning to Pat to do the same.

Gemma held out her hand and she felt an electric bolt shoot through her at his touch. And then he kissed her too, and his other hand, resting on her shoulder as he drew her towards him, moved slightly so he brushed the lobe of her ear very gently. She drew away, trying to convince herself that she'd imagined it. But perhaps she hadn't.

'Nice to meet you, Jono. It's been a pleasure,' she murmured.

'And for me too. I look forward to meeting you again at the fitting.' He stared into her eyes and Gemma stared back.

They stepped out of the house as the studio car drew up. Jono opened the rear door for them and Gemma climbed in first.

Wow, she thought, as she sat back in the soft leather seat of the Lexus, the whole morning had been unbelievable. And even more unbelievable was how lush and fit Jono was in the flesh. Just gorgeous. She'd seen him at the cinema, when in close-up his face had

73

measured about ten metres across, and you would have thought that having seen a bloke's face in that much detail, meeting him in the flesh wouldn't come as a shock. But it had. In the flesh, he was . . . Oh, she couldn't explain, even to herself. Yummy didn't seem right. More scrumptious? No. Knee-trembling? Better. And she wondered what it would be like to run her hands over his naked chest. What did Rowan feel as she caressed and stroked—

'That went well, I thought.' Arabella sounded less frosty than usual.

Gemma almost jumped. She'd been lost in another day dream. 'Yes, fine,' she agreed. She needed distracting from having more thoughts about Jono. 'Tell me, what was their bedroom like?' Arabella's description of the Knightons' boudoir was just the thing.

'Blimey,' said Zoë, her mouth open in amazement. 'And you spent how long there?'

'About an hour,' said Gemma, trying to sound blasé and failing miserably.

'So what's the house like?'

'Well, I wasn't offered the guided tour.'

'No? You amaze me.'

Gemma ignored the sarcasm. 'The bit I saw was unbelievable. The pictures in that article we read the other day really didn't do it justice. It's huge and almost all of it, everything, is white. You can tell they don't have kids. Can you imagine?'

'White? Just shows they have more money than sense.'

'I don't know about her, but I reckon Jono's pretty sensible. He didn't strike me as the sort to give a flying fart about interior design.'

'But he's a bloke, isn't he?'

'He certainly is,' said Gemma, dreamily.

'Oh, for God's sake,' said Zoë in disgust and envy. 'The girl's in lust.'

'Possibly. But he was really nice to me. Asked about where I lived—'

'You didn't tell him?' shrieked Zoë.

'Of course I did. Why ever not?'

'You did say you lived in West Islington, didn't you? Tell me you did?'

'No, I did not.'

'But Gemma, King's Cross is not a good address. Honest. Don't you want to impress him?'

Gemma regarded her friend sadly. 'Zoë, when a bloke is married to Rowan Day, it wouldn't matter if I said I lived in Windsor Castle or Tower Hamlets. Nothing I could say or do would make an impression on him for good or bad.'

'Yeah. Point taken.'

'Actually,' said Gemma, remembering, 'Rowan said something really bitchy to me today.' She recounted the comment about hookers.

'Ooh, mi-aow.'

'That's what I thought, but why? Why would she bother?'

'Maybe she feels threatened by you.'

'Me?'

Zoë regarded her. 'Well, both your eyes face forward and your features aren't too hideous. A bit like Shrek's missus, only dumpier – and greener.' She shrieked and parried a cushion thrown at her by Gemma. 'Seriously, I expect she just hates all other women. She doesn't strike me as the sort who would waste any of her energies wanting to make women like her. Why should she? If I looked like her and could have the pick of every available man on the planet – and probably most of the unavailable ones too – I wouldn't give a stuff about the feelings of other women.'

'Maybe,' conceded Gemma. 'And she was quite sharp with Arabella.' She felt disappointed to think that a star like Rowan could have feet of clay. What she really wanted to believe was that her screen heroine was like the people she had played in her films: warm, friendly, caring, the girl next door, the sort of person you'd want to share a pizza and a DVD with on a wet Sunday evening, the sort of person who would share their make-up tips with you and tell you if your bum looked big because they cared, not because they wanted you to feel bad about yourself. Sadly, Gemma had a nasty sneaky feeling that Rowan, judging by what she'd seen that morning, was really quite a nasty piece of work. Maybe what the papers had said about her recently was true. She really hoped she was wrong, that she'd misinterpreted the bitchy comment and Rowan's rudeness to Arabella had been accidental. She felt Jono deserved better. He'd been so nice and normal . . .

Then she remembered that Jono was an actor too, and perhaps he had just been acting at being nice and normal. After all, she was so low in the movie industry pecking order that she was subterranean. She sighed. She really needed a reality check sometimes. And now was just the right time for one. So what was the reality? Honestly? How could she have imagined he liked her? He probably behaved like that to all the young women on every film he made and she was just one of a long line of sadly mistaken females.

*

A couple of days later, Gemma was lugging several dresses from Butterfly's own store up to the costume department's office to make some minor repairs and alterations. The dresses were long and she was concentrating on not letting their hems get under her feet and trip her up, as well as trying to open a heavy swing door.

'Let me get that for you,' said a voice she recognised instantly.

'Jono! What on earth are you doing here?'

'Aren't I allowed to visit the studio?' He pulled the door open for her.

'I didn't mean that. Of course you can visit here.'

'So pleased to discover I have your permission. It makes all the difference,' he said with a grin. 'Without it, security would be hunting me down and throwing me out.'

'Don't be silly,' replied Gemma without thinking. She saw Jono's eyebrows go up. Girls like her couldn't tell megastars not to be silly. 'No, I mean you're not silly . . .' She felt herself flushing. 'Shut up, Gemma,' she added, shaking her head.

'No, carry on, please. It's a beautifully crafted hole you're digging. I like to see an expert at work.'

She smiled, the tension from her gaffe released. 'I've got a PhD in excavation. Do you want to take notes? I reckon I could even teach Prince Philip a thing or two about it.' Her arms began to ache with the weight of the dresses. She hitched the costumes up into a more comfortable position.

'Let me take those,' said Jono, wedging his foot in the door to keep it open.

'You can't.'

'Why not? Just because I get paid huge sums of money

to ponce around in front of a camera all day, doesn't mean I can't make myself useful from time to time.' He took the dresses out of her arms.

'But—' protested Gemma.

'But nothing. Where are you taking them?'

'Our office.'

'Then lead on.'

Gemma set off, wondering what on earth the reaction would be if one of the studio bosses saw her being followed by their biggest star, trotting along behind her like some sort of lackey. She hoped to God they didn't think the situation was anything she'd engineered. She led the way along the maze of corridors until they came to the big courtyard in the centre of the complex.

'You all right,' she said, worried that he was getting knackered.

'I'm not a complete wuss,' he said, looking aggrieved, although Gemma noticed he was panting slightly.

'It's just up here,' she said at the foot of the metal steps. She wondered what Arabella and Tina were going to say when Jono Knighton turned up in the office. The pair of them clattered up the steps. Gemma opened the door with a flourish and found the place empty. Typical, she thought. Tina's chance to meet Jono and she'd missed it. Well, tough. Serve the sour cow right.

'Thanks ever so much,' said Gemma turning round and holding out her arms for the dresses, but Jono strode past her and dumped them on the counter.

'Your servant, ma'am,' he said with a bow.

Gemma giggled. 'Hardly.'

'Don't you want me to be?'

'You're being silly again.'

'It's your fault. You make me feel young and foolish.'

Gemma shook her head. 'Only because that's what *I* am.'

'You wouldn't have this job if you were. I've already told you people at the studio think you know more about Regency uniforms than is natural for one person. "Young" maybe, but "foolish"? Never.'

'And, if you remember, I said all that meant was that I'm a sad case who needs to get out more.'

'That's the last thing I would think.' He stared at her for several seconds. Gemma felt a combination of bewilderment and longing under the intensity of his gaze. What did this mean? Anything? Nothing?

'Ah, well.' He looked at his watch and the spell was broken. 'And I am about to be late for a meeting.' He took a stride across the office to where Gemma was standing and kissed her lightly on the cheek. ' 'Bye, sweetheart. See you around.'

He left before Gemma could think of anything to say. A couple of minutes later, while Gemma was still standing where Jono had left her, stunned and bemused, Tina burst in.

'You'll never guess who I've just seen,' she said. Gemma thought she probably could, but didn't think it was fair to steal Tina's thunder, tempting though it was.

'Go on, amaze me.' She tried to look as if Tina had succeeded when she was told.

'The toiles have arrived,' said Tina, shoving open the door to their office and clumping into the room. She threw the uniformly cream-coloured prototype costumes on to the counter.

'Great,' said Gemma, getting up and moving over to have a look at them. She held up the toile of Jono's uniform jacket. It looked great. Well, as good as it could look given that it was made out of calico and not the proper fabric, and given that it was a bit creased. 'We'd best get them ironed,' she said.

'We'd best get them ironed,' mimicked Tina in an unpleasant, sing-song voice. 'You're teacher's pet. You do it.'

Gemma stared at her levelly. 'I will.' She took the garment over to the board at the end of the room and flicked the switch by the plug. She filled the iron from the kettle and carefully laid the toile out. She could feel Tina's eyes boring into her back but resisted the urge to acknowledge it by turning round.

She heard footsteps on the metal stairs. Arabella entered the office.

'Good,' she said. 'I heard there'd been a delivery from the makers. What have we got?'

'Jono's cavalry jacket,' said Gemma. 'I don't know about the rest.'

'Tina?'

Tina shuffled through the toiles, looking at the labels attached to them. 'I seem to have Rowan's ball gown, the rest of Jono's uniform, the Duke of Wellington's top coat and a couple of dresses for Lucia and Inez.' She named the two principal female villagers in the film.

'In which case, I'd like you, Tina, to take over the ironing and Gemma, would you get hold of the Knightons' agent and arrange a time for fitting.'

Gemma put down the iron and moved away from the board. She didn't trust Tina not to try something unpleasant with it if she remained in the vicinity. She moved over to the noticeboard where the unit list was pinned up. This was a list of everyone involved in the project.

'The actors and their agents aren't on that,' sniped Tina. 'Don't you know anything?'

Gemma blushed. She'd forgotten and, once again, Tina had been able to draw attention to her lack of expereince.

Jono was in Max's office, which overlooked Soho Square. It was a beautiful room – or rather, if it had been tidy, it would have been a beautiful room. But given that every square inch of space was covered in tottering piles of scripts, there wasn't much of the room's elegant proportions on view. He listened as Max finished a call from the film's producer and replaced the receiver of the phone. Max then mopped his forehead with a large white handkerchief while Jono sat in front of him, swivelling uneasily from side to side in a large leather office chair. Jono had heard enough of the conversation to know exactly what the situation was.

'Are you going to tell her or am I?' Jono said.

'She's going to be tricky about it,' Max said, 'isn't she?'

Jono whistled. 'Tricky? Christ, that's an understatement. Rowan is going to go ape-shit. Bal-fucking-listic.'

'Then you tell her,' pleaded Max.

Jono sighed. It probably didn't matter which of them told her that she was going to be called Martha in the film or they'd get another actor. Either way, she'd take it out on him later. Part of him felt sorry for Max; he wasn't paid enough to cope with Rowan's tantrums. No one was. Shit, even with the millions he'd got from his last film, Jono didn't think that *he* was either. But Max was Rowan's agent and it was really his job to break it to her.

The phone rang again. 'Maybe they've changed their minds,' said Max hopefully.

'Maybe it's Rowan wanting to know what the answer is,' said Jono dourly.

Max's eyes bulged at the thought, then he raised his eyebrows in supplication, his trepidation writ in capitals and underlined on his face. Jono grinned and reached forward.

'Max Samuels's office,' he said, bracing himself for Rowan.

'Can I speak to Mr Samuels?' said a voice that Jono thought was faintly familiar but which he couldn't place. Anyway, it wasn't Rowan, which was all that mattered for the moment. He grinned at Max who sagged considerably. There was a lot of Max to sag.

'May I say who is calling?'

'Gemma from Wardrobe at Butterfly.'

'Gemma, hi. It's me, Jono.' He heard a little squeak and a clatter at the other end. 'Gemma, Gemma, are you still there?'

'Sorry, I dropped the phone.'

Jono smiled even more broadly. 'Flatter me and tell me that I have that effect on you and it wasn't just an accident.' There was a pause. Max rolled his eyes. He'd known Jono since he'd been in a provincial production of *Oklahoma* when he was a shy and gawky teenager with galloping acne.

'I'd have to be made of stone for that not to be true,' said Gemma with her usual candour.

Jono reprised a role of an octogenarian he had once played in rep. 'Bless you, dear heart. You've just made an old man very happy.'

Max gagged and rolled his eyes even more vigorously. Jono heard Gemma giggle on the other end of the line.

'Don't be silly,' she said.

He resumed his normal voice. 'You make a habit of calling me silly. And I'm not, you know. I can be very sensible and grown-up.'

'I didn't mean that, I meant about you being old.'

'Positively antique, actually. Well, I am, compared to you.'

'I'm nearly twenty-three.'

'Exactly. A mere child. Whereas I am ten years older than you.' He saw Max eye him quizzically across his desk. 'Well,' corrected Jono, 'twelve, if I am being honest. So I think that makes me quite old indeed.'

'Hardly.' Gemma giggled again, a noise that reminded Jono of angel chimes.

'So what do you want with old Maxie?'

'I need to ask him when Pat and Arabella can come and do a fitting with you and Rowan and the toiles.'

'Just Arabella and Pat?'

'Probably. I can't think they'll need anyone else with them.'

'Supposing I said they had to be really, really quick. That Rowan and I could only spare them half an hour. Would they need another assistant then? You, for example?'

'Maybe. I don't know. I've not worked on anything like this before.'

'I've had heaps of fittings in my time. I know these things take time. Shall we try?'

There was a pause. Then, 'Why?' asked Gemma quietly.

Why indeed? thought Jono. Because Gemma had cheered him up no end when she had come to the house that day. She'd done it again at the studio. She was honest, open and guileless. God, he hadn't met anyone that natural in months – years, probably. And . . . and he just wanted to see her again.

But he didn't answer her question. Too tricky. Too many issues. 'I'll pass you over to Max. I'll get him to arrange a good time. And to make sure the fitting is done quickly.' He handed the phone over and went and looked out of the window. He looked on to the busy street below, but he didn't see the black cabs and people streaming past. He was thinking about Gemma. He supposed she was pretty in an ordinary sort of way: brown bouncy curls, retroussé nose, small mouth, pointed chin . . . a bit like a tabby kitten, he thought, and smiled. But not a cat, not like Rowan. His smile faded again. 'Cat' was being polite. He dragged his thoughts back to Gemma. Compared to Rowan she would be considered almost plain, but that wasn't what was attractive about her. Her face was alive.

Every thought, every feeling, was on display on her face. She was vivacious and sparkly. And Rowan? No, Rowan was too wrapped up in herself to bother with being vivacious and sparkly.

Gemma replaced the receiver slowly.

'Everything all right?' asked Mary, the production co-ordinator. She was printing off the latest script changes on coloured paper, ready for distribution to all the cast and crew. The first alterations had been on pink, the second on blue, and these were on yellow. Gemma wondered how much of the rainbow they'd get through before the film was finished. The system meant that when people were working from their scripts it was obvious at a glance if someone didn't have the latest alterations inserted. However, it meant an inordinate amount of paper, coloured and plain, was used and Gemma was still astounded by the amount that came their way every day, most of which was irrelevant to them and went straight in the bin.

'Yes, I think so,' replied Gemma thoughtfully.

'You just look rather shaken.'

'Do I?' She supposed she was. She had done a reality check a few days ago and had come to several conclusions, among which she'd decided that Jono was just being kind to her because he was nice and good mannered. If she'd thought that he felt she was someone special that was because she was naïve and he was a good actor. But that didn't explain his actions at their second meeting. He hadn't had to help her. He could have just said hello and whizzed off to his meeting. And now this. Again, he'd gone out of his way to make a point of grabbing a few minutes with her. It didn't add up.

She hadn't *dreamed* him inveigling the situation so that Arabella might have to take her along to help with the fittings. She hadn't *imagined* him saying that she had made him happy. *Happy?* When he was married to Rowan! God, most men would have thought they were in heaven if they woke up next to her each morning. How happy did he want to be? So why on earth . . . ? But then again, she'd seen the sharp and catty side of Rowan when they'd done the fitting. Maybe Rowan was like that with Jono too, and the gilt was peeling off their golden couple status. Perhaps, Gemma mused, perhaps he really *did* like her.

Mary didn't carry on the conversation. She was too busy and had returned her attention to her printing and stapling. Gemma was glad. She wasn't sure she was ready to talk to anyone about what had just gone on. She didn't even think this was something to share with Zoë. Zoë would either think she was exaggerating, or was making the whole thing up, or that she had got the wrong end of the stick again. Now she had started to think about Zoë's likely reaction, Gemma began to doubt everything herself – again.

She went over and over the conversation in her mind as she walked back to the wardrobe department, and the more she pushed her mental 'replay' button, the more she thought she must have misunderstood. She clumped up the stairs to the office.

'So, what have you organised for me?' asked Arabella.

'They can fit you in on Friday providing the fitting won't take more than half an hour,' said Gemma.

'Really,' said Arabella, clearly annoyed. 'There's nothing for it, then. You'll have to come too. I'll need you to help. I can't possibly get the pair of them in and out of

the toiles and pinned and fitted in that time on my own.'
She sniffed angrily.

Gemma felt a whoosh of excitement thrill through her.
She was going to see Jono again. Yesss! And he wanted to
see her. Unbelievable though it seemed, Jono had made
sure their paths would cross again. Gemma closed her
eyes and hugged herself. Jono Knighton liked her and
wanted more of her company. How fantastic was that!
Maybe he wanted to be friends with her and what fun that
might be. Her brain dived into a mad world of fantasy and
imagination where she was invited to his house socially
and got to schmooze other stars. How *Notting Hill* was
that?

Tina watched as Arabella and Gemma left their office, descended the steps and climbed into the car to take them to the Knightons'. She was seething. She would have given her back teeth to go to the Knightons' house and, if Gemma hadn't been such a bitch, she would have suggested that as she had already been once it would be nice if Tina had the chance to go this time. But no, Little Miss I'm-a-Regency-Expert was being a selfish cow. Again! Huh, well, she'd get her comeuppance. If it was the last thing Tina did, she'd show Gemma that she couldn't mess around with the established staff.

Ten years she'd been in costumes, ten years in which she'd worked and grafted her way up, and now Gemma had come along and shoved her right back down again. Just because she knew all about old uniforms. Like the public cared what the cast wore as long as they looked hot. Until Gemma appeared on the scene, Arabella seemed all right with her work but not now. Not now bloody Gemma kept pointing out mistakes, mistakes that only an anal anorak would know or care about. Tina ground her teeth in anger. Well, if Gemma made the least slip, she could forget any support. In fact, thought Tina viciously, if Gemma fucked up, even a tiny bit, she'd make sure everyone knew about it.

And it wasn't just the fact that Tina had lost her place in the wardrobe department pecking order: Gemma was meeting Rowan for a second time when she would like to meet her just once. *Once*. Was that so much to ask? She had dreamed about meeting Rowan ever since she could remember. She'd dyed her hair to make it the same shade as Rowan's, she'd studied the way Rowan did her make-up, she'd even copied some of Rowan's outfits. Rowan was the epitome of perfection as far as Tina was concerned and she longed to be exactly like her. She'd been a fan of Rowan's from when she'd been playing bit parts, from way before she'd made it big. Tina had always known her idol would make the A-list and she'd been proved right.

That said, Tina wasn't entirely sure that Rowan was right for the part in this film – much as it hurt her to admit to herself that her idol might not be completely versatile. But Tina felt that Rowan was wasted on this period drama. For a start, when Rowan was dressed as a camp follower in the film the costumes were hardly likely to enhance her radiant beauty. Tina envisaged Rowan as Natasha in *War and Peace*, or taking the lead in *Romeo and Juliet*, or possibly in a remake of a Fred Astaire and Ginger Rogers extravaganza. But disguised as a peasant? No way. Tina imagined the sort of costumes that would do Rowan justice – the ones Audrey Hepburn wore in *My Fair Lady* would just about fit the bill, as would the ones used in *Gone With the Wind* before the war started. But homespun and linen – never.

Tina wondered what it would be like to be in the same room as Rowan and then her imaginings got more specific and she wondered what it would be like to be Rowan's dresser. She imagined that Rowan would have the most perfect body. She'd been reading about Rowan's daily regime in one of the glossy magazines; how she worked out with her personal trainer every day except Christmas Day and Easter Sunday; how every mouthful of food that she ate was strictly calorie controlled, and how she never ate after six in the evening unless it was absolutely unavoidable; how she practised yoga to de-stress and never drank or did drugs to make sure her skin and her health were always perfect. Tina couldn't imagine having that amount of willpower. It just made Rowan's perfection seem even more unattainable to ordinary mortals. Of course, she'd read the libellous stories in the tabloids about Rowan's drinking but she'd dismissed them. No way would Rowan behave like that; she had far too much self-control. Perhaps if Tina got to meet her she might pass on some of her wondrous self-control tips to her.

Not that Gemma seemed to appreciate her luck at meeting this demi-goddess. She hadn't even said a word about it. And Tina wasn't going to lower herself to ask, despite the fact that she ached to know the details. But no way was she going to give the cow the chance to swank about her encounter. Tina snorted with annoyance as she gathered lists of required outfits together and prepared to go down to the costume store to make an inventory.

She stamped out of the office and thundered down the metal stairs. Shooting at the studio was due to start shortly and things were beginning to hot up. It would really go crazy once the filming did begin, but at least Gemma wouldn't be able to stop her from meeting Jono and Rowan then.

Tina, full of hatred for Gemma, stormed to the rooms

where the hired costumes were being stored. She pressed the right sequence of numbers on the keypad and turned the lock. With the door open she could see the collection of costumes in front of her. Endless rails of empire-line dresses and colourful military uniforms, top coats and cloaks were lined up across the room. Around the edges were shelves of bonnets and boots, reticules, gloves and fans and all nature of accessories and accoutrements to be logged, accounted for, dished out and retrieved. It was no simple task keeping track of so much kit and Tina was currently responsible for making sure that everything was ready for when the costumes were required.

She began going through the dresses against the inventory of requirements and sizes. When shooting started the extras would be directed to their costumes according to their size and height. It was Tina's job today to get the rails organised so that the extras could easily find a suitable costume. In subsequent days she would add accessories that wouldn't need fitting – gloves, bonnets and the like. When the extras finally turned up, they would then be measured for shoes and boots and each would be responsible for keeping their costume together and handing the complete ensemble back at the end of filming each day. Of course, when they got to that stage, she would have minions to help her but she had to get everything ready to rock and roll first.

As she worked, she pinned labels to the dresses and uniforms and moved them to other rails. The work was tedious but not difficult and gave Tina plenty of time to brood on all the wrongs Gemma had visited upon her since she had joined Butterfly.

A draught swept past her feet. Someone had opened the door. Tina stood on tiptoe to peer over the racks of costumes to see who was disturbing her. David, the production manager, had come in.

'Can I help you?' she asked.

'Hi. I just went up to the costume department, but there was no one in. I was hoping I'd find someone here. And I have.' David made his way through the racks, smiling at her.

Tina, still feeling thunderous, was disinclined to smile back. 'Yeah, Arabella's out. Gone to do a fitting at the Knightons'.'

'And Gemma?'

'Dunno. Hardly ever see her.' Tina didn't even bother to cross her fingers. So what, the cow deserved everything she got, including this blatant lie.

'Oh?'

'No, she swans in, does sod all and then swans off. *Research*, she says. Skiving, more like.'

'Oh?' said David, again. 'Arabella hasn't said anything.'

'Well, she wouldn't, would she? I mean, she was responsible for hiring Gemma. She's hardly likely to admit it, is she? She's probably hoping she can sort it out before it becomes too much of a problem.'

Tina knew full well what she was doing and who she was dealing with here. David was responsible for trying to bring this production in on budget and the thousands of pounds that Gemma's wages would cost the team over the ensuing months could make a significant difference to the bottom line. If she wasn't pulling her weight then he would have to do something about it. Tina watched his face harden and knew she'd scored a hit. And she also knew that however much Arabella defended her protégée, the doubt would remain in his mind. Gemma would only have to step a fraction out of line now for her job to be in real jeopardy. Tina had seen it happen before in this business and had no doubt that it could happen again. Especially if she continued to drip-feed poison.

Contrary to popular belief, Gemma was unaware that she was being talked about: she had no shivers, no spooky feelings of any sort, and her ears were a perfectly ordinary temperature – no sign of spontaneous combustion whatsoever. But maybe this was because she was waiting for Jono and Rowan to come into the room and she was ridiculously excited about it. Beside her sat Arabella, who was outwardly completely calm and relaxed, and across the room was Pat who was studying her feet and who had barely said a word since they'd picked her up. Both seemed quite unfazed, but then this was just another day at work for the pair of them. Gemma, however, was having to make a real effort to sit quietly and she was still having a problem getting her head around the whole business of working closely with stars.

Gemma couldn't contain herself any more and got up and wandered – she hoped, nonchalantly – over to the window that looked across the garden and over to Richmond Park. Below her was a terrace that caught the morning sun and on it were some sumptuous bits of garden furniture. Gemma wondered what it would be like to stretch out on the loungers and have your every whim catered for. She wondered which room was beneath the snug and opened on to the terrace. A swimming pool? A sitting room? She hoped it was a pool – it fitted better into the millionaire lifestyle she was vicariously enjoying. She imagined swimming a few laps and then wandering out to the garden to enjoy the sun. Oh, the bliss.

The door opened and Gemma spun round, almost

feeling guilty at the pleasure she had been getting from admiring the Knightons' fabulous surroundings and indulging in a little harmless fantasising. Jono and Rowan entered. Well, Rowan *entered,* Jono walked in perfectly normally. Out of Rowan's line of sight he smiled at her. She smiled back, telling herself that he was smiling out of good manners, that he was a kind man putting her at her ease and it was nothing personal. His smile flicked off as he turned and faced Rowan. Gemma took that as a signal to focus on her, too.

Rowan stood by the door and regarded the three women as if she was trying to make up her mind about something.

'You're the senior costumer designer, aren't you?' she asked Arabella bluntly.

'Yes.'

Rowan appeared to think for a few seconds more. 'Then you can help me into my costume. The girl can do Jono.'

Arabella nodded. She didn't mind one way or the other.

'And I've got another appointment this morning so I'd like to have my fitting first.' She swept out of the room again, leaving Arabella and Pat to rush around collecting up their bags and the toiles and race after her.

Gemma swallowed. She was alone in the room with Jono. Again. Blimey. Nervously, she picked up his toiles and the shirt that had been made to go under it.

'Umm,' she hesitated. 'Um. Could I ask you to change into this?' She put them down on the side table beside him.

'You certainly can,' he said, smiling at her. He undid the buttons of his shirt and shrugged his shoulders out of it.

Gemma swallowed again. Alone in a room with a half-naked Jono. Double blimey. 'Thank you. Perhaps I'd better leave you while you change,' she said nervously as Jono began to unzip his flies.

'I'm decent underneath,' he said, undoing the button on his waistband. 'I've got pants on, you know.'

Gemma could feel herself blushing furiously. She turned away and stared out the window, aware that her heart was crashing about in her chest. Her whole body seemed to be shaking. Good grief, in a room alone with an almost naked Jono Knighton. Wait till she told Zoë about this! This sort of thing didn't happen to kids just out of fashion college who lived in a seedy part of London.

'You can turn back now,' said Jono. She could hear the amusement in his voice. 'You'll have to pin these trousers, though. No fly buttons.'

Gemma came forward and gulped. She'd have to put one hand down the front – touch Jono – if she didn't want to prick him. She grabbed her pin cushion and took a deep breath. Tentatively, she pushed the fingers of her left hand behind the waistband of Jono's breeches and as quickly as she could, stuck a pin in to secure them. She looked up, relieved to have managed the job without mishap.

Their eyes met. Gemma froze, overwhelmed by his presence and proximity. Then Jono leaned forward and kissed her, very softly, on the lips.

Gemma jumped as a jolt of electricity sparked through her, and shot backwards.

'I'm sorry,' said Jono.

Gemma was dumbfounded and confused. This was all wrong. She gulped and tried to regain her composure. Now what? Should she pretend it hadn't happened? Get angry? Laugh it off? Was he serious or was he teasing? She turned away and fiddled with her pin cushion while she tried to get her thoughts in order.

'That was bang out of order,' said Jono, looking as confused as she felt. 'I shouldn't have done it.'

'No, you shouldn't have,' said Gemma, staring out of the window and wishing she was a bit more sophisticated. She didn't have a clue what to do and she felt incredibly awkward and embarrassed. She knew she was blushing again.

'I couldn't help it, Gemma, you're irresistible.'

No she wasn't. What was he on? And he was married to Rowan, who really was beautiful. But part of her really wanted to believe that he meant it. Not that it seemed possible. Perhaps he was lying or teasing or it was something he said to all the girls he came across to see if he could score. Maybe that was it. Whatever the answer, she didn't like it. She felt anger rising up. She spun round.

'Look, Mr Knighton, I don't know what your game is, but you're messing with me. I don't know if you find it amusing to lead on a nobody like me, but I don't. I don't have a clue what you're up to, but I think you're being mean and so I'm asking you to stop. Stop teasing me, or patronising me, or whatever it is you are doing. Please.' She felt quite out of breath when she'd finished her little speech.

Jono looked contrite. 'I'm sorry. I really am. What I did was wrong and whatever I say now – well, you're not going to believe me, are you?'

'Probably not, no.' Gemma took a deep breath. She needed to put this in the past and to get on with the present. She shrugged. Trying to sound calm, she said, 'This isn't getting the fitting done, is it?' She picked up the shirt and handed it to him at arm's length and then crossed her arms defensively across her chest.

Jono slipped one shirt sleeve on and then reached back

to shrug himself into the other one. Gemma saw him wincing as he stretched his arm behind.

She might be angry and upset with him but she couldn't just stand around and watch the poor man struggle. 'Let me help,' she said. She went round behind him and guided his hand to the sleeve. Blimey, that was one helluva bruise on his shoulder. And it looked like teeth marks too. She was glad she was standing behind him so he couldn't see her expression. For a sordid moment, she wondered what sexual antics he and Rowan got up to together.

'Pretty, isn't it?' said Jono.

Again, Gemma wasn't quite sure how to respond. 'It's certainly impressive.'

'It looks worse than it is,' he added lightly.

'Have you put any arnica on it?'

'Arnica?'

'Yeah. It's a herbal remedy for bruises. Works a treat.'

'Really?'

'Sure. You ought to try it. Although it works best if you put it on before the bruise really comes out.'

'I'll try some. And maybe I ought to keep some handy.'

'Why, do you bruise easily?'

'Not easily, but often,' said Jono with a grimace.

Gemma was out of her depth again and she pretended she hadn't heard the last comment. What the hell went on in Jono's private life? Nothing that was any business of hers, that was for sure.

She finished helping Jono into the shirt and then his jacket. She pinned the front of this too, but this time she stood a bit further back – out of kissing distance.

'Once bitten twice shy, eh?' said Jono.

Gemma ignored that remark too.

'Though I seem to be the only one to get bitten around here.'

Gemma looked up. She might have been deluding herself about a number of things regarding Jono, but the bitterness in his voice was completely obvious. Quickly, she looked back to the front of his jacket and got on with the pinning. She reminded herself that Jono's private life was nothing to do with her.

'Have you finished with Jono?' asked Arabella coming back into the room. 'Pat is just finishing with Miss Day. She'll be along as soon as she's done.'

'Yes,' answered Gemma. Completely, she added under her breath, and let's hope he's done with me.

Arabella mentioned that Gemma seemed unusually quiet as the three of them rode back to the studio in the car.

'Am I?' Gemma shrugged.

'Starstruck, I expect,' she said, smiling at Gemma.

Gemma smiled back. If only you knew the half of it, she thought.

Gemma tossed her payslip on to the sitting-room table.

'Get a load of that,' she said to Zoë.

Her flatmate picked it up and scanned it. 'Fuck-a-duck,' she said.

'Not elegant, but it just about sums it up.' Gemma tried not to sound too smug but it was tough. She'd been living pretty much on a shoestring since leaving college and now she was in funds. Serious funds.

Zoë fanned herself with the piece of paper. 'Not being mean, but are you . . .'

'Worth it?' Gemma raised her eyebrows in amusement. 'Yeah.'

'Don't know, don't care. But I tell you what – we're going out on the lash tonight. For months, I've had to be careful, stay in and watch crappy DVDs because I've been too broke to even think about having a good time, but not any more.'

'Yee-ha! Just us?'

'Don't be silly. Let's ring round the girls. See who else can come.'

The 'girls' were their mates from fashion college with whom they kept in touch from time to time, mostly by text – for cheapness. Mostly, the texts consisted of questions about employment or prospects that came back with negative answers. Of the six of them who had been almost inseparable at college, only Zoë and Gemma now had jobs they were both truly happy in. Victoria was working in a video shop, Freya was stacking shelves in a supermarket, and Danielle had landed a job as an assistant buyer for a chain of department stores – to the envy of all the others – but the chain had been the victim of a takeover bid, and she'd been out on her ear a month later and now, like Sian, she was on the dole.

'But they're all skint – like you were last week. Remember?'

Gemma slumped; Zoë was right. Just because she was no longer broke didn't mean things had changed for her mates. But she was going to have money for a bit, at least six months if the shooting schedule was to be believed, and life was short. Fuck it.

'My treat,' she said. 'Tell the girls that I'll pay.' If she wanted to celebrate she might have to put her new-found riches where her mouth was. Well, so what? And what was more, she needed to go out and not stay in and brood about the morning's events. Jono had said he found her irresistible. She couldn't get his words out of her head and she still couldn't work out what his game was. And, despite the anger and confusion she'd felt earlier, she couldn't help but be flattered, too.

Zoë was already hitting the phone and ringing their friends. Gemma watched Zoë as she began to spread the good news about her flatmate's largesse. She wondered about sharing her news about what Jono had said but something made her hold back. For a start, Zoë probably wouldn't believe her and even if she did, Gemma knew that Zoë would probably make some quick remark about Jono needing a carer or glasses, which would spoil the possibility that maybe, just maybe, he did find her irresistible.

Gemma tried to crush that idea. It was mad. He was married to Rowan. One of the world's most beautiful women. And anyway, even if he did find her faintly attractive – Gemma really couldn't quite believe that 'irresistible' rubbish – what would Rowan do if she got wind of it? That didn't bear thinking about and Gemma was pretty certain that she wouldn't take it lying down. Not if the bruises on Jono's back were anything to go by.

She went into the kitchen to make them both tea while Zoë continued her calls. As she waited for the kettle to boil and then the tea to brew, Zoë shouted updates from the sitting room as to how things were progressing.

'Vict is up for it. She'll meet us at the bar we used to go to in Upper Regent Street.'

'Great,' shouted back Gemma. She mashed the tea bags about in the pot. She let her mind drift back to the morning again and felt that sudden surge of heart-stopping desire when she found herself being kissed. Was it for real? Was he acting? Did he find her special? Or was he like that with every woman he met? She leaned on the work surface and tried to work it out, her heart thudding with longing. Supposing he *really* fancied her? said her heart. But that was absurd, her brain answered. He was a star and she was a nobody. Yes, her heart argued, but they were both people.

'And Danielle says she can come but she thinks Sian has gone back to Cardiff to live with her mum for a bit.'

'Oh, right. Good.'

'Good? That Sian has buggered off?'

'No – er – good that Dani can come.' Gemma poured in the milk and carried the mugs through. She put them on the table while Gemma finished her conversation with Freya.

'. . . Yeah, I know. Great, isn't it? Just don't get her started on the subject of Jono, though . . . Yeah, just don't tell her how envious you are.' Zoë ducked the cushion that was chucked across the room. 'Right. See you at about seven thirty. It should be a great one. 'Bye.' She turned to Gemma who was pulling a face at her.

'I don't bore for Britain about Jono – do I?'

'Not really. Well, no more than I would if I were in your shoes.'

Gemma grinned. 'So all the gang except Sian. Great. And I promise I won't say a thing about Jono all night.' No, but I'll think about him, she thought to herself. Think about him all the time.

'I should think you'll get lynched if you keep that promise. The girls have only agreed to come if you dish the dirt. Oh, that and offering to pay for the booze.'

The second bottle of white wine seemed to be dispensed with even faster than the first. But, thought Gemma, with five of them tucking in, it was hardly surprising.

'I'll get another,' she shouted over the racket of the packed bar.

'Don't you think we ought to have something to eat first?' yelled Vict, back across the table, leaning forward slightly to get closer to the other girls. The noise was deafening.

The others nodded. Gemma didn't want to seem mean,

but it was one thing supplying the booze for their night out, but food as well? She was going to be broke for the rest of the month – even with her fat paycheque – at this rate.

'We can all cough up for that,' shouted back Dani, to Gemma's relief. 'Dutch treat. Let's go and find a pizza or something.'

'We can have another bottle with our food,' bellowed Gemma, not wanting to be seen to renege on her promise.

''Sides,' shouted Vict, 'it's too loud to chat properly in here. Can't hear myself think.'

The girls gathered up their bags and grabbed their mobiles off the table – where they had placed them so as not to miss a call or a text, because there was no chance of hearing them ring in that racket – and followed Gemma out of the door. Giggling and chatting, the girls wandered along the back of Oxford Street until they found a cheapish Italian restaurant that fitted their bill. They piled into the place, called for a bottle of chilled house white, and rearranged themselves exactly as before; their bags on the floor under their feet, their mobiles close to hand – just in case a friend or parent chose to call or text.

'So,' said Dani, as they perused the oversized menus. 'What's he like? Is Jono really completely lush, or is it done by make-up and camera angles?'

'Wrong question,' said Zoë. 'She'll tell you now. Every pore, every hair follicle . . .'

'Like we don't want to know?' said Vict. 'And Rowan? Is she really that beautiful close up? Tell me she's got spots.'

Gemma stared at Vict who had flawless skin, long blond hair, and was no slouch in the looks department herself. What could she say about Rowan that was the truth and yet wouldn't make Vict feel like something out of a horror movie? How could you describe Rowan's beauty to anyone and not make them feel utterly inadequate? She was still considering when Zoë spoke.

'Rowan's a bitch.'

'What?' Three jaws dropped in perfect unison.

'Tell them,' said Zoë.

Well, that was one way of solving the inadequacy problem. Cut to the chase, why don't you, Gemma thought. So Gemma, feeling a little disloyal, recounted her first encounter with Rowan and the hooker comment. 'But I probably misunderstood her. You know, it's easy to do.' Three heads shook. 'But she *is* stunningly beautiful,' she added, as if this forgave bitchiness. And she certainly wasn't going to mention her vicious temper if her assessment of what had happened to Jono's back was anything to go by.

The waitress came and took their order, which caused a certain amount of hiatus as none of them had given a thought as to what they wanted to eat. Finally, the waitress left, promising to bring garlic-and-cheese bread and more wine 'pronto'.

'And Jono?' asked Freya. 'You haven't told us about him.'

'He's lovely,' said Gemma simply. 'Just nice. Sweet.'

'Sweet?' her friends chorused, definitely *not* wanting to think of him in those terms. Definitely not a macho thing for him to be.

'Well, kind,' qualified Gemma. 'I had to do his fitting today . . .'

Four jaws dropped again in unison. Gemma wondered if there was an event in the Olympics for synchronised jaw-dropping. Perhaps there should be. These girls would be a shoo-in for gold.

'What? You were right up close to him?' Vict swooned.

Gemma blushed as she remembered quite how 'right up close to him' she had been, what with her hand down the front of his trousers and then that kiss.

Zoë noticed the flush. 'I think we can take that as a "yes", girls.' She grinned wickedly at Gemma. 'How close, Gem?'

'Close. Touching. *And*,' she emphasised the word heavily, 'you have to understand that I was acting entirely in my professional capacity here – I had to ask him to get undressed.'

Vict pretended to faint and fell forward on to the table. Then she sat up a bit and fanned herself with her hand. 'Oh my, oh my. Naked. Wow.' She grinned lasciviously.

'No, only semi-naked,' Gemma corrected, but she wasn't sure any of them noticed. Just as well I've sworn not to tell them anything else, thought Gemma.

'That's so unfair,' said Dani from across the table. 'Did you pull your clothes off too, and offer him your body?'

If only you knew . . . thought Gemma. 'No. Besides, the door was open and anyone might have walked in on us.'

'You mean it was just the two of you. *Alone?*' squeaked Freya.

Gemma nodded. Keep it light and frivolous, she told herself. They'll never guess what really went on.

Her phone trilled, signalling an incoming text. She put her hand out to grab it but Zoë got there first.

'Could this be Jono wanting an assignation?' she said wickedly, brandishing the phone just out of Gemma's reach. 'Your phone doesn't recognise the number,' she said, pressing the key to read the text out loud. ' "*Got ur number off unit list im really sorry honest.*" What the hell does that mean, Gem?'

Gemma willed her voice to stay steady. 'Fuck knows. Some random who can't dial properly. Let's have a look.' She took the phone off Zoë and appeared to study the message. Of course she knew what the unit list was but she wasn't letting on to the others. Her heart was thundering as the implications of the text from an unknown number sank in. She swallowed and prayed her voice would be steady when she answered. 'Someone's probably got a wrong number. Load of rubbish, anyway. Unit list – unit trust. Probably some banker.' She threw her phone back on to the table, trying to appear casual, then hid her hands on her lap under the table because she knew they were shaking again. The conversation around her began to speculate about whether or not *banker* was an old cockney rhyming-slang word. The wine appeared and was poured out, which distracted the girls from the subject of the mystery text, and Gemma was able to withdraw into her own thoughts.

It had to be Jono texting her. Especially considering what had happened earlier? Who else could it be? Or was someone just mucking her about? She wished she knew. And how could she find out?

There was nothing she could do about it this instant. If she made the excuse of going to the loo right now and took her phone with her they'd smell a rat. Oh, why had she said they'd all go out tonight? If she was alone at home she could answer straight away. The conversation, like the wine, swilled around the table and the girls were too busy exchanging news and gossip to notice that Gemma wasn't joining in.

The waitress appeared carrying several pizzas at once

and the girls rushed to clear the table to give her room to put the hot platters down. Gemma used the opportunity to shove her phone in the pocket of her jeans.

'Just going to the loo,' she said, hoping it sounded nonchalant. The others hardly noticed her slip away. She shut herself in a cubicle and pressed the buttons to recall the message. She read it a couple of times. It could be from anyone. There was nothing at all to say it was Jono. But something was driving her to find out. She hit 'reply'.

Who r u. She hit send. About five seconds later the phone trilled.

Jono.

Gemma felt herself go hot. Then she pulled herself together. Bollocks, it was probably one of her friends playing a prank. But it couldn't be. If they texted her, it wasn't their numbers that came up, but their names. This message was coming from a number not programmed into her phone – a number unknown to her. Jono's number?

Y r u texting me.

2 say sorry properly.

She heard the outer loo door squeak. Then someone banged on the cubicle door.

'You all right, Gem?' asked Zoë. 'Just that we're getting worried about you.'

'Fine. Sorry, didn't mean to be so long.' Hurriedly, she switched her phone off – she didn't want it to keep on announcing incoming messages. The girls might get curious and she wasn't prepared to risk them hijacking her mobile again. She stood up, flushed the lav and unlocked the door. 'I just got a bit hot in there. Probably too much wine too fast. Felt I had to cool down,' she said as she came out and dabbled her fingers under the tap.

Zoë looked at her curiously. 'Sure you're all right? I

mean, if you're feeling rough, we can call it a day as soon as we've paid the bill. The girls have had a great time already. They won't mind.'

'I'm fine. Honest.'

Zoë gave her another hard stare. 'Well, if you're sure.'

Gemma caught sight of her reflection in a mirror above the basin. She was beetroot. No wonder Zoë was giving her the third degree as to her health. She splashed some water on her cheeks. 'Honest. Just a bit hot. Really.'

'If you're *sure*.' Zoë didn't sound convinced.

'Positive.' Gemma pushed her way through the swing door and back into the restaurant.

'We were just wondering if you'd done a bunk to leave us with the bill,' said Freya.

'Nah. Zo caught me going through the window and hauled me back. Got to be quicker next time, or wear looser jeans.'

They all laughed and Gemma's short disappearance was completely forgotten. In no time they were on to the next topic of conversation, which was which club they were going to go on to. Gemma's phone remained in her jeans pocket – switched off.

It was late on Saturday morning before Gemma remembered she ought to switch her phone on again. And even then the effort seemed almost too much to bear. Her head throbbed and her mouth seemed like the mudflats of the Thames with the tide out – sticky, repellent and possibly toxic. She suspected her breath was probably the same.

So much for Jono fancying me now, she thought. Jono! Those messages! She crawled out of bed to retrieve her jeans. She ferreted in the pocket to find her phone and pressed the 'on' button. 'New Message' flashed at her on the screen. She hit a button.

R u still cross appeared on the message screen. *U didnt answer.*

No, she sent back. She flopped back on her bed, the effort of having moved her thumb over the keypad having proved too great. The messages hadn't been a product of her drunken imagination after all. But, she reflected, it could have been someone else, purporting to be Jono, who had sent her several messages. Well, now she had been proved correct – she had had messages last night but, the thing was, had it really been Jono? Anyone could text back the word 'Jono'. It didn't prove anything. Except . . . who else felt they owed her an apology? Didn't that mean it really did have to be Jono? *Sorry*, she sent. *Phone died.* It was a lie but it explained her silence if nothing else. Meantime, she had to work out a way of confirming beyond doubt that it was Jono who was texting her. Until then, she was going to keep her phone switched off.

11

'Hiya, Gemma. You're in early for a Monday,' said Mary in the production office. 'What can I do for you?'

Gemma had been hoping to find the office empty if she got in at the crack of dawn. It had come as a bit of a shock to find Mary there when she opened the door so she had to think quickly if she was going to get the phone number she wanted so badly. 'Got a bit of a problem,' she lied smoothly. 'Arabella needs to get hold of Jono urgently about a fitting and his agent won't pick up his phone – too early for him, I expect. Can I have his mobile number please?' She prayed that Mary didn't decide to check with Arabella first before she gave out such information. Or offer to ring herself. She was relying on the fact that Mary was one of the busiest people among the entire crew and had virtually no one to help her. The phone rang and Mary picked it up, gesturing to Gemma not to disappear as she rummaged on her desk.

'Yes, sure, David,' she said, tucking the phone under her ear to free up her other hand. 'Yes, yes. I'm working on it now. Yes . . . Yes . . . Ah, here it is.' She fished a piece of paper out from under a pile. 'No, not you,' she explained to her caller. 'Just a mo.' She put the receiver on her desk and handed Gemma a sheet of numbers. 'And I want it back immediately after you've finished with it.' She turned back to her call. Gemma legged it before she got cold feet at her subterfuge.

She dodged along the corridor to the ladies' loo and darted into a cubicle. She got her phone out of her bag and pulled up the number the messages had come from. Then, having shut her eyes for a second or two to try to compose herself, she turned her attention to the sheet. She compared Jono's number with the one she had. They matched. Slowly, she lowered the sheet and the phone. So it really had been Jono texting her. She felt her stomach lurch with the shock. Shit. Now what?

She sat there for a moment or two while she composed herself. Then, making a decision, she pressed the buttons to save the number she now knew for certain was Jono's on her phone. 'JK', she typed in when it asked her who the number belonged to. Pretty ambiguous, she hoped, should anyone else get to her phone like Zoë had on Friday.

She switched her phone off – she didn't want any embarrassing texts while she was at work – then dropped it back into her handbag and flushed the loo. Hiding in bogs was becoming a bit of a habit lately, she thought as she unlocked the cubicle and took the telephone list back to Mary.

'Get him?' asked Mary.

'Yes, thanks,' said Gemma, trying to sound really casual.

'Good.' Mary shoved the list back in the tray on her desk and carried on stapling some papers together.

When Gemma got up to the office only Tina was in.

They ignored each other as usual. Gemma sat at her workspace and got on with checking lists of costumes received against what was still outstanding. Tina was rummaging around in their stationery drawer muttering about not being able to find any drawing pins. Gemma found a discrepancy on her list and, try as she might, she couldn't get the two lists to correlate.

'Bugger,' she said under her breath. 'If anyone wants me, I'm just going down to the costume store to check something.'

Tina looked up from her rummaging with her usual you-think-you're-talking-to-someone-who-gives-a-fuck expression on her face. Gemma shrugged and ran down the stairs, lists in hand. It didn't take her long to find the mistake. It was, as she had assumed, sloppy accounting; probably, she guessed, by Tina, but there was no point in remonstrating or complaining. It would bear no fruit and furthermore it would only make Tina even more bad tempered – as if that were possible. By the time she got back, Tina had disappeared.

'And good riddance,' muttered Gemma to herself.

'Did Arabella get Jono's fitting organised okay?' asked Mary to Tina when she appeared in the production office in search of some more drawing pins a couple of minutes later.

'Fitting?' repeated Tina, confused.

'Yes. She sent Gemma down earlier to get Jono's mobile number.'

But Arabella wasn't in yet and she hadn't phoned. So why had Gemma lied to get it? Tina was sure she was up to something, but what? She replied. 'Yeah, yeah. No sweat.'

'Good,' said Mary. 'Now, what can I do for you?'

'It doesn't matter,' said Tina. 'Forget it.' Getting another packet of mapping pins to shove some designs on their noticeboard with was the last thing on her mind now. She had much bigger fish to fry. She returned to the costume office and pretended to carry on with her allotted tasks for the day while she considered all the implications of the interesting little tit-bit Mary had let slip. The two of them worked together in their usual stony silence. However, while she mended and pressed, stitched, altered and made occasional phone calls to suppliers to wrangle about delivery dates, Tina's brain was obsessed with Mary's recent, casual comment. Why on earth did Gemma want Jono's personal number? And the more she thought about it, the more she found that only one answer kept popping up in her head. Gemma had the hots for Jono and thought she was in with a chance. As if!

Tina cast a glance at Gemma and wondered what the cow would do if she told her she had rumbled her sad little fantasy. Deny it, probably. Well, you would, wouldn't you? It was completely lame to think that a fit guy like that would go for a freak like Gemma. Especially when he already had Rowan.

Tina was besotted with Rowan: her looks, her figure, her hair colour were all objects of veneration for Tina and, as far as Tina was concerned, Rowan was too beautiful for any man – even Jono. Tina didn't like the idea of some bloke – even if the bloke was Jono Knighton – pawing and mauling her idol. There wasn't a man on earth who deserved perfection like that. And the thought that Jono would *ever* give up All That for anyone else was simply not credible.

No, thought Tina, there was no way Gemma's mad delusions would ever pan out. But the fact that they were doomed didn't excuse anything Gemma might have planned for Jono – like sending sad little infatuated messages. It amused Tina to think that Gemma might be stalking Jono by text, but what other reason could she have? After all, if it was a two-way thing and Jono had wanted to talk to Gemma, he'd have given her his number. But *that* idea was too ridiculous to even contemplate. Not when he had the glorious Rowan. No, it had to be Gemma being obsessed with him. It was like something out of *Fatal Attraction*. Perhaps she fancied herself as Glenn Close but, Tina thought, she was more like the boiled bunny – all big, brown, staring pop-eyes.

She wondered what sort of barking messages Gemma was sending him. What wouldn't she give to get hold of Gemma's phone and see what she was saying! The idea of getting hold of Gemma's phone gathered momentum and appeal. If Gemma was pestering Jono and if he didn't like it, it was all the ammunition she needed to get the snub-nosed weirdo off the film. Tina felt quietly smug as this thought crossed her mind. Gemma could laud it about all she liked for the next few days because Tina had made a small bet with herself that she could get rid of her before shooting started.

'I'm going back down to the costume store,' said Gemma.

And Gemma's point was? She wanted applause? Tina didn't even bother to respond, although her heart gave a little skip of delight. Maybe this absence of Gemma's was going to be serendipitous for her. She waited until she'd heard Gemma's footsteps go all the way down the stairs before she pulled open the bottom drawer of the filing cabinet. Yup, there was Gemma's bag. But was her phone in it? She cocked an ear to listen for anyone coming up the outside stairs. Sometimes there were real advantages to working where they did. It might be perishing cold in the winter but no one could sneak up on you.

Deftly, she unzipped the bag and rummaged through it. Eureka! There it was. She hoped Gemma didn't realise she'd left it behind and come rushing back. But just in case, Tina put the bag back in the filing cabinet drawer, gaping open so she could drop the phone in it and kick the drawer shut in a flash. Smiling at how clever she was being, she switched it on and got busy with the buttons.

'JK'. Huh! If Gemma thought she was being clever then she was even stupider than Tina thought. And who was JK likely to be? Ms Rowling? She found the text messages sent and received. *Got ur number off unit list im really sorry honest*, she read. She sat down and reread the message, stunned and bemused. But there was no doubt about it – Jono had instigated the texting. Christ, the man might be fit to look at but he was obviously blind and stupid. She looked at Gemma's reply.

Who r u.

Jono.

So if she knew who was sending the texts, why on earth did she want Mary's list with Jono's number if she already had it? So Gemma was ugly *and* thick, thought Tina. Poor kid, she really didn't have anything going for her. If Tina didn't hate her so much she might almost feel sorry for her.

Then Tina's mind went through the self-same process as Gemma's. Anyone could text the word 'Jono' – maybe that's why she wanted to check the number out. Hence getting hold of it from Mary this morning. Angrily, Tina jabbed at the buttons to close down the list of messages and threw Gemma's phone in her bag. She slammed the drawer shut with a resounding clang and flounced over to her space.

What on earth did a lush guy like Jono see in a freak like Gemma? And how dare he play fast and loose with Gemma when he was married to Rowan. Tina was almost throbbing with rage and indignation, partly with jealousy and partly on behalf of her idol. The cow waltzes into her job, she seethed, and goes on a fitting to the Knightons' that, by rights, should have been hers . . . Tina should have had the opportunity to get to know Rowan. She would have shown Rowan the sort of respect she deserved; made sure the measurements were all done perfectly. Gemma couldn't possibly be trusted to do it properly. Gemma wouldn't understand the importance. Tina raged inwardly at the injustice of it all and raged all the more when she thought of the phone and the incriminating messages. And then, *and then*, she gets Jono in her claws. Hah! Scheming little minx. Tina wanted to throw something, she was so angry. Arrgghh! She picked up the heavy fabric shears and stabbed them into the counter. She wished the surface was Gemma's face. She stabbed down again and again. Bitch, bitch, bitch.

'What on *earth* do you think you are doing?' Arabella's voice cut across their office like a scythe.

Tina dropped the shears and looked up. She'd been so mad with rage she hadn't heard Arabella climbing the metal steps. Tina felt the colour rise in her face and her stomach plunge with guilt. She'd been caught in an act of wanton vandalism and she had no excuse. Well, not one she could use. Christ, if Gemma hadn't . . . Yeah, it was *her* fault. She'd get her for this. She would.

'I'm waiting.' Arabella had her arms crossed and was tapping her foot. Shit, she looked livid.

There was only one way to play this, thought Tina. She lowered her eyes and hoped she looked contrite. 'I'm sorry, Arabella. I really am. I had a rotten weekend and then I had a message from a friend that their car had been smashed up and everything just seemed so bad. I don't know what came over me.'

Arabella came over and ran her fingers over the surface of the counter. 'You've made quite a mess here, haven't you?'

Tina breathed a little easier. She didn't sound quite so mad. 'I am so sorry. I'll go and speak to the chippy. I'll see if he can fix it.'

Arabella turned her attention to the heavy fabric scissors. The points were bent and ruined. 'And these are wrecked too.'

'I'll replace them. Honest. I'll go out in my lunch hour and get us a new pair.' And that's money I can ill afford, she thought. Another black mark she held against Gemma.

'Well . . .' Tina could tell that Arabella was softening. 'You'd best get along to the carpentry department and ask them to send someone up. But if they can't fix it properly you'll be responsible for a replacement. You'd better hope they can.'

'Yes, Arabella. Sorry, Arabella.' Three bags full, Arabella. I'm tugging my forelock now, Arabella. But as for you, Gemma Brown . . .

By the time Gemma got back, the chippy and his orbital sander had worked their magic on the big wooden counter that ran the length of the office. Apart from a faint smell of wood shavings, there was nothing to show for the previous incident. As neither Arabella nor Tina said anything about it – the matter being closed – Gemma was completely unaware that anything out of the ordinary had occurred while she had been away. It was only when she went to get her bag to go on her lunch break that a moment's suspicion flitted across her mind. She always left her bag zipped up, didn't she? She took it out of the cabinet drawer and wondered. But then the discovery that Jono actually had been texting her – not some random nutter pretending to be him – had put her in such a flurry this morning that she might have done anything. She zipped it shut and went to lunch.

Jono was pacing up and down the pool room in the basement of the house. Beside him the limpid water was mirror calm and outside he could see the team of gardeners making sure that not a blade of grass was out of place. Rowan, he knew, was being put through the mill by her personal trainer in the gym on the second floor so he was certain of being undisturbed for a while. For once, he was grateful for Rowan's obsession with her body: there was something to be said, after all, for being married to a woman whose only interest was herself. There was no way she would allow any interruption to her daily routine of keeping her body in immaculate condition – well, outwardly, anyway. Christ alone knew what her liver was like.

He pressed the button on his mobile to bring up the list of numbers. He paused; what was he doing? He was married and he was phoning another woman behind his wife's back and yet he couldn't help himself. He kept telling himself that he just liked Gemma. Nothing more.

That it was all innocent. Just good friends. But he knew, deep down, he felt more than that for her. And if he was truly honest, he felt a great deal more for her than he did for Rowan these days. In fact, now he was being *really* honest with himself, he felt nothing at all for Rowan. However, they were married, and Rowan had no one else to look out for her. She needed a responsible adult in her life and as her husband, it was his job. Jono sighed. It was a bugger having principles.

He scrolled down till he came to the initial G. He shoved all thoughts of disloyalty and infidelity to the back of his mind and hit the 'call' button. Please make her answer this time, he pleaded silently. All weekend he'd been trying to get hold of her and each time he'd reached her answering service. After about the fifth attempt he'd given up. Was she blocking his calls deliberately? Was there something wrong with her phone as she had said? He wished he knew. He lifted his phone to his ear and listened. At least this time the phone was ringing. Then he heard her voice.

'Jono?'

'Gemma,' he said with relief and gladness. 'Yes, it's me. Who did you think it was?'

'Well, this is a bit unexpected. I mean . . .' he could hear the hesitancy in her voice. 'I mean, this is all a bit surreal. I only found out this morning that it really was you texting me. It could have been anyone.'

'Yeah, I didn't think. Sorry. But it really is me. Honest.'

Gemma didn't answer.

'Are you there? Is this a good time to call? Can you talk?'

'Yeah, I'm in the canteen, having lunch.'

So that explained the faint hubbub in the background.

'That's good. Not that I'm interrupting your lunch, but that you can talk.'

There was another pause before she spoke again. 'Look, Jono, I can't say I'm not hugely flattered by all this. What girl wouldn't be?' She gave a nervous laugh. 'But you're married, you're a big star. I'm a nobody.'

'You're saying you don't like me.'

'Don't be ridiculous,' he heard her snap.

Jono smiled. It was a long time since anyone had spoken to him like that. God, Gemma was so natural. She was so refreshing. Not many people in the movie business were, he'd discovered. He bet himself that if he asked her about his films she'd tell him exactly what she thought. He didn't think she would say the standard 'Oh, you were marvellous, darling' comment that he got from all the sycophants that hung about the premieres and the studios.

'I really don't want you to think that I'm the sort of actor who just sleazes on to the younger crew, so I want to apologise properly for taking such an appalling liberty. I want to make it up to you, somehow. Take you out, buy you a meal, perhaps.'

'I don't think that's a good idea.'

'Why not?'

'For all the reasons I've already given you. Anyway, I never date married men.'

'Please.'

'Oh come on, Jono, think about it.' She sounded completely exasperated. This wasn't the reaction he'd been expecting. 'This really isn't on. It would just be better if both of us forgot all about it. Besides, I don't think Rowan would appreciate the fact that you're even phoning me, let alone anything else.'

'I know it's not right, but I just want to see you. Rowan and I are all washed up,' said Jono quietly. Since her last binge and subsequent fit of violence – the one that had left the mark Gemma had noticed on his back – he'd decided he had to get out of his dreadful marriage. But this was the first time he'd actually voiced his decision. Saying it out loud made him more determined to sort out his life and stop living a lie.

There was another pause. 'The "my wife doesn't understand me" line doesn't work on me, Jono,' she said quietly.

'No. You're too sensible for that.'

'And neither does flattery.'

Jono laughed bitterly. God, this girl was sharp.

'So,' Gemma continued, 'if you and Rowan are "all washed up" as you say, why do you stay with her?'

'Because I've only just decided to go. And no – it doesn't have anything to do with anything, outside the fact that she's become too difficult to live with. Trouble is, she's incredibly fragile. The least thing and she goes to pieces and then she is so wild, I can't cope with her. I used to love her but she's made it impossible for me to do so any more. But because I did love her once, I can't go till I know she's going to be all right on her own. I need to get her dried out. Maybe wait till she's found some other guy or her career gets a lift. Hopefully, this film we're both working on might do the trick. But I have to move on or I'm going to go mad.'

'If she's so very fragile, you phoning another woman behind her back isn't going to help matters, is it?'

'She doesn't know. She won't find out,' said Jono.

'No. Jono, as I said, I am *hugely* flattered. I am finding it very hard to believe, even now, that I am having this conversation with you, but this is going to stop right now. It wasn't such a big deal. Goodbye, Jono.'

The connection was abruptly severed. Jono pressed redial but Gemma had her phone switched off again. Damn, damn, damn.

12

Gemma stared at her phone. She couldn't believe what she had just done. Since when did girls like her tell superstars where to get off? She felt sick. Supposing she'd really pissed him off? That could be as bad as pissing Rowan off and could be just as fatal for her career. Oh, fuck. Why did this have to happen to her? Apart from actively going after the job, she'd done nothing to court any of this. Glumly, she thought of something her mother was always saying: 'Be careful what you wish for, you might get it.' Well, she had wished for a job in films so as to be close to some glamorous stars and to be involved in something she really loved but she'd never wished to be quite as close to a star as it now seemed she was.

God, this situation was such a mess. She had to admit to herself that she was amazed and flattered that he seemed to have feelings about her, but he was married! And if she saw him outside of work, what would that make her? Lots of unattractive names flitted through her head. Even if they just went out for a drink, as mates, could any encounter between them really be that innocent? And what if they got found out? What if someone spotted them? Well, her job would be a goner. Gemma sighed. She wasn't going to risk that. She'd worked too hard to get the job to lose it now because of a stupid attraction to a bloke out of her league, an attraction that probably wouldn't last five minutes after shooting finished.

She pushed her plate of congealing chilli away from her. At least Jono had called her at a time when she'd been able to take the call without being overheard. The canteen was always noisy and no one ever paid any attention to her, sitting on her own in a corner, like she always did. Tina brought in sandwiches – anyway, the idea of she and Gemma enjoying cosy lunches was just laughable – and Arabella had her own clique of friends with whom she ganged up at lunch. Gemma didn't mind. She quite enjoyed her own company and, besides, once the production really got up and running she had no doubt she'd find a whole bunch of other newbies, drafted in like she had been, with whom she could share a few minutes of conversation in the break. How tricky it would have been, though, if Jono had rung her while she was still in the office!

Rung? Gemma realised something with a shattering feeling of horror. Her phone had *rung*. She remembered distinctly switching it off before she left the lavs after programming in his name. And she had been sure she'd zipped up her bag, too. She was certain of it. She remembered quite clearly, now. And phones just didn't switch themselves on again and bags didn't unzip either. So who had been tampering with both? Well, there was only one answer to that. Tina. But why?

A cold, clammy feeling crept over her. Was Tina snooping on her? And if she was, had she read those text messages? And if she had, what would she make of them?

Between Jono fancying her and Tina prying into her private life things had taken a completely surreal turn. Maybe she would tell Zoë about it this evening. Perhaps a bottle of wine and some advice from her best friend would help things to become clear in her head.

Feeling sick with worry, Gemma returned to the office. She was glad Tina wasn't there, like she normally was, chewing on her sandwiches and oozing malevolence. The more Gemma went over events in her head the more she was certain that Tina had been spying on her. And the more certain she became, the angrier she got. What right, *what right* had Tina to do this? None! And how could she be sure, if the trollop had been in her handbag, that she hadn't done more than just spy? Frantically, Gemma checked her purse. As far as she could tell, her cash was intact, but Tina could have copied out her credit card details – anything.

Gemma took a deep breath. She was over-reacting. Getting paranoid and twitchy. And what good was it doing her except making her angry? It wasn't as if she had any proof. She just knew she was right. What a bitch. What a cow! She wasn't sure she would be able to stop herself from having a confrontation there and then. But with no proof of any wrongdoing it would probably only do more harm than good. The question now was, would she be able to get through the afternoon without taking Tina to task? She really didn't think so. And if she didn't, the rage was going to erupt out of the top of her head like it did in the cartoons.

In the event, the question didn't arise as Arabella took Tina off with her to Angels – the theatrical costumiers – to discuss shipping costumes to Spain for the location phase of the shoot. Just as well, thought Gemma, but it didn't lance the throbbing boil of her rage. She crashed around the office fixing fittings, organising shoes, ordering fabrics and sorting out the specialist to bring the jewellery to the shooting of the ball scenes. She tried to be professional and to keep her personal feelings out of her work but she was aware that she had been terser than was entirely necessary when dealing with some suppliers.

She was still churning with anger as she turned off the lights and locked up the office for the night, and she knew she would probably have to address the problem in the morning. Being so angry had exhausted her, and wearily she walked to the Tube and began her journey across London to her flat. She was so wrapped up in her thoughts that she was oblivious of the discomfort and crowds and crush. By the time she got to King's Cross she was still no further forward in her machinations: should she confront Tina? And, if so, how? Or would it be better to ignore the whole matter?

Feeling fed up, worried and tired, Gemma hit a local store on the corner of her street to get something filling but effortless for supper. A large ready-made pizza and a bottle of Soave seemed to fit the bill admirably. Sod the 'five fruit and veg a day' governmental advice; what she needed was comfort food. Besides, she reasoned, as she stood at the checkout, she was getting three in this meal – tomatoes, mushrooms and grape juice.

Five minutes later she was in the flat, with the pizza in the oven and the wine in the ice compartment of the fridge.

'How was your day, Gem?' said Zoë, coming out of her room on hearing noises around the flat.

'Don't ask,' replied Gemma, glowering.

'Let me guess. Tina, right?'

'In one.'

'She's a cow, so it's a given. What's she done now?'

'Nothing.'

Zoë made a spluttering sound. 'Yeah, right.'

Gemma decided that she was too wound up to talk about it just yet. If she did, she'd sound paranoid. She'd let herself calm down a bit before she spilled the beans to Zoë. Perhaps when the wine had kicked in. 'I don't want to talk about it – well, not yet. Later, maybe.'

'Okay.' Gemma liked that about Zoë; she didn't pry. 'Is that supper in the oven?'

Gemma, thankful for the change of tack, nodded. 'And there's a bottle of plonk getting cold.'

'Enough for two?' asked Zoë hopefully.

'Pizza? Yes. The wine? Not sure. Crap day. I feel like getting wasted.'

Zoë hitched herself on to the stool by the fridge. 'It won't solve anything.'

'Maybe not, but from where I'm standing it seems like a good idea.' Gemma flipped down the oven door and peered in to see how the pizza was doing. A gust of warm air, smelling faintly of cheese, wafted into the kitchen.

'Well, if you're hell-bent on self-destruction, maybe I should make a contribution.'

Gemma slammed the oven door shut and straightened up. 'In what way?'

'I'll get a bottle in too.'

Gemma was still in too bad a mood to be easily bought. 'Don't feel you have to. I'm quite happy going on a bender on my own.'

'Whatever. I'll go and get one.'

'Just don't go getting any ideas that this is going to be a jolly girls' night in. It isn't.'

But Zoë had already gone out of the door. Gemma seethed inwardly; not at Zoë going to buy booze, but at the general unfairness of life and the specific nastiness of Tina. Metaphorically, a cat was in danger of a good kicking.

Zoë was back in the flat, brandishing a bottle of cheap white, just as Gemma was getting the bubbling pizza out of the oven. Her bottle of slightly chilled plonk was already uncorked with a couple of glasses beside it.

'There's a bloke downstairs asking for you,' said Zoë casually. Gemma paused in slicing up the pie.

'What?'

'There's a bloke downstairs . . .'

'Yeah, I heard you. Why?'

'I dunno. Ask him.'

Gemma shook her head in bewilderment. This was mad. Who on earth would call on her? It wasn't as if she even had a man in tow at the moment – she hadn't for almost a year. And she didn't know any other men in London – well, none who would know where she lived. Of course she'd had boyfriends; loads when she'd been at college, but all except one had been very casual and she'd been happy that they weren't out for commitment as she certainly wasn't either. There would be plenty of time for that when she got her career sorted out. The one that hadn't been casual had been rocky, intense and ultimately disastrous and it had been Gemma who'd wound up hurt. She wasn't prepared to go through that sort of mill again. It had been quite therapeutic when she realised that at Sew Wonderful she was unlikely to meet any men as she needed time to recover from the last bruising. Her job now kept her so busy that she hadn't made the effort to get out into the marketplace again so, as far as she could see, there weren't any blokes at all who might make a sudden reappearance into her life.

'Well?' said Zoë.

'Well, what?' snapped Gemma. She really didn't want to be sociable this evening; she didn't want anything from the evening except a quiet night in, trying to put a vile day behind her – being polite to some random guy off the street was the last thing she wanted.

'Well, are you going to leave this guy hanging around in the stairwell?'

'Oh, for God's sake,' said Gemma, throwing down the pizza wheel. She had to do something about him. Tempting though it was to just abandon him until he got fed up and pissed off, she really couldn't. She strode out of the kitchen to the door of the flat and flung it open. The random bloke was standing right outside the door.

Gemma gazed at him. He was a nerdy, geeky-looking type with bum-fluff on his chin and thick glasses. But he was smart. Nice clothes, she noticed. But who the fuck was he? Oh shit, she thought, it's some God-botherer come to make her see the light. She'd show him the light, all right!

'Yes?' she snarled. The day was crap and now this. Per-fucking-fect.

'Gemma,' said the geek as if he knew her.

'Yes?' Gemma was perplexed; the voice was familiar. Where on earth . . . ? The nerd removed his glasses. Oh. My. God. Recognition dawned.

'Bloody hell,' whispered Gemma.

'Surprise!' said Jono.

Gemma felt her stomach lurch. How did this guy have such an affect on her? But she knew she mustn't fall for it. She had to make him keep his distance although her treacherous body didn't want to play along. Her confusion quickly turned to anger. She grabbed him by the arm and hauled him inside the flat.

'What the fuck do you think you're playing at?' she hissed as she slammed the door behind him.

Zoë, hearing the slam, appeared from the kitchen, plate of pizza in one hand and a glass of wine in the other. 'Are you all right?' she asked. Then, seeing the look on Gemma's face, she said, 'Hey, what's going on?' Gemma didn't answer. 'Gemma?' Her increasing concern was obvious in her voice.

'It's all right, Zo. Just an unexpected and *unwanted* visitor.'

Zoë put her plate and wine down on the small table by the kitchen door and came closer. 'Anyone I know?'

Gemma shrugged. 'Not really. Not as such. Zo, this is Jono Knighton.'

Zoë stumbled. 'Fuck me!'

'Nice offer,' said Jono, 'but not one I'll take up till we've been formally introduced.'

'Christ,' said Zoë, recognising his distinctive voice, even though his face, hidden by wispy whiskers, wasn't ringing bells. 'It really *is* you.'

'Large as life and twice as natural,' he said with a mock bow.

'And just as amazing,' said Zoë, awestruck.

'Amazing and *pushy*,' said Gemma. 'And about to bugger off again.'

'You can't talk to him like that,' said Zoë, horrified.

'Just have.' Gemma stuck her chin out. 'Jono, we've had this conversation about you and me. Remember what I said?'

'If I recall, you said a lot of things, among which you said you don't date married men.'

'Give this man a coconut.'

'I'm not asking for a date.'

'No?' Gemma's eyebrows were in danger of getting tangled in her hairline they went so far up her forehead. 'Then just what are you doing here? Stalking me?'

'Gemma?' said Zoë. 'I really don't think that you ought to talk—'

'Shut up, Zo. And yes I can. I can talk to Jono anyway I like. He may be a big star but he still understands English. And I told him to leave me alone only this morning.' A thought crossed Gemma's mind. 'And where does Rowan think you are right now?'

'She thinks diddly-squat. She's on a plane, flying over to the States with Max to discuss making a TV series with Magnum Opus Studios.'

'How handy for you. And while the cat's away . . . Is that it?'

'Please, Gemma. I just want to do something to make up for making you so angry the other day. Buy you a drink or a meal. Just something.'

Zoë's jaw hung slackly. She couldn't believe what she was hearing. Her mate Gemma was being asked out by one of Britain's biggest stars and she was playing hard to get. The girl needed sectioning – care in the community at the very least.

'Look,' said Zoë, 'far be it for me to butt in, but if you just want someone to go for a drink with—' Gemma shot her an evil look. Jono shouldn't be going for a drink with anyone except his wife. 'I'm only offering,' said Zoë, defensively.

'You're about to eat,' Gemma reminded her.

'It's only pizza,' said Zoë.

'Pizza!' Jono's face lit up. 'I can't remember the last time I had pizza.'

'Oh, for God's sake,' said Gemma, getting even more fed up. 'Some of us mere mortals can't afford caviar, you know.'

'And caviar is thoroughly overrated, if you ask me. But pizza? Mmmm – food of the gods. Especially with mayo and tomato sauce.'

'We can do mayo and tomato sauce with it,' said Zoë before Gemma had a chance to stop her. 'You can have my share. I can pop to the corner shop and get another one.'

'Do they do garlic bread too?'

'No,' Gemma said loudly. 'No, they don't. And I bought the last pizza. So there.'

There was a pause of a couple of seconds. Then Jono said, with a wicked grin, 'We could order in.'

'Great idea,' said Zoë.

This was the last straw. And Zoë was encouraging him. How could she? Gemma stormed into the kitchen and slammed the door. Hot tears were burning her eyes and she felt angry and betrayed. What was wrong with Zoë? Couldn't she see beyond her screen idol to notice that this was all wrong? Didn't she care that this man was supposed to be happily married and that he had no business pitching up like this? It was probably going to land them in all sorts of trouble. To say the least, if this got out, she'd be sacked on the spot. And the tabloids would have a field day.

And Christ only knew what Rowan would do. If she was as fragile as Jono implied then the consequences didn't even bear thinking about and Gemma wasn't going to have a film star going completely off the rails on her conscience. No siree.

It wouldn't be so bad if she didn't fancy him like crazy. She was trying so hard to be strong, so hard to do the right thing, and the pair in the sitting room were treating the whole business like some massive joke. But it wasn't. There was so much at stake and what she really needed was encouragement to resist, not the pair of them plotting a cosy little get-together. The tears spilled and slid down her face but she didn't know if anger, frustration or self-pity was behind them.

She waited a few minutes till she felt calmer and her tears had subsided. Then she wiped the palms of her hands across her cheeks to brush away the traces of how upset she had been and straightened her back. Her mind was made up. Jono was going home.

13

Standing tall and snapping her shoulders back to give herself an aura of self-assertiveness that she didn't feel, Gemma opened the kitchen door and looked out. She shook her head in disbelief. Zoë was offering Jono a bite of her pizza and his face was like that of a little boy getting a bike on his birthday – a huge gleeful grin was spread over it. Gemma felt like spreading the pizza over it too.

'When you have quite finished . . .' she said coldly. She was determined not to be swayed now that her mind was made up.

'Oh, lighten up,' said Jono crossly, his voice muffled by mozzarella and dough.

'I suggest you page your chauffeur – or whatever – and get him to come and pick you up.' Gemma was equally cross, if not more so.

'Come on.' Jono swallowed his half-chewed pizza noisily. 'I'm just offering you a drink or something. It isn't a date. It's just two friends sharing some time together. That's harmless enough, isn't it?'

Which it was, put like that. But Gemma, despite her recent resolve, wasn't sure that it would be 'just two friends'. Jono was far too attractive and charismatic for her to think that if she spent time alone with him she could stay strong. And the last thing she wanted to do was weaken. She – and he – had too much at stake. But, if she really, truly made up her mind to keep her distance, to be strong and to just go out with him on a purely social basis, what harm could there be?

'And if you're worrying about anyone recognising me, it's hardly likely, is it? said Jono. 'You didn't. The paparazzi aren't hanging around your door snapping your every move. And I doubt if the local watering holes in this neck of the woods are frequented by the rich and famous, so they won't be hanging around those either.' At this point, Zoë let out a very unladylike guffaw. 'I'll take that as a confirmation that I'm right,' said Jono, grinning. 'No one is going to expect an unknown girl – albeit a very attractive one – to waltz into her local pub with a film actor in tow now, are they?'

Zoë's eyes flitted from one to the other. It was obvious that Gemma was weakening.

'That's all very well and you're right, no one around *will*, in all probability, recognise you. But it's not just a case of complete strangers twigging what's going on. I've got a dreadful feeling one of my colleagues is spying on me. Haven't a clue why, but I'm sure she's been going through my handbag and reading my texts.

'I don't believe it,' squawked Zoë. 'You said she was a cow, but really!'

'Why?' asked Jono.

'I've no idea. None. But she doesn't like me. She makes that very obvious.'

'But that doesn't affect the here and now. Back to tonight.' Gemma wondered if he was always this persistent. 'Since you have admitted that no one round here will see through my cunning disguise – heh, heh, heh,' Jono gave an evil, pantomime laugh, 'there can be no more excuses as to why you can't come out for a drink.' Gemma opened her mouth but Jono held his hand up. 'And before you say "I don't date married men" again, this *isn't* a date.'

Gemma felt worn down. She'd tried, she told herself, she'd really tried, but honestly, it was going to be easier just to give in and get it over with than to keep on fighting him. And it would be something to tell the grandchildren. And he was hugely attractive. Well, he was when he wasn't looking like an escapee from the Rutherford Laboratory. And, deep down, she really, really, longed to get to know him better. She'd been replaying over and over the moment when he'd kissed her at the studio . . . And the kiss at his house . . . She felt her insides go mushy with longing at the memory.

But, meanwhile, back in the real world . . . She pulled herself together. She mustn't let herself fall for him or let him fall for her. Who was she kidding? He would probably be bored with her company after about an hour – they were hardly going to have much in common given the difference in their incomes and lifestyle – and then he'd never want to see her again. Except that he'd have to on a professional basis, but she wouldn't hold a grudge when that happened. So what if he couldn't wait to get shot of her at the end of the evening? It was to be expected really. Once he'd got what he'd wanted, an evening with her, and the novelty had worn off, that, in all probability, would be that.

'Oh, all right,' she said grudgingly.

'Yee ha!' yelled Jono.

Even Zoë bounced around looking excited.

'So where are you going to take me?' said Jono.

'Me! Take you?'

'Metaphorically.'

Gemma calmed down. 'Oh. There's a wine bar around the corner.'

'Does it do food? Pizza?' added Jono hopefully.

'Ah – no. Their cuisine only runs to salt and vinegar crisps. And pickled onions on high days and holidays. But there's an Italian not too far away. Their pizzas are okay, aren't they, Zoë?'

'Very nice,' confirmed Zoë.

'Hey,' said Jono. 'Why don't you come too? I think Gemma would feel safer with you around.'

'I don't think so,' said Zoë, although it was obvious to anyone she longed to join them. 'I am not about to start being a gooseberry.'

'But you wouldn't be,' insisted Gemma.

'Not at all,' agreed Jono.

'Come on, Zo. I insist,' said Gemma.

'No, I . . .' She didn't sound very convincing.

'If you don't come with us,' said Gemma. 'Then I shan't go either.'

'Oh, all right,' Zoë conceded, grinning broadly and grabbing her coat. 'Come on, Jono, you've pulled.'

The stewardess showed Rowan and Max to their seats on the top level of the jumbo jet and helped Rowan out of her coat.

'And hang it up properly,' snapped Rowan as the girl took it away. 'It probably cost more than you earn in a year,' she muttered as the poor woman departed.

'I'm sure she will, darling,' said Max. In the relatively

confined space of the cabin he could smell the booze on her breath. She must have poured a load of hooch down her throat before he caught up with her in the first-class departure lounge. He wondered if many of her fellow travellers had noticed how much she'd tipped back while she was waiting. It was the sort of thing that only took one video clip on a mobile phone and Rowan's reputation could be even more shredded than it was already. Studios didn't like employing stars who needed rehab, no matter how glamorous or famous they were. He didn't think Magnum Opus would be any different and Rowan really didn't need to be blown out of yet another deal.

'And when are they going to start serving the champagne?' she complained.

'Any minute now,' soothed Max, as if she hadn't had enough already. This had all the makings of being a long trip. But it was probably safer to keep her in booze now than to try to shut off the supply. He knew exactly what she could be like when she had too much to qualify as being anywhere *near* sober, but not enough to knock her out. The last thing he needed right now was for Rowan to throw a major tantrum in a confined space.

He risked a glance across the width of the cabin at her. She looked petulant – like a spoilt five year old about to throw a major strop. Muttering that he needed the loo, he eased himself out of his seat and went back to where not only the loos were situated, but also the galley. Checking, with another quick look, that Rowan was sizing up the quality, fame and bank balances of her fellow travellers and not watching him, Max cornered one of the senior stewards and explained succinctly that if she wanted a quiet and uneventful trip then a timely 'welcome' glass of fizz to seat 2A might get them off to a good start and save them all a lot of trouble in the long run.

'Mr Samuels . . .'

'Max, please.'

'Mr Samuels,' reiterated the stewardess, firmly, 'this airline has a very strict policy when it comes to the behaviour of our passengers and drunkenness is frowned upon. Are you suggesting to me that I should encourage Miss Day to drink?'

'Not encourage – she certainly doesn't need that!' said Max smoothly. 'How about we look at it rather as "humour" her?' The stewardess gave him a steely stare. She obviously thought he was pulling a fast one – or just trying to get more of his share of complimentary champagne. 'Have you met Miss Day before?' asked Max.

'I don't think I've had the pleasure,' replied the stewardess. Max noticed that she had a name badge that announced she was called Anne.

'I think, Anne,' said Max, confidentially, 'that "pleasure" isn't a word you would use if you had – met her, that is.'

Anne looked surprised. 'But aren't you a friend?'

'I'm her agent and that doesn't mean I can't tell the truth,' said Max with a broad grin. 'Now, if I promise to try to make her behave, will promise to help me?' He could sense from her body language that Anne was unbending slightly.

'It's not really within company guidelines,' she said with hesitation.

'Well, if I'm prepared to put my balls on the block by accompanying Miss Day to the States and making sure she doesn't disgrace herself or ruin the travel experience for all your other passengers, I do feel that it would be a terrific help if you could meet me halfway. I can only do so much,' he added, hoping he looked mildly helpless.

Anne opened her eyes wide and looked shocked. Max wondered for a second if he had overstepped the mark with his fruity language.

'I think that'll be very hard for me to achieve,' said Anne. 'Seeing as I don't have any. She smiled at Max. 'Balls to put on the block, that is.' She reached for a bottle of champagne and began to take off the foil.

'That's a shame,' said Max, relaxing, 'because I think you'll need them if you're going to be ministering to Miss Day for the next twelve hours.'

'Not if she passes out, I won't.'

Max could have hugged her, but instead, feeling that it might be construed as sexual harassment or some other PC crap, he just blew her a kiss. Anne winked back at him in return.

By the time the flight to LA was over Ireland, Rowan had her seat in the fully reclined position and was snoring gently and Max was able to relax over an extremely enjoyable meal of several courses including an excellent lobster thermidor.

14

The pizzas being munched by Jono, Gemma and Zoë weren't quite up to the same culinary standard as the first-class catering on Max's transatlantic flight but were, nonetheless, hugely enjoyable. Jono had wolfed his one down in record time and had then cadged morsels off his two companions using his years of deprivation as an excuse. Their fellow diners ignored the small group – they certainly didn't seem to recognise Jono in his nerdy disguise – and the only looks the trio got were from a few people who seemed to be wondering how such a weedy-looking bloke had managed to be out with two such very pretty girls.

The girls were obviously having a good time with the bloke, judging by the way the conversation was flowing. The quality of their banter was manifested by the gales of laughter that rocked the table's occupants every few minutes. The slightly plumper one of the two girls seemed to dominate the conversation for a while and if any of their neighbours in the pizzeria had listened, they would have discovered that she was able to make the business of selling fabrics and haberdashery funny.

In exchange for a sizable portion of the girls' food, Jono in turn made them roar with laughter at his imitations of various megastars with whom he had come into contact over the years.

'I can't believe', said Gemma, wiping tears from her eyes after a particularly cruel but funny bit of mimicry, 'that he is really that camp. The guy always comes over as *so* butch! Incredibly macho.'

Jono's wrist flopped. 'But that's what acting', he said in a voice that spookily resembled Kenny Everett's Cupid Stunt, 'is all about – hiding the real me from my fans. Anyway, it's all done in the best possible taste.' The girls fell about.

'So, who is the real you?' asked Gemma, straightening her face.

'This one,' answered Jono, looking Gemma straight in the eye. He would quite like to be on his own with Gemma now. Zoë's presence had served it's purpose; Gemma had relaxed, had stopped seeing him as some sort of Casanova intent on cutting another notch on his bed post, and he wanted a chance to get to know her properly. He'd thought for a fleeting second that perhaps she wanted to get to know him, too.

'I can't see why, just because Rowan doesn't like to eat pizza, you have to suffer,' said Zoë, realising that Jono had eaten rather more of her pizza than she'd intended and completely missing the momentary intimacy between Jono and Gemma. And with her comment the intimacy was gone.

'Yeah, well. Let's just call it family solidarity. And the thing is,' said Jono. 'I think she *would* like to eat pizza and it's easier for her if I don't.'

'Blimey,' said Gemma, 'I don't think I could be that self-sacrificing for anyone.'

Jono was just finishing up the last of the cheesy garlic bread and eyeing the dessert menu hopefully when Zoë's mobile rang.

''Scuse me,' she apologised as she fished it out of her pocket. She glanced at the number and frowned, then pressed the button to take the call. 'Hello? Yes . . . Yes, of course . . . Can't you? Damn.' She glanced apologetically at her dinner companions. 'Okay . . . I'll be there in about twenty minutes. See you there.' She severed the connection. 'Sodding alarms.'

'What's the matter?' said Gemma.

'The flaming shop alarm has been triggered. The cops can't get hold of Jean and, as the other keyholder, they want me over there to check the premises and to switch the bloody thing off. How fucking typical; tonight of all nights.'

'Is the shop far?' asked Jono. 'I have a car on call. Shall I page the driver?'

Zoë looked up gleefully, her irritation at having to trek over to Sew Wonderful now subsumed by her delight at a ride in Jono's limo. 'Cor, that would be fab!'

Jono whipped out his mobile and made a swift call. 'What's the address of this place?' he asked, holding his phone away from his mouth. 'And the shop Zoë has to go to?' Gemma told him and he relayed it. 'The driver will be here in about five minutes. And I wouldn't get excited, the car is nothing special. It's from a cab firm I use because it's discreet.'

Zoë's smile faded rather. Ah well, a cab would be better than walking. 'That's okay,' she said. 'But a cab? Don't the drivers recognise you?'

'Yup, but it's not a problem. I'm a customer like anyone else. They drive all sorts. Now, Zoë, I don't wish to get rid of you, but I suggest you go and get your coat so you're ready for the car. Parking doesn't look much of an option round here. It might be helpful if you were ready and waiting for him.'

Zoë nodded in agreement. 'And get the driver to drop you back at the flat. I should imagine we'll have finished here by the time you're done,' added Gemma.

Zoë bounced off, still looking remarkably pleased for someone who had been called away from a meal with a film star by the police.

'So,' said Jono, 'where were we?'

'You were about to order a pud,' said Gemma.

Jono pulled the menu towards him and quickly scanned it. 'Actually, I have a much better idea. How about we cut straight to coffee?'

'Sounds good to me,' said Gemma. 'I'd love a cappuccino.'

'I was thinking that you could make coffee back at your place.'

Gemma rested her elbows on the table, clasped her hands, and lent her chin on them. She stared across the table at Jono.

'Is that wise?' she asked.

'No,' said Jono cheerfully. 'I've had a great evening, the food was fab, but the ambience . . .' he waved a hand at his surroundings. 'I mean, it's hardly intimate, is it?'

'No,' agreed Gemma. 'That's what I find rather reassuring.'

'I won't jump on you, if that's what you're worried about.'

For some curious reason, Gemma found herself experiencing a feeling of disappointment. She hoped it didn't show. 'Good,' she said lightly. 'Nothing worse than having a bloke think of you like some sort of trampette.'

'Trampette? Is that a bijou tramp? A tramp that's only a bit homeless and quite fragrant? Or,' Jono was warming to his subject, 'when applied to the female of the species, one who is only partially free with her favours and just a little slutty?'

Gemma found herself smiling against her will. 'Well, thanks very much.' She tried to sound cross and knew she'd failed miserably. 'On balance, then, I think I'll be fragrant and homeless.'

'Sure?'

Gemma nodded, laughter bubbling up inside her.

'I'll get the bill, then,' said Jono.

'Do I look like I'm going to fight you for it?' asked Gemma.

'Oooh,' said Jono. 'Wrestling. Now there's a thought.'

Gemma shook her head. This bloke was incorrigible. 'I didn't say anything about wrestling.'

Jono signalled to a waiter to bring the bill.

The waiter brought it and disappeared discreetly. Jono glanced at it, whistled, and took a couple of notes out of his wallet.

'Was it horribly expensive?' asked Gemma.

Jono looked at her with a puzzled smile on his face. 'Expensive? Shit, no. I've spent more than that on tea at the Ritz.' Then he coloured slightly. 'Sorry, that sounded incredibly big-headed. I didn't mean it to. I haven't eaten food that I've enjoyed quite so much, in company that was quite such fun for so little cost since . . . I can't remember that far back.'

'I wouldn't worry about it,' said Gemma soothingly. 'A lot of people have a problem with their memories as they get older.'

Jono grinned. 'I asked for that. Now about that coffee.'

'All right,' said Gemma. 'Seeing as Zoë and your car should be arriving back at the flat in the not-too-distant future. But it's just coffee. Understand?'

'Crystal,' said Jono, grinning.

Gemma grinned back. She seemed pleased and happy to be spending time in his company, thought Jono. He didn't want to spoil it by making any sudden move so, as they walked back along the street to Gemma's flat, Jono resisted the temptation to take Gemma's hand and made sure he didn't crowd her on the pavement. The last thing he wanted to do was ruin what they now had by pressuring her. He wondered, as he walked, how he was going to convince Gemma that his marriage to Rowan was now meaningless. In fact, it was worse than meaningless, it had degenerated into a hideous nightmare.

Jono sighed quietly to himself as they walked along the pavement in amicable silence.

'Penny for them,' said Gemma.

'Not worth that.' He grinned at her; he didn't want to ruin the light-hearted mood with any hint that he had other worries.

Gemma let them into the block and ran up the stairs ahead of him to unlock the door.

'Sorry it's not more luxurious,' she said, eyeing the cramped space and clutter with outsider's eyes. Basic didn't even come close – and compared to his fabulous mansion on Kingston Hill, well . . . The paint was grubby, the carpet worse and horribly worn as well, the windows were grimy, the sofa clearly needed replacing and she couldn't even bear to think about the stained bath and the dated kitchen. Still, it wasn't as if he hadn't already clapped eyes on the place once that day, only then she'd been so taken aback by his presence that she hadn't thought about what a come-down their flat was for him.

Jono glanced about him. 'I haven't always been rich, you know. When I started out as an actor, the digs I lived in were far worse than this.'

It was Gemma's turn to raise an eyebrow.

'They were,' protested Jono. 'You have no idea how grim some theatrical digs can be.'

'I believe you,' said Gemma, but Jono could tell from the tone of her voice that she didn't.

She bustled into the kitchen and began to get out mugs and milk and fill the kettle with water.

'Sugar?' she called through to him.

'Please.' Jono moved over to the door to the kitchen.

'Don't come in here,' said Gemma, catching sight of him watching her. 'Max'd have a fit at the thought of his client putting his life in mortal danger. There are probably more bugs in this kitchen than in an NHS hospital – and that's saying something.'

'I reckon my immune system can cope with the bugs. It's you I don't seem to be able to shake off.'

Gemma felt her stomach flutter but desperately tried to keep it light. She snorted crossly. 'That makes me sound as though I'm a nasty virus; that I'm the one doing the clinging. I think we've established that I don't . . .'

'Yeah, yeah,' said Jono. 'I know. You don't date married men. But the truth is, Gemma, I just can't get you out of my mind.'

Gemma rested her hands on the work surface and took a deep breath. Jono moved forward to put his arms around her.

'No,' she yelped.

Jono backed off. 'What's the matter? I'm not going to hurt you.'

Gemma shook her head. 'It's not that.' She turned round to face him. 'Look, I have a real problem with all of this.' She held a hand up to stop Jono from interrupting her. 'It isn't just Rowan. It's you. I said it on Friday and I meant it. Guys like you don't go around dating girls like me. And I'm scared that I'm the one who is going to end up a mess. The last man I went out with made all sorts of promises but then dumped me because he found out my dad's a docker.' She stared belligerently at Jono as if daring him to make a comment. 'My background wasn't good enough for him. So, do you see why I can't get my head around this and why I'm scared? I'm scared that you're acting, that this is just a part you're playing. And if it isn't, I'm scared that if I let myself, I'm going to fall for you. It would be so easy.' She smiled hesitantly and Jono wanted to fold her in his arms and kiss her face all over. 'But I just know I'd be the one who'd end up getting hurt – again. It might work in films like *Notting Hill*, but I don't think it does in real life. Our worlds are poles apart.'

'They're not so different, really. My folks weren't swanky. And now it just comes down to money.'

Gemma snorted. 'When you don't have much of it, it makes a *real* difference, believe me.'

'I keep telling you that I know what being broke is like. And it's not so long ago that I was in rep and earning buttons and so skint I could afford either supper or a drink after the show but not both. And what's more, it wouldn't surprise me if I didn't wind up broke again one day. I am sure that someone is going to rumble me one day soon; work out that I can't act, that I'm not worth the money, that my looks are nothing to write home about. Oh, and my breath smells so the leading ladies don't want to kiss me.'

'I can't make a judgement on the first three of your worries but the last one . . . Your breath is fine,' said Gemma.

'Are you sure?' said Jono, moving a fraction closer.

'Positive.'

He leaned in and their lips met. He felt Gemma jump very slightly as he touched her, then she relaxed and let her body rest against his. He circled his arms around her and gently probed his tongue against her mouth. Her lips parted and he kissed her long and deep. She tasted clean and sweet and he let his tongue slick across her teeth and explore her mouth. He heard her give a little sigh and felt desire pulse through his blood. He could feel her heart drumming and he could sense that she was feeling the same.

'My God, Gemma, I have wanted to kiss you like this from the moment you first walked into the snug at home. You are just so fresh and pretty and natural. So unlike the painted fakes I spend my life around.'

She drew away from him fractionally. 'This is wrong. So wrong,' she murmured. 'I'm breaking all the rules.'

'What rules? How can rules apply when it all feels so right?' said Jono gently. And he kissed her again.

Rowan stirred in her bed in first class. She remembered reclining the seat and snuggling down but not asking for a duvet, nor putting it over herself or loosening her jacket. The sour-faced stewardess must have sorted her out. Or possibly Max. For an agent, he had his uses, she thought. She pressed the button to ease the seat semi-upright but her head pounded. She winced. Fucking cheap champagne! That had to be it. Of course she hadn't had too much to drink, she told herself, certainly not enough to merit a hangover like this. No siree. And you'd think that at these ridiculous prices, the airline would at least have the courtesy to provide bubbly that didn't leave you feeling lousy after just a few glasses. Rowan sighed angrily. She'd write and complain.

She pressed the call button for the stewardess then tapped her fingers angrily for the five seconds it took the girl to appear.

'I'd like my dinner now. And take this away.' Rowan plucked ineffectively at the duvet over her, as if she didn't have the strength to lift it off herself.

The stewardess, the one whom Rowan thought was sour-faced, gathered up the bulky bedding. 'Would you like a blanket instead, for your knees? You may find the cabin temperature just a little chill.'

'Yes. That would be nice.' But Rowan said the pleasantry without smiling.

'I'll bring you the menu as well.'

'Do.' Rowan shot her an icy smile. 'And the wine list.' A hair of the dog was what was needed. She reached for the button with a perfectly manicured nail and selected the 'seat upright' setting again, buttoned her jacket, and decided that a trip to the john would be timely. Besides, she could get a good look at her fellow first-class passengers as she made her way aft. She'd only been able to take note of a couple earlier on, as the others had been obscured by the seats around her. And even Rowan knew that it wasn't good manners to rubber-neck at one's fellow travellers when in first. That was the sort of thing the nouveau-riche and the socially inept did. And Rowan's background might not have been top-drawer but she was savvy enough – and a good enough actress – to assume the mien of someone of far better ancestry than her own.

She tugged her jacket down and smoothed her hair, then took a compact out of her bag and checked her make-up. It would do, she decided. Knowing that despite a drink-induced sleep of several hours she still looked hot, she stood up and strolled towards the toilets. Of course it was the turbulence that made her stumble and lurch a couple of times. She fixed a smile to her face as if daring any of her fellow passengers to think the cause of her unsteadiness could be anything else.

Perhaps she needn't have worried, though. About half of the dozen passengers in the cabin seemed to be dozing or asleep; a couple were working on laptops, and the remaining three were reading. No one seemed to be paying any attention to her at all.

Rowan stared at the sleeping travellers and, apart from Max, obviously, recognised none of them. The business-men on their laptops she ignored – she didn't know anyone in business, unless you counted studio bosses – but those reading she paid attention to. The man at the back of the cabin, nearest the galley, looked familiar. Then the light dawned. He was Pete Montgomery, the lead singer with Quikfire, one of the biggest bands in recent years. She remembered his name from when they'd been introduced at an industry bash – or perhaps it had been a private party, a couple of years previously. There had been mutual respect and admiration for each other's success in their chosen field of the entertainment industry. And, more impressive, in Rowan's view, he was a hot guy; devastatingly good looking. And rich – if Forbes's rich-list and a slew of celebrity magazines were to be believed. Mega-rich. Loaded. Absolutely minted. And Rowan was impressed by money. She'd been brought up without it and never underestimated its power or importance.

Back in her childhood, her mother had entered her into beauty pageants because the cash prizes that Rowan won allowed them to eat decently for a week or so. But Rowan had loathed the contests as most of the other girls came from families who were rich enough to have their pageant dresses specially made, their hair done in salons, and tutors employed for elocution and deportment. All Rowan had was her great natural beauty and the other girls, wild with jealousy, had never failed to remind her that she came from the wrong side of the tracks. She would have refused to enter the contests if her mother hadn't pressured her that they needed the money. And each time she'd paraded she'd felt as if she was selling herself and it had sickened her. She'd loathed everything about it, from the jibes of the other contestants to the leers from the old-man judges. The only thing that made it bearable was hearing everyone say how beautiful she was. Now, if her mother hadn't have been dead, she might have returned to the hick town one day and hired the flashest car she could, just to rub those other girls' spoilt little noses in it and show them what wealth *really* was.

Still, the bloke in front of her wasn't going to be impressed by a flash hire car. In fact, there was nothing she could do that would impress him. Except . . . She remembered her last encounter with Pete Montgomery. He'd definitely wanted her on that occasion. She'd got hot thinking about his incredible wealth and he'd made it obvious he fancied her, too. They had ended up in the garden trying to tear each other's clothes off. If it hadn't been for Jono seeking her out like some sort of fucking sheep dog she reckoned she could have had Pete back then. Well, maybe tonight was the chance to see if he still fancied her. She needed something to prove she still had it – that someone still thought she was worth loving. Jono didn't seem to love her any more. All Jono did was bitch at her about being nice to people and keeping off the booze. Why shouldn't she enjoy a drink now and then? Hell, it wasn't as if they couldn't afford it. He didn't seem to talk to her these days unless he wanted to have a go at her. Not like in the old days when they had first got it together. She'd loved him then. He'd been fun then. Now he was always on about 'the public perception' and 'image'. Shit, couldn't he lighten up once in a while? Let his hair down? She was fed up to the back teeth with him. Maybe Pete would be more fun.

'Pete?' she said hesitantly, stooping forward to show her impressive cleavage off to its maximum advantage and allowing her silvery-blond hair to sweep down like an alluring curtain. 'Pete Montogmery?' she enunciated his name carefully. She didn't want to slur.

The bloke looked up from his paperback. Rowan noticed that his expression of surprise turned to pleasure when he realised who was talking to him.

'Rowan. Rowan Day! Well, I'll be— What a pleasure. My, but it's been a while since we last met.'

'A couple of years,' said Rowan.

'But I see you all the time – on the screen.'

'Likewise,' agreed Rowan. 'Your career is so going places.'

'Thank you, ma'am,' he drawled in his Texan accent. He got to his feet, which Rowan thought was a charmingly old-fashioned gesture from someone who was considered one of the bad boys of rock and roll.

Rowan decided to slightly exaggerate her southern

accent. 'My, my. So, when was the last time we met? The MTV awards?' Then she said, as if it had just come to her: 'No, it was at that crazy party at the Osbourne's. It was a fun night. Well, you and I had a heap of fun in the garden.'

'Yeah, I remember now. That was some night.'

Rowan could see by the look on his face that Pete was remembering exactly the same as she was. She lowered her voice to make it even more husky. 'Just wild.' She saw the stewardess take a rug and the menu forward to her vacant seat.

'Now look, darlin',' she said, breathing huskily, 'I've just got to pop to the bathroom and then I'll be right back. Why don't we see if old Max – my agent – will swap with you, then we can have a nice littl' ol' gossip while I have my dinner? And maybe we can talk about old times and think of something we can do together' – she deliberately let the word 'together' hang provocatively – 'to help the time pass.' She could see Pete hesitating, looking at the reclining form of the slumbering agent. 'Now don't you worry your head about disturbing old Maxie – I pay him so he does as he's told.' She laughed her little-girl laugh so as to sound less demanding, less spoilt. 'Anyway, you think about my offer while I'm gone.' And she waggled her finger at her new friend as she continued on her way and thought happily to herself that at least now she would have something much more entertaining to occupy herself with than watching some crappy films chosen by a spotty youth at the airline's head office.

When Rowan exited the lavatory having, apart from attending to the call of nature, swilled a good slug of mouthwash to disguise any hint of alcohol on her breath, she found Pete stretching his legs in the big space at the back of the first-class cabin. The stewards were nowhere to be seen and the other passengers were snuggled down in their comfy, fully-reclining armchairs.

'A welcome party. For me – and I've only been gone a couple of minutes. How sweet.' She fluttered her eyelashes at him. 'Couldn't you wait any longer for my company, then, big boy? And did you think about my offer?' Rowan lowered her lashes and licked her lips in a gesture that she knew drove men wild. She looked up coyly and saw that Pete was no exception. She moved towards him until her body was almost touching him. She meant her body language to be unequivocal and it seemed she'd succeeded. Pete raised his hand with his index finger extended and traced it along the inside edge of her jacket lapel, barely brushing the soft smooth skin of her breast where it was visible in the V of the fabric, a smile just teasing the corners of his mouth upwards.

'So Jono's not travelling with you?' he asked in his deep Texan voice.

'Not this time, darlin'. I just got Maxie-baby to act as chaperone – and he don't care none. As I've already said, I give him his paycheque – he knows what's good for him.' And she leaned forward a fraction and flexed her knees then slipped her hand between his thighs and slid it upwards until it was nestled in his crotch. Pete's eyes widened, then his smile followed suit.

He pulled Rowan around by her shoulders so her back was squarely to the cabin and the entrance to the galley, then he flicked open the buttons to her jacket. It fell open revealing that underneath there was no blouse – only a wisp of expensive lingerie.

Rowan watched Pete's nostrils flare as he eyed her magnificent breasts, barely covered by the gauzy fabric of her bra, with lust and admiration. Glancing over his shoulder, he eased one out of its covering and flicked his thumb across the nipple.

'Cut to the chase, why don't you, honey?' drawled Rowan, breathlessly, her pupils dark pools of lust, as she arched towards him.

'Do you want to fuck?' asked Pete in a voice thick with sex and desire.

'Sure do, honey. But not here.' She dragged him into the bathroom and pushed the door shut, her inhibitions, few though they were, now completely suppressed by drink. A flicker of a frown crossed Pete's face. Maybe she'd called his bluff, thought Rowan wickedly. Maybe he wasn't such a bad boy as he liked to make out he was. Maybe he wanted to wait till they landed. Well, she couldn't. The thought of doing it here, in first class, was part of the thrill. It was working better than an aphrodisiac.

'I didn't mean right now. What about the cabin crew?' he asked.

Yup, the boy was chicken but she wasn't going to let him cool off. Not now. 'What about them, lover-boy? They know what's good for them. If word of anything that goes on in first class ever reached the press, they'd have their sorry little asses sued from here to Kingdom Come. Or have I got you all wrong? Do you want them to join in too? I expect a couple would agree if we asked.' She glanced up and saw the horror on Pete's face. 'Only joking, honey. Only joking.'

She was busy undoing Pete's shirt buttons as she spoke. She bent forward and fastened her beautiful lips around one of his nipples and gave it a sharp nip with her teeth. She heard Pete draw in a gasp of breath.

'You like that?'

In response, he dug his fingers hard into her buttocks and pulled her against him. 'I'll show you what I like,' he growled.

15

When Zoë bounced back full of gripes about the police and the burglar alarm system and the time it had all taken, and even fuller of her ride in Jono's hired Lexus, it took her several minutes to detect the huge shift in atmosphere between Jono and Gemma. She'd left them at the pizzeria as nothing much more than 'mates' and now . . . Now things had moved up a gear or two. Something had definitely happened while she'd been away. Her stream of chatter puttered to a stop like an engine running out of fuel. She looked from one to the other and then shut up completely.

'So,' said Gemma to Jono in the silence, 'as your car is here, I suppose you'd better get going. Mustn't keep the driver waiting,' she added brightly. 'You don't want him getting scared in this rough area.'

'No.' But Jono didn't move.

'I'll see you down, shall I?'

'You sound as if you're trying to get rid of me.'

'Not at all.' Zoë was ignored, forgotten, as the exchange between Jono and Gemma continued. 'Of course I'm not. It's just . . .' Gemma now faltered to a stop.

'It's just . . . ?'

'It's getting late. I have to be at the studio early. It's beginning to get frantic at work – really mad.'

'Of course. I'm sorry, I didn't think.' Gemma followed Jono downstairs to the door. There he leaned forward and kissed her gently on the lips. 'I'll be seeing you.' He turned to go.

' 'Bye,' called Zoë from the landing.

Jono glanced over his shoulder. 'Yes, 'bye, Zoë,' he added in an obvious afterthought.

Gemma closed the door behind him and leaned against it.

'So?' asked Zoë when she returned upstairs again.

' "So" what?'

'Oh, come off it, Gem. You know exactly what "so" means.'

'Nothing.'

Zoë's eyes widened and she put her fingers to the tip of her nose. She pulled them away to indicate it lengthening. 'Yeah right, Pinocchio. I may only be a shop girl but I'm not stupid. And I've got eyes.'

'It's late. I've got to be up at dawn.'

'Did he kiss you?' asked Zoë, pursuing Gemma to the door of her room. 'Properly?'

'What is this, the Spanish Inquisition?'

'Well, that's a "yes" then,' said Zoë with a grin.

Gemma spun round. 'It was just a kiss. It meant nothing. Honest. Just a kiss. And if a whisper of this gets out then I shall know exactly who to blame.'

Zoë backed off crossing her heart. 'Come on, Gem. You can trust me. I'm your mate, remember? Mates don't do that to each other.'

Gemma shook her head. 'I know. I'm sorry. It's

just everything is going so fast and I don't understand what's happening and I'm shit-scared and . . .'
She stopped and took a breath. 'And now I'm going off
on one.' She shot a grin at Zoë. 'Tell me I'm not going
potty, Zo?'

Zoë tilted her head on one side. 'We-ell . . .'

'I thought as much.' Gemma leaned against the door-
jamb. 'Not surprising, really, given that this is a crazy
situation. I mean – why? Why me?'

Zoë smiled broadly. 'At the risk of sounding like
a bitch, but the same thought was crossing my mind.
I mean, Rowan Day is in a different league from most
of us.'

'Jono says she's not very stable.'

'How?'

'He wasn't very specific but I believe him. I think she
can be violent. He's got some shocking bruises and I
swear I saw a bite mark when we were doing the fitting
the other day.'

'Blimey. There's *not stable* and being a fucking psycho.
Shit, no wonder he's looking elsewhere for a bit of love
and kindness.'

'Yeah, maybe,' said Gemma thoughtfully. Then she said
goodnight to Zoë and went into her room. Perhaps that
was all it was, perhaps all he wanted was someone who
wouldn't turn loco at the drop of a hat.

Max came to with a jolt as Rowan shook his shoulder
brusquely.

'Hey, Maxie. Wake up.'

'Huh, wha . . . ? What time is it? What's the matter?'

'Max. It's me.' Rowan leaned into his face. Max could
see right down her jacket, past her lacy bra, all the way to

her navel. That sight woke him up with the effectiveness of a cup of cold water in the face.

'Yes, Rowan,' he said, trying to sound alert and rubbing the last vestige of sleep out of his eyes. 'Problem?'

'Nothing you can't help with. I'd really appreciate it if you could swap seats with Pete here. We've got some serious catching up to do and he's seated right at the back.'

Max tore his gaze from the view down Rowan's gaping jacket and switched it to look over her shoulder. He saw a long-haired guy with a couple of facial piercings whom he thought looked faintly familiar. The guy grinned at him and shrugged his shoulders as if to imply that this wasn't his idea. Max knew only too well just how persuasive Rowan could be. And just how bloody she could get if she was thwarted.

'Max, this is Pete from Quikfire. Pete, Max.' As introductions went this one was barely even perfunctory but Max wasn't about to complain. Rowan often didn't bother with social niceties where he was concerned. As a mere agent he didn't expect her to waste her time trying to impress him. However, Max was intrigued to meet Pete Montgomery. And surprised. He didn't know Rowan knew any musicians.

'Pleased to meet you,' he said.

'Likewise,' said Pete.

They both knew that neither of them really gave a stuff but manners dictated that they appeared to.

'So, Maxie?' said Rowan, getting impatient.

'Yeah. No sweat. Just let me gather my kit together.' Max pressed the button to get his seat back to upright and then busied himself with stuffing his belongings in his overnight bag. Rowan tapped her nails on the back of his seat to make sure he didn't slacken his pace.

The sour-faced stewardess came forward. 'Is there a problem?' she asked.

'No,' said Rowan. 'Max is just swapping with Mr Montgomery.'

Max noticed Anne shoot Rowan a glance of scarcely veiled disdain. He hoped Rowan was too wrapped up in herself and Pete to notice. He didn't fancy Anne's chances of continuing her employment if Rowan got a whiff of how Anne felt.

'Let me give you a hand?' the senior stewardess offered.

'Max can cope,' snapped Rowan.

'I'm fine,' said Max. 'Honest.'

'I'll put fresh linen on the beds,' said Anne, through tight lips.

'Yeah, do that,' said Rowan. The two women exchanged cool stares. Max scuttled out of the way before things turned nasty.

Anne bustled about with quiet efficiency as she, with the help of one of the other stewards, sorted out the change of linen for the two beds with the minimum of fuss and disturbance for the other passengers. It was only a couple of minutes before she informed Max that his new bed was ready for him.

'Thanks,' said Max. 'Rowan likes to get her own way,' he added *sotto voce* so none of his fellow travellers would hear. 'Anyway, it's nice that she has a friend to talk to, to while away the hours.'

'So I gather,' said Anne. 'And she and Mr Montgomery seem to be on *very* friendly terms.' She didn't exactly finish her sentence with nudge, nudge, wink, wink, but Max got the idea.

He was sure he'd only been asleep for a few minutes, but he knew Rowan of old. And this wouldn't be the first time Rowan had behaved like a cheap tart.

'Really?' Max tried to sound as if he hadn't understood the implication. Better that than the 'Ohmigod, not again!' response, which was the one he'd had to bite back. He wondered how hard she'd had to work to snare this bloke this time. Or maybe she hadn't had to work at all. Maybe he was as randy as she was. Maybe he was flattered by her attentions. And if he was, thought Max, it could only be because he didn't know how easy she was, nor what a long list of predecessors he had. Max sighed when he thought about Rowan's infidelities. Just as well Jono was unaware of most of them if not all of them. He'd be destroyed if he knew quite how free Rowan was with her favours. Max had done his best to protect him from the ugly truth, but couldn't be sure he'd succeeded.

Why on earth couldn't she have the decency to wait until she got to the privacy of her suite at the Beverly Hills Hotel? Why did she have to take such gawd awful risks by getting her leg over almost in public? Inwardly, Max seethed at the stupidity of his client and wondered, not for the first time, what would happen when the public finally got to find out exactly what the real Rowan Day was like. And also, not for the first time, he wondered why on earth Jono stuck with the difficult, manipulative nymphomaniac.

Max turned his attention back to Anne. 'Well, I think they're old friends,' he said with a sheepish grin as if that would explain everything.

'I see,' said Anne.

'And it is only *you* with any idea of what might have . . . allegedly . . . ?' he mumbled, embarrassment making him unable to finish the sentence coherently.

'Any idea of *what* exactly?'

He swallowed. 'The other passengers didn't see anything. Did they?' he added, hopefully.

Anne shook her head. 'As far as I know, no. But unless some of them were deaf, I suspect they *heard*. I can't be sure, of course.' She shrugged. 'Maybe they were listening to music or watching a movie, or asleep. But if not . . .'

Max couldn't suppress a groan of despair. Anne smiled another of her tight, disapproving smiles. 'I can't be sure. I mean, when two passengers disappear into the lavatory together, and there is a certain amount of thumping and noise before they reappear simultaneously, you don't have to be Mastermind to work it out, do you?' She was clearly angry and embarrassed. And so she might well be. Rowan had used her first-class cabin like some sort of bordello and it was obviously the sort of behaviour that irritated Anne because of the upset and embarrassment it would cause her other passengers.

'She might have had something in her eye,' suggested Max weakly. 'The guy might have just been helping her.'

Anne looked at him as if he had just suggested that the earth was flat or that the sky was falling. Withering distain didn't even come close.

Max shrugged in embarrassment. 'Well, if it is only you who actually saw anything, could you keep it that way?'

'Mr Samuels, it is not my practice to be indiscreet.' She enunciated slowly and clearly as if she was talking to a small child or a foreigner. 'I respect the privacy of this airline's clients and I'm not about to change my habits now.' That was telling him, thought Max, but all the same he breathed a sigh of relief. 'But although Miss Day can rely on my discretion, I don't think she can on that of the other passengers, should any of them have noticed something. Of course, they may not have done, but I think you ought to warn her to be more careful in future.'

'Easier said than done, Anne. Easier said than done.'

16

Jono lay awake in the massive double bed in the pristine bedroom he shared with Rowan, when she permitted it, and thought about Gemma. To his right, the amber glow of London filtered through the designer drapes that Rowan had spent a small fortune on and, on both sides of the bed, acres of equally pricey cream carpet disappeared into the gloom of the dark room as Jono lay restless and alone.

What was it, he wondered, that was so attractive about Gemma? She wasn't sophisticated, or beautiful, or tall, or blonde. Sure, she was pretty. And she had a great sense of humour. And she was uncomplicated and not up herself at all. But it still remained that she was none of the things that he normally found attractive in women and yet he couldn't get her out of his head. Everything about her drew him in like a magnet. He wondered if it was her sense of mischief that he had found so attractive; her straightforwardness; her sheer freshness. Jono turned on his side and pummelled his pillow, but still an image of Gemma remained in his mind. Images of Gemma laughing at his jokes, of slurping strands of mozzarella cheese into her mouth, of licking her fingers greasy with garlic butter, of being natural and uncomplicated and fun. The fun was there in the way her eyes sparkled when she laughed, the way the top of her tilt-tipped nose wrinkled when she smiled, the way her curls quivered when she giggled. Jono sighed. There were no two ways about it; she was adorable.

Fun wasn't an adjective that anyone would apply to Rowan these days. Her idea of fun now was getting blind drunk. She'd been good company a few years ago, before the drink had got to her. Back then, she'd also been focussed and determined but she'd enjoyed a joke and had been good company. He wasn't quite sure which had gone wrong first – the drinking or the slide in her career – but it was certain that the two were now intertwined and she'd become vicious, bitchy and violent. But fun? Nope. Then Jono wondered if perhaps he was being unfair. There had been something about Rowan, other than her extra-ordinary beauty, that had made him fall for her in the beginning. And if he were being scrupulously honest, she had had a certain *joie de vivre* back then. She had lived life to the full, certainly; working, dancing, going out, partying, but perhaps it had all been an act. Rowan Day in *The Good-Time Girl*. Rowan Day in *Fun-Loving Female*. Jono could almost see the neon lights shining out, and he'd bought tickets to the show. That was the trouble with goddamned actors, thought Jono. You never knew when the play was over, the curtain lowered and the make-up and costumes had been stripped off; they carried on in character even though it was all false.

Gemma had complained of exactly that. She'd said that he'd been putting on an act of fancying her so she'd be flattered and fall for him. Jono sighed. As if it were as easy as that. If he could make someone fall for him by just acting, he could have had half a dozen leading ladies swooning over him. But they hadn't because there'd been no chemistry. You couldn't act chemistry. He'd have to remember to tell Gemma that next time he saw her.

Sleep was eluding him completely and Jono decided to give up the struggle and make himself a hot drink. Hot drink? He could almost hear Rowan mocking him. What you need is a slug of bourbon, she would have said. But what Jono wanted now was comfort – not oblivion.

He slid across the wide bed, grabbed his dressing gown from the foot of it, and thrust his arms down the sleeves. From habit, he also picked up his mobile from the bedside table and slipped it in his pocket. In bare feet he padded across the thick carpet and on to the landing. The house was silent apart from the ticking of a clock somewhere.

Jono made his way down the sweeping stairs to the kitchen. The red light of the deactivated infrared burglar alarm winked as it watched him move through the quiet house. Jono felt as guilty as an intruder as he tiptoed across the huge hall and through the heavy door that led to the domain of their live-in housekeeper. The door swung slowly shut behind him, restrained by its heavy spring. Jono felt to his left and flipped on the light.

The startlingly bright, recessed spotlights flashed into life. Jono blinked as his eyes adjusted. The expanse of the kitchen stretched before him. Gleaming, pristine work surfaces and clinical cabinets lined the walls combining with the immaculate, mark-free floor to look like an ad from a lifestyle magazine – the sort that Rowan would flick through while she tried to decide if her happiness would be improved by the acquisition of a new suite in their drawing room or if complete redecoration was the only answer.

Not for the first time, Jono wondered what on earth anyone would want with a kitchen this size. It was big enough to cope with the demands of a fully booked cruise liner. And it wasn't as if they ever entertained at home these days. Rowan was far too unpredictable to allow that. Besides, what was the point? The vast majority of their friends were so self-obsessed with their body image that their eating habits were now completely dominated by this or that new food fad. Normal eating didn't seem to apply to fashionistas and movie stars any more. Rowan insisted that they ate salads and wholemeal pasta and poached chicken – nothing he really liked or enjoyed. And it wasn't as if he got the remainder of his daily calorie intake from booze like she did.

Bollocks to that, thought Jono as he strode across to the fridge on the far side, his bare feet slapping on the specially commissioned designer tiles. He liked pizza, and bacon and egg, and roast beef and Yorkshire pudding, and tiramisu and doughnuts. In fact, with Rowan away, he should tell Janet to make him stew and dumplings for supper one night.

The fridge was a monster. Like all the appliances in the kitchen it was overlarge and probably over-priced. He hoped their housekeeper appreciated them as he didn't think Rowan had clapped eyes on them since she'd chosen them in the Chelsea showroom. How different from the tatty, cracked lino and shabby fittings in Gemma's kitchen. And Gemma's kitchen might have been shabby and tatty but at least it was used, and smelt of cooking. The kitchen here smelt of cleaning products and looked as shiny as the day it had been fitted.

He pulled out a plastic bottle of milk – skimmed, of course, Rowan wouldn't allow anything full-fat – and rummaged in a succession of cupboards until he found a pan – which was far too big, but there didn't appear to be anything more suitable. He slugged some milk into it and then put it on the hob of the massive stainless-steel range that dominated one side of the room. He studied the rank of knobs that ran down the side of the appliance and tried to work out which one lit each burner. In the end he gave up and twisted the closest – then moved the pan to the flame.

While he waited for his milk to warm through – hardly rock and roll but it was his mother's answer to sleeplessness and it had worked before – he wandered over to the window above the sink and pulled up the blind. All he could see was the reflection of the kitchen and himself, staring morosely at the glass.

Behind him he heard the milk begin to fizz against the hot sides of the pan. He turned back to the stove to watch it. The bubbles grew bigger and joined up and the centre of the liquid began to pucker as a thin skin began to form. He switched off the gas and poured his milk into a mug, then stared at it. Was this what he really wanted? Truth to tell he didn't have a clue what he wanted at all any more.

He gazed about him; at his state-of-the-art kitchen which he barely set foot in, at his vast house, which was devoid of life and laughter, at all the visible trappings of wealth and success, and what did it all signify? Diddly-squat in the great scheme of things.

Yet he'd dreamed of this when he'd started out; that one day he'd make it big. From the first time he'd got a part in a school play, he'd known that acting was the only thing he wanted to do in life. He'd joined the local am-dram theatre group and his parents had blamed the time he spent there for his appalling GCSE results. His father, a civil servant, didn't really approve of theatrical types and, as far as he was concerned, Jono's results just confirmed everything he'd ever thought. It had gone down pretty badly when he'd got a job in rep and then he'd met Max, who had suggested he should audition for RADA – 'and come and see me again when you graduate. I'll take you on.' His father, predictably, hadn't shared his excitement. His mother had been proud, though, and now – now he'd proved that he was good at what he did – his father had come round too. Maybe the holiday home in France that he'd bought them, the one they'd always dreamed about owning, had helped too.

So, his parents were happy, Gemma – full of life and laughter – doing the job she'd always dreamed about, certainly was. Her friend Zoë, who worked in a fabric shop and earned peanuts, seemed utterly content. So what had he to be discontented about? He had a stellar career, a beautiful house and a huge income. And yet he wasn't happy. He smiled to himself as he thought what Gemma's reaction would be to his dissatisfied introspection. He could almost hear her saying, 'Ah, diddums.' Which was what he deserved, no doubt.

Carrying his milk, Jono made his way down a level to the pool. He switched on the lights at the bottom of the spiral stairs and walked over the textured tiles to the water's edge. He swished his toe over the surface to break up the mirror calm and sipped his milk as he watched the ripples spread over the surface to the far side. Even as he gazed at the artificially blue water, the chemical smell of chlorine twanging in his nose, the ripples stopped and the mirror returned. He shattered it again. Maybe, he thought, this was what he should do with his own life. Suppose he was to do something drastic like leave Rowan? Although he knew the question wasn't 'if', it was 'when'. The ripples would wreck things for a while but they would settle down and then life would continue. And life with Gemma would be so different, of that he was certain.

Jono finished his milk and returned his mug to the kitchen before retiring back to bed where, eventually, he drifted off into a fitful sleep.

In the morning, he awoke to the normal sounds of his household starting work. Outside he could hear one of the gardeners whistling and the sound of someone raking the gravel paths. Through the open door to his bedroom drifted the faint noise of a distant vacuum cleaner being pushed around while the smell of freshly brewed coffee had him reaching for his dressing gown for the second time in a relatively short space of time.

Slinging on his robe, he padded down the stairs and into the cavernous kitchen. In daylight, and occupied by the housekeeper, one of the several girls who came in daily to clean, a gardener and the pool man, it didn't look half as big as it had the previous night.

'Morning,' he greeted the slightly startled assembled company. 'Is that coffee I can smell?'

'Mr Knighton, good morning,' said Janet in her soft Scottish accent. There was just a hint of disapproval in seeing the master of the house in her domain, Jono could tell. This was hardly the 'downstairs' of a Victorian drama, but Jono knew that his presence was out of the ordinary and, perhaps, not entirely welcome. 'I'll bring some coffee to you in the breakfast room.'

'Coffee would be fine. I fancy a swim.' Jono glanced at the pool man. 'Is that okay?'

'Your pool,' said the technician easily. 'Besides, I'm just here to check the chlorine level and I can do that without getting in your way.'

'Great.' He took the mug of coffee being proffered by Janet. 'And I could fancy some scrambled eggs for breakfast. And bacon, and white toast.'

'White toast,' repeated Janet as if unsure of what she'd heard. Rowan disapproved of refined carbs.

Jono nodded. 'In about half an hour?'

'Half an hour, Mr Knighton. They'll be ready for you then.'

Jono carried his mug down to the pool room and sipped his coffee while he shrugged off his dressing gown, stepped out of his pyjama bottoms, and slid on a pair of trunks. Gulping down the last mouthful, he dumped his empty mug on the cane-and-glass table by the rattan lounger and then dived into the water. It felt rather less than lukewarm but as he struck out in a steady crawl he began to warm up.

He swam steadily for thirty laps and then hauled himself out of the water, panting slightly. He sat on the side of the pool, his legs dangling in the water as he got his breath back. He could hear the phone extension chirruping at him. Jono padded round the edge of the pool and checked the caller ID.

'Max,' he said cheerfully, feeling invigorated and virtuous following his swim.

'Hi, boss.'

Even with a less-than-perfect signal from Max's phone and six thousand miles separating them, he could tell Max wasn't a happy man.

'Okay. What's up?'

'Rowan.'

Jono's good mood just dematerialised in a nano-second. Fuck, he thought. 'What's she done now?'

'It's "who", not "what",' said Max.

'How do you mean?' said Jono, although he thought he could probably guess. Rowan had a knack of causing offence or upsetting people and in the close confines of a jumbo jet she was quite capable of going stir crazy. There was silence at the other end of the line. Jono wondered if the connection had been broken. 'Max? Max?' Jono heard a sigh. Max was apparently wondering how best to break the bad news.

'I wouldn't have told you anything but the LA press seem to have got a whiff of it.'

'A whiff of what, Max?'

'Rowan had an encounter on the flight.'

Jono was beginning to lose patience. What had Rowan done this time, he wondered. Had she hit someone? Quite possibly. Had a row? Got drunk and ugly? Even more likely. He needed to know. 'What sort of encounter, Max? Just give me the details. However gory.'

'She met this guy. Pete Montgomery. He's got a band.'

'A band.'

'It's called Quikfire.'

Jono had heard of them, but he didn't know that Rowan had. 'And?'

'And it seems they have met before.'

Even at this distance, Jono could hear the embarrassment in Max's voice. And the phrase 'who, not what' she had done suddenly made hideous sense. He came to his rescue. 'Let me guess,' he said, shutting his eyes and breathing out slowly. 'She and this Pete guy now know each other a whole lot better. Am I right?'

'That's about the size of it. But someone tipped off the

press; the cabin crew say it was probably another passenger. They swear it wasn't them. We were met by a posse of hacks at the airport who all seemed to know what went on. No one was interested in the contract she's due to sign with Magnum Opus, or the film she's going to be shooting with you. All they could ask questions about was Rowan now being a member of the Mile High Club. One of them even mentioned that the local police were talking about her being indicted for lewd behaviour.'

'Oh, for fuck's sake.'

'I'm doing my best here,' said Max. 'There are no witnesses – not as such. Another passenger is intimating that she saw them enter the bathroom together and leave together and heard noises, but obviously there's no proof as to what went on in there. Also, the airline isn't interested. They take the view that as there were no witnesses and, whatever went on was between consenting adults and done in private, so what? And as far as I can tell, the incident took place in international air space so I think it'll be a five-minute wonder. I wouldn't have told you, Jono, but I didn't want you reading about it in the press.'

Jono knew that Max was generally very discreet and was only trying to protect him from the worst of the things his wife got up to. However, it irritated him slightly to think that Max might know about other indiscretions of Rowan's and not be telling him simply because the press weren't aware of them. That had certainly been the implication in his last sentence. Jono realised that he was beyond caring whether or not his wife cheated on him, but it still stung his male pride that Max knew things he didn't. Well, so be it, although Jono thought that, these days, he was unlikely to be shocked by anything Rowan did.

'Meantime, the shit is hitting the fan and Rowan . . . ?'

'Is hitting the bottle.'

'Already? You must have just landed.'

'You know Rowan.'

Jono sighed again. 'Do you want me to come out?'

'I don't think it'll be necessary. As I said, it'll blow over in a couple of days.'

Jono bade farewell to Max and ended the call. Almost immediately, his phone rang again.

'Mr Knighton?' asked an unknown voice.

'Yes,' said Jono guardedly.

'This is the *Sun* here. Would you like to comment on the news that your wife was caught *in flagrante* on a transatlantic flight?'

Gemma stepped out of the Tube station near the studios and had her eye caught by a headline in a late edition of the *Sun*: ACTRESS IN MILE HIGH SEX ROMP, it blared. Gemma was about to look away – so what? – when she realised that the picture beneath was Rowan's. She stopped dead, causing a swearing commuter to cannon into her back.

'Sorry,' she mumbled as she rummaged in her bag for the necessary change to buy a copy. Grabbing one off the newsstand, she skimmed the story, then, having got the lurid gist, she tucked the paper under her arm as casually as she could. Outwardly, she looked like any of the millions of people across the capital commuting to work but, inwardly, she was fulminating against the crass stupidity of her friend's wife.

That stopped her in her tracks for a second time and caused another rear-end shunt from another swearing commuter. He wasn't just a friend now, was he? Not since that second kiss – the one in the kitchen. And it wasn't just the goalposts that had now been moved, the whole pitch had shifted. Being Jono's friend wasn't an especially complicated place to be. This new development was a whole different ball game. In fact, she thought, as she walked swiftly along the grubby pavements towards work, she would rather be his 'friend' than anything more tricky.

However, after the previous night, their relationship had moved on to decidedly tricky ground. Or it could if she allowed it to. Jono had indicated that was where he wanted it to go. Did she? What the hell would happen if Zoë was indiscreet, or the papers got wind of things? And then there was the issue of Rowan. Gemma sighed as she strode through the commuting crowds. She wasn't equipped to deal with these sorts of problems, she was only human after all.

Gemma reached the security gate at the Butterfly Films offices and picked up her pass. Making her way past a gaggle of women sporting curlers and too much make-up – extras for a new drama about members of a chorus line during the Second World War – she ran lightly up the metal stairs to the costume department.

Tina was in ahead of her.

'Morning,' said Gemma coolly, still angry that Tina had been snooping on her.

Tina glowered a greeting.

Suit yourself, thought Gemma, and sat down at the workbench. No longer was she going to drop her bag into the bottom drawer of the filing cabinet. She would now keep it by her at all times. She hoped Tina would notice and work out the reason why.

She ran her eye over the list of jobs still to do before shooting started the following week; there were about three dozen pairs of hand-made shoes to be chased up, two of Rowan's dresses hadn't appeared, and Gemma also had to task the jewellery specialist to organise the transport and insurance for the stuff used in the ballroom scene. On top of that a couple of script changes had knock-on effects as to costume requirements and there were all the final fittings to be done for the minor characters. Even with all the team working flat out, Gemma doubted if she would be getting away before six that night – or any other night for the foreseeable future.

'Have you read that muck?' asked Tina.

'What?' Gemma looked round.

'That.' Tina was pointing a pair of scissors at the paper next to Gemma's handbag.

'Why?'

'It's not true, of course.'

'You were there, were you?' asked Gemma.

Tina looked at her colleague as if she was mad. 'But it stands to reason. Of course Rowan wouldn't go off with' – she sneered and pointed her scissors at the inset picture of Pete Montgomery – '*that.*'

'Well, he's not in Jono's league,' agreed Gemma. 'Maybe Rowan likes a bit of rough.'

Wrong thing to say. Very wrong. Tina's face contorted with rage and she moved towards Gemma, her scissors still in her hand. 'Don't you dare say that,' she snarled.

Gemma backed off. Tina and scissors. Not a good combination. 'Sorry, sorry. I didn't know you felt so strongly.' Blimey, psycho or what! 'Perhaps the paper got the wrong end of the stick. Mind you, if they have, I imagine Rowan will sue their socks off.' Would that placate the cow? Gemma certainly hoped so.

'I hope she does,' spat Tina. 'There should be a law against printing such lies.' She stabbed her scissors at the picture making Gemma jump. Under the circumstances, Gemma thought it wise not to get involved in a discussion on the existing powers of the libel laws. She let the matter drop and hoped that Tina would do the same, along with the scissors.

Tina retired back to her corner where she lurked like a spider in the corner of a web, ready to shoot her venom at some poor unsuspecting passing fly. Gemma returned to her work, aware of Tina's brooding presence behind her. She got out a list of phone numbers and made a note of people she was going to have to call to get the most urgent of her current problems sorted out. From the depths of her handbag, her phone trilled to tell her she had a text. Gemma reached in and looked at the display. 'New Message from JK,' it said. Resisting the temptation to glance at Tina or to hide the fact that she was receiving a message from Jono, Gemma pressed the button to read what he had to say: *Thanx 4 last nite. C wot I mean about u no who. Cant believe wot she did. Xx.*

Gemma wondered what on earth she could say by way of reply. Is it true that your wife really is such a slapper? Not to worry? Do you mind? Has she done this kind of thing before? She sighed. She thought it was unlikely the papers would print a story unless they were pretty sure it would stand up, so the chances were it was true. Poor old Jono. She couldn't think of anything to say that wouldn't be trite or banal. The poor guy must be going through hell. She hoped he had someone who worked for him who could take his calls and protect him from the worst of the inquiries from the press.

Gemma dismissed all her initial thoughts of how to respond to Jono's news as crass or tactless. But she had to say something. She had to offer the poor bloke some sort of support. She decided to think about it for a minute or two. Perhaps something would inspire her.

The sound of high heels on the metal stairs announced the imminent arrival of Arabella. She breezed in, shaking her head and taking off her jacket.

'Well,' she said, as she hung her expensive coat on the back of the door, 'that's put the cat among the pigeons.'

'What has?' asked Gemma, without thinking.

Arabella looked at her as if she had just said something obscene. 'This business about Rowan. *They* are not happy.'

At least Gemma knew who she meant by *they* – the studio owners and producers of this movie. 'It's probably someone trying to screw money out of the papers with a malicious story,' she said. Arabella looked unconvinced. 'It's a storm in a teacup,' added Gemma.

'Maybe. There's talk of sacking her and finding someone else.'

'Surely not. But the dresses? The shoes?' Gemma was horrified, and saw Tina's expression change at the awful thought of her idol being sacked.

Arabella hooked a stool out from under the work bench and sat on it. 'Realistically, they probably won't. By the time the film comes out it'll be old news. No one will remember the incident unless she does it again.'

Gemma was aware that in the corner Tina had picked up her scissors again. Without thinking she picked up her bag and held it across her chest like a shield.

'So what do we do now?' she asked.

'I suppose we carry on. If Rowan is sacked, then we'll have to start from scratch with the leading lady's costumes and whatever we do over the next few days will make not a blind bit of difference. If she stays, then we need to be ready. My only worry is that if she is sent packing, will Jono go too?'

Gemma hadn't thought of that. She felt a stab of anxiety. Not Jono? She felt Tina's eyes on her and instinctively glanced across at her. She looked triumphant. Gemma looked away. Tina mustn't see that this mattered to her. She mustn't confirm the cow's suspicions. Tina had no proof that she and Jono were anything but casual acquaintances and she was determined that it stayed that way.

Jono paced around his house unsure of whether he wanted the phone to ring or not. He was desperate to hear from Max and to discover what the hell was going on with Rowan out in America but equally he dreaded the calls from the press. He had the answering machine switched on so he could screen his calls but the press were undeterred and asked intrusive and rude questions followed by a number so he could call back with his answers. As if! Did these hacks really think that he would get back to them with the sort of intimate soul-baring they were after?

The staff crept about the place, all of them now aware of the scandal in which Rowan was embroiled. They weren't scared of Jono like they were of Rowan, he knew that, but he also understood that they worried about intruding on his angst and unhappiness. The trouble was, with the staff leaving him alone, he not only felt unhappy but lonely, too. In the absence of Max, he needed someone who wouldn't be intimidated by his fame and who would give him some straight-talking advice. Someone like Gemma. In fact, not even 'like' Gemma. What he needed was Gemma in the flesh.

He pulled his mobile out of his pocket and texted her again, wondering, as he did so, why she hadn't replied to his first text. Surely she knew the hideous mess Rowan had got herself into yet again? Surely Gemma would understand that he needed her common sense and sympathy? Irritatedly, he kicked at the carpet as he paced back and forth in the snug awaiting her reply, staring at his mobile, willing her to get in touch and getting angry with her for ignoring him. Perhaps he should call her. Perhaps that was the answer.

Then he realised that, unlike him, she had a day job and it might not be appropriate for her to get back to him straight away. Stamping around his house in a strop of impatience meant he was acting like the worst sort of spoilt movie types he despised. The ones who bitched because the soft furnishings in their trailers were the wrong shade of cream; or that the water on offer was Perrier when it should have been Evian; or that the low-carb-high-protein food they had demanded last week was now the last thing they wanted. And so it went on. The self-obsessed rantings of a class of people who had too much money, too much time and not enough self-awareness. Please, God, if he ever got like that Max would give him a shake and tell him to 'get a grip'.

His phone bleeped at him. Gemma at last.

Wot can i say. Do u want 2 talk.

Yes get a cab here after work ill pay.

Now all he had to do was get through the day till he could see Gemma, if she could make it.

'We haven't got time to text our friends,' said Arabella crisply.

'Sorry,' muttered Gemma, guiltily stuffing her phone back into her handbag. She'd been so wrapped up in making arrangements with Jono that she hadn't heard her come up the metal stairs.

'I would have thought that you, of all people, had more than enough work to be getting on with.'

'Sorry,' said Gemma again. She grafted her socks off till lunch, when she was able to text Jono again to get his address on Kingston Hill. She didn't think she'd impress a cabbie by wanting to be taken south of the river with only a vague idea of exactly where she was heading when she got there. She hoped there weren't going to to any paparazzi on the pavement outside.

Her getting snapped going into his house wouldn't help matters. Maybe they wouldn't be interested in Jono and they certainly wouldn't be interested in her – a complete nonentity if ever there was one. After all, it was Rowan who had been caught playing away from home – not Jono.

Rowan paced about her sumptuous suite, from the huge plate-glass windows, overlooking the yellowy haze of smog that veiled LA, to the grand piano by the opposite wall with the vast vase of lilies on its lid. Her tread was soundless as the thick carpet absorbed sound like blotting paper did ink.

'Sit down,' said Max, losing patience.

'But I feel like I have to do something.'

'What? I told you, never apologise, never explain. So sit tight and do nothing. Besides, you've made your bed, now lie in it,' Max added deliberately.

Rowan glared at him. 'You sure there's no proof?'

'No, I'm not sure. It's a gamble. But no one could photograph you in the john and you're pretty sure no one was anywhere near when you went in or out. Anne, the stewardess, has sworn the story didn't come from her . . .

'Huh!' snorted Rowan.

'Well, I believe her,' said Max coldly. 'So, all in all, I think that you and Pete demanding that the paper retract the slur might do the trick. All they've got are the stories of two unconnected passengers who were on the flight.

The noises they heard might have been coincidental. That's what I've told the paper and I've told them that unless they can prove otherwise then they have to print a retraction.'

Rowan paced across the carpet again, then stopped before the huge window and stared morosely at the murky view of LA in the smog. Perhaps Max was right. Perhaps it would blow over. But what if it didn't? 'Get me a drink, Max.'

'No. Today you're going to stay sober.'

She whirled around. 'I don't take orders from you, Max. Now get me a goddamned drink.'

'I promised Jono . . .' he began.

Rowan mimicked him. 'I promised Jono . . . Well, he's not here, I am, and I want a fucking drink.'

'Then I'll quit.'

'You wouldn't dare.'

Max picked up his briefcase and headed for the door.

'But what about tomorrow's negotiations with Magnum Opus?'

'What about them?'

'You need to be there to cut the deal.'

'No, I don't, Rowan. *You* need me to be there to cut the deal. I don't need to be there at all. Not if I couldn't give a flying fuck about the ten per cent. Which I don't. Frankly, my dear, in words you should understand, I don't give a damn. You're not my only client. Sure you've been one of the more lucrative ones, but you're slipping down the list. I'm not going to starve without your business.'

Rowan stared at him, horrified. This wasn't the reaction she'd been expecting and she realised that she didn't have the guts to call his bluff.

'Get me a soda,' she spat, trying to maintain her dignity and the upper hand.

'No,' said Max. 'You want a drink, you get it. I'm your agent, not your servant.'

Rowan screwed her eyes up as she tried to think of some sort of comeback and, failing, just screamed and flounced into her bedroom, slamming the door behind her.

It was almost seven before Gemma got away from work. Things were getting truly frantic now with many of the minor stars coming in for costume fittings to say nothing of chasing up missing items and getting two huge lorry-loads of clothes ready to be shipped out to Spain for the location phase. They would get more assistants to help with dressing the cast and maintaining the clothes once shooting actually started but at the moment there was more work for Tina, Gemma and Arabella to do than they could cope with.

Gemma managed to hail a taxi shortly after leaving the production offices. The driver grumbled predictably when she gave him the address but Gemma was too knackered to care or argue back. She just flopped back on the slippery rear seat in exhaustion and hoped that the journey didn't take too long. What she really wanted was to get home to sleep and this mercy mission to hold Jono's hand was not going to allow her to get to bed on the right side of midnight. But that's what friends are for, she told herself.

The taxi, caught up in the last of the rush hour, ground its way through Fulham and over the river at Putney Bridge. Gemma tried not to glance at the dial showing the fare payable. It was clicking upwards at alarming speed.

She hoped to God Jono wouldn't forget his promise of paying. Thirty pound-plus cab fares weren't the sort of thing she could afford. And then there was the question of her return journey. Would she get away before the trains stopped running or would she have to get another cab? She was going to be skint at this rate.

The cab sped along through Roehampton, the traffic now thinner, and down the A30 towards Kingston. Not far now, thought Gemma, remembering the big roundabout from her previous visits to Jono's. She leaned forward and told the cabbie that the house was at the top of the hill on the right. He nodded his acknowledgement.

'This one,' said Gemma. The gaggle of paparazzi clustered outside the gates were more of a clue that she'd found the right address than anything else.

The cabbie swerved the taxi across the road and through the open gates. Gemma wondered if they had been left open for her as flashlights blossomed on either side of the vehicle as it rushed past the ambushing snappers. She hid her face as best she could with her handbag and hoped that her utter lack of fame would be a better shield.

The driver drew up outside the big portico and Gemma got out.

'That lot after you?' asked the cabbie as she got out a couple of twenty-pound notes.

Gemma shook her head. 'I think they just snap away at everyone,' she said lightly. 'I'm a nobody and yet they still took my picture.'

The cabbie handed her the change and Gemma ran lightly up to the front door and rang the bell. It was opened almost immediately and Gemma was let in.

'You must be Miss Brown. Jono's in the snug,' said a

middle-aged woman whom Gemma hadn't met before. One of the Knightons' staff, apparently. She wondered how many staff there were.

'Thank you.' She hung about awkwardly, not sure if it was okay for her to wander through the house alone or if she should wait for an escort.

'Do you know the way?'

Gemma nodded. It was her cue to set off through the rooms that led to the back of the house.

The door was open when she got there and Jono was lounged on the sofa, remote in hand, flicking through the channels on the TV. He looked miserable and every one of his thirty-something years. It had obviously been a tough day for him. However, he jumped up when he saw her, his face changing from looking morose to ecstatic in a second.

'Gemma, Gemma. I thought you'd got cold feet and decided not to come.' He held his arms open and Gemma came forward for a hug.

'I'm sorry I'm late,' she said into his shoulder, her voice muffled by the strength of the embrace. 'I got held up at work. Everything is mad at the office.'

'You can blame Rowan for that,' said Jono grimly.

'Actually, Rowan's not really the problem, well, not for the costume department. There's a lot to do. Of course, if she does get taken off the movie it'll be—' Gemma stopped. Perhaps this wasn't something she should be saying. Maybe the studio hadn't discussed it with Jono.

'If she gets taken off the movie it'll be no more than she deserves, but it'll screw up a lot of people who don't deserve to be screwed up. God, what a mess.' He released Gemma from the embrace and pulled her over to the sofa. He zapped the TV off and then ran his hand over his face.

'Have you eaten? You must be famished. What would you like?'

Gemma raised her shoulders in bewilderment. 'Yeah, some supper would be nice. Umm, what is there?'

Jono looked as bewildered as she did. 'I don't know. Whatever you fancy. Janet will get you what you want.'

Gemma was flummoxed. Did he really mean this? Surely his cook or housekeeper, or whoever Janet was, wouldn't be able to rustle just any meal up out of thin air. 'I don't know. A sandwich or a salad. Maybe an omelette.'

Jono got up from the sofa and pressed a button by the fireplace. 'Let's ask Janet what she can produce, shall we?'

Gemma nodded. That sounded much more sensible. The middle-aged woman who had let Gemma into the house reappeared.

'What can we get Gemma to eat, Janet? The poor kid is famished.'

'I've a nice coq au vin cooking for your dinner. Would you like that, Miss Brown?'

'Sounds delicious,' said Gemma. Her stomach joined in with a small rumble of hunger.

'Will you have that too, Mr Knighton?'

He nodded. 'And some of your wonderful mashed spuds. And a salad?'

'That's fine,' said Janet. She went towards the door then paused. 'Do you want to eat here or in the dining room?'

'Let's be slobs and eat here tonight. You don't mind, do you, Gem?'

Gemma looked at her jeans and sweater and shook her head. 'Bugger,' she said. 'I forgot to get my tiara out of the vault, so I guess I'll have to slum it.'

Janet grinned and left, closing the door discreetly behind her.

'Here's money for the taxi,' said Jono, handing Gemma two twenties. 'Is that enough?'

'That's great, thanks,' said Gemma, feeling slightly awkward suddenly. But Jono soon put her at ease again.

'Now, a drink for you. What would you like?'

'What have you got?'

Jono pushed a panel in the wall and a door swung open to reveal an enormous bar. 'Does that answer your question?'

'A glass of white wine would be lovely.'

Jono poured her drink and a gin and tonic for himself and took them over to the sofa.

'I got papped on the way in,' said Gemma as she accepted the drink with a smile.

'Shit. Gosh, I'm sorry.'

'I mean, I know I'm a nobody, but do you think they might use it?'

'Two things. One, you're not a "nobody" to me, you're far more than that and, second, I very much doubt it. Besides, even if they do, Rowan is hardly in a position to cast the first stone, is she?'

Gemma shrugged and sipped her drink. 'From my point of view, I'll just have to hope they hit the delete button. From your point of view, I don't want to make things difficult for you.'

Jono put his drink down on the table. 'So what are we going to do next?' he said.

Gemma's forehead creased. 'I'm not with you. How do you mean?'

'You and I. Us. What are *we* going to do next?'

Gemma still felt bewildered. 'About what? Rowan?'

'Shit, Gemma, for a bright kid you can be dumb

sometimes. I think that Rowan knows that I can't – *won't* – ignore this. I shall probably wait until things die down a bit and we've finished shooting the picture, then I'll suggest that she and I split up.' Jono took Gemma's hands. 'In the meantime, I want to think about life after Rowan. For me that means *us*.' He stared deep into her eyes. 'You can't tell me you don't have feelings for me.'

Gemma suddenly felt very scared. She'd been trying to convince herself that all Jono wanted was someone 'normal' as a friend, but since the previous evening there had been a shift in the whole fabric of the relationship. And what he was saying now left her in no doubt that things hadn't shifted back again. It was as if she had just stepped into some sort of parallel universe where the sort of rules that usually applied to ordinary girls like her had ceased to exist. 'I do but . . . Jono, it isn't as easy as it would be if you weren't so famous.'

'I could become a nobody. I could quit this and get a job in Woollies or a bank. How about that?'

Gemma smiled and shook her head. 'But you're an actor. You'd shrivel up and die inside if you did that.'

'Maybe, but I'd have you.'

'Not until the issue with Rowan is resolved.'

Jono sipped his drink thoughtfully. 'I worry about her, all the time. She dominates most of my waking hours. But I don't love her any more. She is utterly self-obsessed and completely off the rails. And I can't abandon her, or not yet. I think if I left her now she might have a total breakdown, do something drastic. And if she did . . .'

Gemma nodded. 'But can't you get her help? I mean, aren't there places for people like her? Like the Priory?' she added, picking the only one she had ever heard of.

'And can you imagine the publicity she'd get? Every

time her publicity gets worse she reacts by drinking more and behaving even more badly so the publicity gets ever worse . . . it's a downward spiral.' Jono looked beaten and he rubbed his hand over his face. 'And don't think I haven't tried to help her. We all have. Me, Janet, Max, her publicist, the studios . . . But it's as if she doesn't want to be helped. I tell you, Gemma, I'm at the end of my tether. I am just praying that she meets someone who can cope with her and who makes her happy because I know I can't and I don't. Maybe this Pete Montgomery is the sort of guy she needs.'

Gemma doubted it. From what she'd read in the papers it sounded more like some drunken one-night stand than a meeting of soul mates. But it wasn't for her to comment.

'So the question is, Gemma, what are *we* going to do?'

Gemma took a deep breath. This was a toughie. 'I think,' she said slowly, 'we should do nothing. I couldn't live with myself if you and I having an affair tipped Rowan over the edge. And I don't think you could either. I care for you very much. I can't believe what is happening to me, not that you feel the same way about me, but we can't rush into this. Perhaps—' Gemma stopped. This was the hardest decision she had ever made. 'Perhaps we oughtn't to see each other, except professionally, until you and Rowan have resolved things.' Jono looked stricken and opened his mouth to speak but Gemma held up her hand to stop him. 'That way we can both be absolutely honest if anyone asks any awkward questions. I'm a rotten liar and I can't act for toffee. And anyway, I don't date—'

'Married men,' finished Jono. He looked sad but understanding. He sighed. 'You're right, of course.'

'I am sure it'll work out for the best. It's just a question of being patient.'

'**O**ut with Jono?' asked Zoë suspiciously the next morning, clocking Gemma's bruised-looking eyes and pale skin as they made tea and toast in the kitchen.

'Just a bad night,' said Gemma, comforting herself that at least she didn't have to lie too much. Anyway, she hadn't been *out* with Jono; they'd stayed in all evening.

'So why didn't you come home after work?'

'I went out for a drink with friends.'

'Not Arabella and Toxic Tina?'

'As if. No, some of the others. Then we had something to eat. You know how an evening can get away from you.' She hoped this would be enough of an explanation to shut Zoë up. And it was very close to the truth.

She got the third degree again from Arabella when she got into work.

'Too much bed and not enough sleep?' her boss asked acidly as Gemma yawned widely.

'Sorry, Arabella, I had a bad night. Couldn't sleep.'

Tina sneered from the corner. 'Guilty conscience?'

'No. Why?'

'Just wondered. You obviously had an assignation last night – going off in a taxi after work.'

Gemma felt the muscles in her stomach clench in anxiety. 'Why should going off in a taxi mean I had an assignation? I was just in a hurry.' Gemma tried to sound confident but she knew her face was flushing. Had Tina been spying on her and reading her texts again? Did she know something? Gemma whizzed back through the previous day and was sure she'd never let her bag and her mobile out of her sight. Surely Tina knew nothing about the most recent text from Jono? Even so, Gemma felt sick at the thought. At least it confirmed that her decision not to see Jono outside work until he and Rowan had got their marriage sorted out one way or another was the right one. Although, it would make seeing him professionally purgatory. Gemma wondered how she was going to cope over the next weeks and months of the filming.

'Hi, Jono, darling. It's me, Rowan.'

'Hello. How's LA?'

'Oh, you know, busy, expensive, smoggy. I thought you'd want to know how I got on at Magnum Opus.'

Actually, thought Jono, he didn't give a toss. But perhaps it wouldn't be a good idea to say this. 'Of course. And how did it go?'

'I got the contract. And the money is fab. I mean really hot. I'll be up in the big league with this.'

'That's great, baby. I'm thrilled for you. Great news.' Jono tried to sound genuinely pleased. He was an actor, after all; he should be able to cope with something as basic as this. And, realistically, this was good news for Rowan and maybe it might be what was needed to get her back on an even keel again. Please, God, it would help. And if she got stable it might make it easier for him to find a way of moving on.

'There's just one small thing.'

'What's that?' He just knew there had to be a catch. No such thing as a free lunch.

'The filming schedule for this series is really frantic. I'm going to be working flat out for months over here. Honey, I think we're going to have to move over here while I shoot this series. I don't want to be all on my own for that long and with this kind of money we can afford to get a dream house. I rang a realtor and he's got some really wonderful properties we could look at. We'll be the envy of everyone. Think of the parties we'll be able to throw. It'll be such a blast. And the weather will be decent. I'm fed up with the rain in England.'

Rowan wittered on about the monetary advantages her new job would bring, all the 'things' they would now be able to afford and Jono felt his whole body sag. No. Surely not. He loathed America but, even more, he loathed LA. Everything about it was anathema to him; from the shopping malls to the exclusive boutiques, the ridiculous parties and social climbing, the climate, the cars, the egos . . . All the pointless, material stuff that now seemed to mean so much to Rowan.

And it would mean leaving Gemma.

'Right,' he answered slowly. He injected a note of forced brightness into his voice. 'Well, we don't have to think about this immediately. We can discuss it when you come home. And there's something else we need to discuss then too.'

'Oh yes, what's that?'

'Just what happened on the plane?' Jono was proud of how calm he sounded when he asked that question. He wondered how many men would have managed the degree of control he'd just exercised if they had read about their wife having a quickie with a near stranger in the loo of a jumbo jet.

'Oh, that.'

Yes, THAT, he thought, having to will himself not to shout at her.

'It was nothing, Jono. I swear. Some silly people got the wrong idea.' He heard her little-girl, southern-belle tinkly laugh. Yeah, like making fun of the sordid story was going to make it go away. 'Max has made the papers retract everything and I've promised I won't sue. See, nothing to worry your li'l old head about.'

Jono, breathed out slowly and knew there was no point in asking if it were true or not. She'd lie – like she did about her drinking and taking coke and all the dozens of other things she didn't want to admit to him about. Or even to admit to herself.

They ended their conversation and Jono hung up. He flopped back on the sofa feeling even more betrayed and determined to end his marriage as soon as he could. Rowan had promised him, when they first made it big, that she never wanted to live in the States again, that she loved London and England and that she felt so much safer here than in the US. And recently, when Jono had said he wanted to get back on the stage again, she'd vowed she wanted the same. 'That acting on the stage was the real deal.' Now it appeared that the only 'real deal' Rowan wanted was to sell herself to the highest bidder.

Jono got up and went over to the panel to reveal the bar. He poured himself a generous gin and added a splash of tonic. He had a couple of days before she came back from LA and in that time he felt he had to make a decision.

Maybe the contract she'd been offered in LA was the perfect excuse to split. He could refuse to accompany her; perhaps Max could line something up for him here, something too good to turn down. After a few months of separation, he didn't think the divorce issue would be much of a problem.

Gemma stared at the call sheet and felt a huge frisson of excitement fizz through her. This was it. Shooting was about to start. Tomorrow they would be on the set with the stars, the extras and the costumes and she would see how a film was made. She would be part of the making of a film. She'd get a credit. A tick in the box. It would be something to put on her CV and it might mean that she got more work. No more working in a haberdashery or doing crappy sewing-machine demos. It wasn't just the excitement of filming here that was gripping her; it also meant that in a month she'd be high-tailing out to Spain for two months for the location shoot there. She knew it was probably going to be hot and difficult and hard work, but she didn't care. Her dream was just about to come true – and how many girls of her age could boast that.

She read through the sheets of paper in her hand. It was the first time she'd seen a real-live call sheet – one with her name on it. It detailed everything from the pick-up times of the stars by the studio cars, to when each star had to be in wardrobe and make-up, to the order of shooting for the day, the crew required for each scene, the time allowed for setting up each shot, official visitors to the set and the catering arrangements ... Blimey, she thought, it even detailed the time of sunrise and sunset – which, she supposed, might be important if they were shooting outside. It looked more like a plan for a military operation than something to do with entertainment, and she was enormously impressed by it. The logistics of the whole thing were immense, as were the costs and, as Arabella had explained, the better the organisation, the better the chance of the film coming in on budget.

'Not that it happens that much,' she added. 'There's always something unexpected that puts the costs through the roof.'

'At least we don't have to remake all the costumes for a new leading lady,' said Gemma.

Arabella shook her head. 'At least there's that. As long as the silly woman doesn't go and do something else sordid.'

In the corner of the room, Toxic Tina glowered. They were dissing her idol again.

'And you're all right to get here for five in the morning?' said Arabella.

'I'll have to be,' said Gemma. 'I'll get the night bus in. They're pretty reliable.'

'Just don't be late. The minibus will leave on the dot. We have to be at the house ready for the stars as soon as they pitch up. Time is money in this game.' She bustled off to supervise the despatch of the gowns for the ballroom sequence, which was being filmed at a stately home just outside London. Then she and Tina were going to the big house to carry on organising their part of the operation at that end. Tina and Arabella had already spent several days there making sure that the costumes were all ready and in order, that the big marquee, erected for use by the extras, was properly kitted out with mirrors, hanging rails and dividing screens to provide a modicum of privacy. Gemma couldn't wait to join them tomorrow, even if it did mean a hideously early start. Shooting was due to start at ten but before then they had to get the cast dressed and made up, and, given the numbers involved in these scenes, it was going to be quite a task.

A team of assistants for wardrobe and make-up had been hired in to help with the dozens of extras. Gemma had been warned that it would be absolutely manic and that at the end of the day she would be wrung out with exhaustion, but she didn't care. This was what she had longed to do since she'd won a place at fashion college and the icing on the cake was that she might get the chance to catch a glimpse of Jono. She had no intention of doing anything more than that. It would be too dodgy to make proper contact with him, beyond a possible polite 'hello', with so many people around.

The day whirled past with phones ringing, orders being frantically given and received, tempers being lost, and stress levels rocketing. And that was just in Gemma's attic sanctuary. A phone call from Arabella at the location indicated that things were even more frenetic there, as behind Arabella's imperious voice Gemma could hear shouts from the gaffers, the riggers and the chippies. She could barely make out what Arabella was saying to her over the bedlam of bangs and thumps as lighting rigs and ramps were put together in the grand ballroom of the house.

'What?' shrieked Gemma, for about the third time, into the phone.

'Hang on,' said Arabella. There was a pause, then, 'Is that better?'

It was. Gemma couldn't, for the life of her, imagine why Arabella hadn't phoned from somewhere quieter in the first place.

'I said,' repeated Arabella, 'don't forget to bring the

sewing machines and the sewing box when you come tomorrow. Someone is bound to put a heel through a hem.'

'I won't,' said Gemma, although she already had it on her list of stuff to lug with her to the location. Once they started shooting everything could stay there until they moved back to the studios. 'What about the ironing board and iron?' And the kitchen sink, she felt tempted to add.

'No, we've got several set up here. Right, I'll see you tomorrow, bright and early.'

'Indeed,' said Gemma, thinking that she would be early but unlikely to be bright at that hour. And she was so excited about the whole thing she thought it unlikely that she was going to sleep very well that night, but was it just excitement that shooting was about to start, or was it that she might see Jono? His name was on the call sheet so he was definitely going to be there. She felt a little swoop of joy at the thought.

She staggered into the flat at nearly nine that night. Last-minute hitches and problems had kept her hard at it at the office until way past eight.

'Blimey,' said Zoë. 'Is it going to be like this every day? You're going to end up a wreck if it is.'

'It explains why the pay is good.' Gemma kicked off her shoes and flopped on to the worn, stained sofa. 'Be a honey and make me a cup of tea.'

'And how about a sandwich – or some toast?'

Gemma felt almost too tired to eat but knew that she was simply being foolish if she didn't. 'That would be brill. Sandwich. Cheese and pickle?'

'If we've got any, it's yours.' Zoë went into the kitchen

and Gemma listened to her filling the kettle and opening and shutting drawers and cupboards before shutting her eyes – just for a minute or two.

'Hey. Eat this, then go to bed. I'll run you a bath.'

Gemma dragged herself out of her slumber. She felt as though she'd been buried alive by dust or sand; her mouth felt all gritty and her eyes were heavy and itchy and all of her senses seemed to have been dulled and abraded.

'Yeah?' she yawned.

'Cheese and pickle toasted sandwich and tea.' Zoë eyed her sternly. 'I'll run you a bath while you eat it and then you must go straight to bed. What time did you say you have to be up in the morning?'

'You foun li my muvver,' mumbled Gemma, through bread and cheese.

'And your mother would say exactly the same as I am – if you're to be up early, you need an early night,' said Zoë crisply. 'You'll make yourself ill at this rate.'

Gemma rolled her eyes and chewed off another bit of her sandwich while Zoë went into the bathroom and turned on the taps. 'I won't. It'll get sorted. Not everyday will be as bonkers as this. It's just because it's the start. And when we get to Spain, I won't have to worry about commuting. That'll be a doddle after this.'

'Huh,' billowed out of the bathroom along with some steam. Gemma took her sarnie and went into her room to get undressed. When she reappeared in her dressing gown, Zoë, pink in the face, emerged from the bathroom.

'Do you want a hot-water bottle?' she asked.

'Zo, I'll be fine. Honest. I'm tired. I'm not ill. And I can sleep on the minibus to the location tomorrow.'

'Make sure you do,' said Zoë, pushing her into the bathroom.

Ten minutes later it was Gemma emerging pink faced. 'Night, night,' she mumbled as she fell on to her bed. She shut her eyes and didn't even hear Zoë switch off the light.

And sleep on the minibus was exactly what she did until she was shaken awake by one of the make-up girls.

'Get a load of this,' said Janine.

Sleepily, Gemma rubbed her eyes and stretched. It took her a second or two to get her bearings and to work out where she was. Then she focussed properly. Out of the windscreen of the minibus she could see a stunning Georgian mansion complete with portico and a sweep of steps up to the front door. On either side of the bus was what looked like a caravan park full of huge trailers, trucks, lorries and cars. At the edge of this was a large truck with a queue of people stretching away from it. The ones at the head of the queue were having mounds of eggs and bacon shovelled on to their plates. The smell of breakfast drifted into the minibus and Gemma's stomach rumbled loudly. A snatched lunch and a cheese and pickle toastie had been all she'd eaten the day before and she was famished.

The bus braked and its passengers gathered together their belongings. Gemma staggered off the vehicle with a large sewing basket over one arm. She'd have to come back for the two sewing machines. Pack mule she wasn't. She looked around to find out where she was supposed to go. The clue was in the pink fluorescent sign that had 'costume and make-up' on it in bold capitals and which pointed the way to a marquee behind the trailer park. Gemma hitched the sewing basket more firmly over her arm and walked towards it.

Despite the fact that it was only just after dawn there was hustle and bustle all round her. Men carrying lengths of scaffolding or planks headed purposefully towards the house. A length of track for the cameras was being laid in from of the steps and across the gravel drive. A cherry-picker was being manoeuvred into position and everywhere men with radios were instructing others about the placing of lighting rigs and cameras.

Gemma picked her way carefully over the cables that snaked across the grass and tried to ignore the delicious smell of frying bacon that followed her. She ducked through the door flap of the marquee. Inside, it smelt of trodden grass and damp canvas and all around her were racks and racks of clothes, all carefully labelled with bags of shoes and accessories tied to the hangers.

'There you are,' said Arabella, looking and sounding fraught and with her arms full of Regency evening dresses. 'Where have you been?'

'The bus has only just got here.'

'Put the sewing basket down and make yourself useful. These costumes here need to go to the dressers over there.'

Gemma had rather been hoping to have been told to get herself some breakfast and a cup of coffee, not to start work immediately, but she didn't dare argue. Instead, she relieved Arabella of the gowns, and trotted over to the corner of the marquee that Arabella had indicated. She handed the costumes over and helped hang them up.

Behind a couple of screens that looked as though they might have been past props from a medical drama, a number of female extras were already being hauled into corsets to give their bodies the right sort of shape to look good under Empire-line dresses. There were squeaks and squeals as the dressers pulled on the laces. Some of the actors were slightly on the plump side and the dressers were going to be hard pressed to get a slim silhouette – if that was what they were after. Gemma thought that if they bunged her in a corset, because she hadn't eaten properly for so long, they would be able to get the two sides to close up completely on her and get her waist down to a hand span. Her tummy rumbled again as if in agreement.

After collecting the two sewing machines she'd left on the bus, Gemma returned to Arabella with the intention of asking if she could go and get herself a coffee.

'Good,' said her boss, before Gemma could form her request. 'Now I need you to take these dresses into the main house, to the dressing rooms we have made in there for the principal artistes. They're on the far side of the ballroom – you can't miss them. Tina has asked if she might be allowed to dress Rowan. I didn't think you would have any feelings one way or the other.'

Gemma kept schtum. She did have feelings but she certainly wasn't going to admit them to anyone – let alone to Arabella or Tina. Anyway, this suited her just fine. Apart from anything else, as far as she was concerned, Toxic Tina and Rowan the uber-bitch deserved each other.

Gemma left the marquee, flung a longing glance at the catering truck, and headed up the steps into the stately home. The black-and-white marble-tiled hall was chaotic with a scaffolding rig in the middle of it carrying lights and cameras and yet more cables snaking over it like malevolent black liana vines in a jungle. The sound of hammering reverberated around the space making Gemma's ears ring, so she crossed it as quickly as she could and headed deeper into the house to try to find the dressing rooms for the stars. More activity seemed to be coming from a door to her left so she peeped round it. Perhaps this was the ballroom.

It was. Huge and elegant, with a high ceiling and massive portraits hanging against the walls. Five long windows graced one wall, each window dressed with fabulous curtains. The floor was polished wood and at one end was a small gallery. Gemma reckoned that originally it had been intended for musicians to use; now it was chock-full of lights and a camera. More lights were suspended from rigs up near the ceiling and there were huge circles of silver fabric strategically placed in various corners to reflect lights back into the room. And everywhere there were the ubiquitous cables to be stepped over and avoided.

Gemma made her way cautiously across the space and out the door at the far end. Goodness only knew what the room beyond had originally been but now it was filled with prefab partitions to form a series of rooms off a central corridor. In the space closest to her was Tina, carefully ironing the amber-coloured dress that was to be Rowan's for the ballroom scenes.

Tina put the iron down, shook out the dress and put it back on its hanger.

'Hi,' she said sullenly.

Gemma smiled. Just because Tina didn't have any

social skills, there was no need to fall to her level. 'Where should I put these?' she asked, inclining her head to the pile of dresses in her arms.

'Check the labels in the dresses to see who they are for. The names of the artistes are on the doors. You need to iron them before you hang them up.'

'Fine,' said Gemma. No offer of help, she noticed. But then, it was Tina she was talking to.

She dumped the dresses on a nearby rail and began checking the labels. She found the names of the actors sewn inside the neck. Right, now to match them up with the dressing rooms. Gemma spent the next half-hour taking each gown, ironing it, and then hanging it carefully in the correct makeshift dressing room. She had just finished and was thinking longingly of coffee and bacon butties again and wondering if she could slip away for just a tick when Arabella appeared.

How does she do it? thought Gemma. All she'd needed was five minutes. Oh well, if she looked on the bright side she might yet make it down to a size eight. Arabella had yet another list of things for Gemma to do. As she was talking she snuck a glance at her watch. Only seven o'clock! And yet she'd been up for hours.

Gemma worked flat out organising costumes, dealing with minor alterations, and making sure that the extras weren't planning to go on the set wearing their watches or inappropriate earrings when Arabella appeared yet again.

'Jono and Rowan have arrived. David is bringing them through to their dressing rooms.'

A little burst of happiness flowered like a firework inside Gemma but she made a big effort to keep her face impassive. There was a small flurry as the stars' entourage arrived. Rowan, as always, made an entrance. David, the production manager, and Jono kept a pace or two behind her to allow her her moment of carefully engineered adulation.

'Gemma,' said David, 'good to see you at work. Makes a change, I hear.'

Gemma was completely wrong-footed. What on earth was he on about? She was always at work. Fucking hell, getting *home* was the trick at the moment! She shrugged. Frankly, she was too busy right now to try to decipher what he meant. Besides, she had more to worry about than one of her superiors having hold of the wrong end of the stick. Perhaps he'd confused her with someone else.

Arabella stepped forward and introduced Tina to Rowan. Gemma noticed that Tina's face was transformed. She'd spotted from comments and events back at the production offices that Tina seemed very keen on Rowan, but Gemma was slightly stunned by the look of rapture that now lightened her usually surly features. She also looked as if she was about to curtsey. Gemma turned away to hide a smile – and found herself face to face with Jono.

'Hi, Gemma,' he said, gazing into her eyes.

Gemma's pulse rocketed. If she'd been a cartoon character her heart would have been thudding visibly out of her chest and bells would have been clanging around her ears. 'Mr Knighton.' She prayed she sounded cool, not the emotional mess that she felt. Jono raised an eyebrow of acknowledgement. Perhaps she did.

Beside her, Tina was fawning and gushing and Rowan was apparently impressed. She was certainly smiling. Maybe that was the way to treat stars. Shame, thought Gemma, because she really didn't think that sycophancy was in her psyche.

'I'll show you to your dressing room,' she offered.

'Thank you.' Jono moved forward, followed by Rowan, and David came too. Gemma wished they'd bugger off. She wanted just a second or two with Jono – alone. But, at this rate, it was going to be something else, along with breakfast, that she was going to be denied today.

She opened the door to Jono's room; a larger MDF-built space than most and with a sofa, a TV, a bowl of fruit and flowers. His uniform and accoutrements and accessories were hanging up ready for him and the lights were on around his mirror.

'Thanks,' said Jono.

'Is there anything else we can get you?' asked David.

Gemma guessed that for 'we' he actually meant 'Gemma'.

'I'd love a coffee. And perhaps something to eat? Rowan?'

Rowan shook her head and pointedly sipped at the bottle of water in her hand.

'Of course,' said Gemma. 'Coming right up.' She almost skipped out of the room. She'd get him a bacon buttie and maybe one for herself. One for you and one for me, she thought.

She wolfed hers down by the catering truck and wiped away all traces of grease from around her mouth before she returned. She knocked and went into Jono's dressing room with his buttie and his coffee. She balanced the tray on the flat of one hand and carefully opened the door.

'Oh, it's you,' said Rowan frostily as she entered.

'Just bringing Mr Knighton some breakfast,' explained Gemma.

'White bread and bacon! For heaven's sakes. Take it away. And caffeine? Ohmigod!'

Gemma began to back out of the door again. Shit. Jono

hadn't seemed averse to junk food and caffeine when they'd had a pizza together, but mentioning that was hardly going to be politic. This was Jono's battle and she wasn't going to get involved.

'Actually, it's *exactly* what I want,' said Jono, grasping the tray and taking it from her. Rowan shot him a look. Gemma slid out of the dressing room and shut the door. From over the top of the MDF partition she could hear Rowan start on Jono about his diet and his health. That's rich coming from you, she thought venomously. At least his liver is probably in a lot better shape than yours!

Arabella pitched up again. 'Can you and Tina get Jono and Rowan along to make-up? Then, as soon as they have finished there, you and Tina need to get them into their costumes. David and the director are having fits about starting off as we mean to go on – and that means getting everyone on set on time.'

'Yes, Arabella,' said Gemma meekly.

Arabella tapped her foot. 'So what are you waiting for?'

'Miss Day is with her husband.'

Arabella tilted her head and listened to the raised voices drifting over the partition.

'Ah, I see,' she said. 'Well, perhaps we can afford to wait for five more minutes.'

Gemma hung around outside make-up while the girls there worked their magic. No heavy pan-stick or any other sort of obvious make-up for film stars. With cameras getting so close that every pore was visible, the make-up experts had to ensure that Rowan and Jono looked natural while enhancing their features and skin tones incredibly subtly. Gemma idly wondered if they would teach her a thing or too about the tricks of the trade.

As soon as they were made up and Rowan's wig was in

place, Gemma and Tina took them back to their dressing rooms. The two stars were dressed in luxurious bathrobes. Now it was up to Tina and Gemma to finish the transformation and make them into the characters the public would see at the cinemas. Gemma had to whiz off to pick up Jono's jacket from where one of the assistants was pressing it. When she returned and knocked on Jono's door, he opened it already dressed in his breeches and shirt.

'Do you require any help?' she enquired politely, aware that she had no idea who might be listening as these partitioned rooms only gave privacy from eyes not ears.

'Absolutely,' said Jono, opening the door wide.

Gemma stepped inside and hung the jacket on the rail as Jono shut the door behind her. She could see he was just about to say something to her when she gestured frantically to the open ceiling of the room and shook her head in warning. He nodded.

Silently, he wrapped his arms around her. Gemma stiffened and tried to pull back, but Jono held her close. She'd promised herself that she would keep Jono at a distance until he and Rowan were sorted out and yet . . . a hug was pretty innocent. It was just a friendship thing. Gemma rested her head against his chest. Then, the door burst open without warning. Gemma leapt back as if she'd been touched with a cattle prod. And there was Rowan.

Gemma turned away, sure her face was either white or crimson. The way she was feeling there was no way it could have been 'normal'. Luckily, they were almost behind the door when it flew open and thus shielded from view so it was possible Rowan had seen nothing. Even so, she might have noticed something. Gemma dared to look back to see Rowan's reaction but she didn't seem to be aware of anything out of order. She felt her knees sag with nerves and relief. That had been a close shave. What on earth had she been thinking of, letting Jono hug her like that with Rowan around? She must have been mad. Well, she thought, it wasn't going to happen again. Whatever risks Jono was prepared to take, she wasn't.

'Darlin',' said Rowan, 'you've got to get Max on to this. My dressing room is just not good enough. I tried telling David but he said he was sure I could cope. But I can't, honey. I can't.'

'Why don't *you* talk to Max?'

'Oh, honey, you know he and I don't see eye to eye. We had the most terrible row in LA. He'll listen to you.'

And why did Max despise Rowan? thought Gemma.

Would it be because she was a spoilt, overbearing egotistical cow, with the morals of an alley cat and the self-restraint of a two year old? The only reason Max would help Jono out on this would be to give everyone else a quiet life. Judging from the look on Jono's face, this was what he thought, too.

He sighed. 'Okay,' he said, 'I'll give him a ring when Gemma has finished with me.'

'Make sure you do that, honey. I'm going to get cabin fever in that little place. I just know it.' She shot a glance at Gemma as if she was daring her to contradict what she'd just said and swept out.

'Let's get this jacket on then, Mr Knighton, shall we,' said Gemma breezily and loudly for the sake of Rowan who would surely still be able to hear every word from the other side of the door. One of them had to act at being normal. As Jono didn't seem inclined to do so, it left things up to her.

Jono sighed and rolled his eyes, but Gemma ignored him and held out the jacket ready for him to put his arms down the sleeves. She slipped it on to his shoulders and smoothed the fabric across them, brushing off a couple of tiny stray threads. The fit was perfect.

She walked round to the front to help him with the buttons but as she went to fasten them he held her wrists in his hands and pulled her to him again. She shook her head vehemently. Her heart was still thumping from the last close call with Rowan. She didn't think her system could cope with another fright like that.

'No,' she whispered. 'Are you mad?'

'Just mad about you,' said Jono softly.

Gemma's stomach went into freefall. And she was mad about him. There was no denying it. She was miserable when he wasn't around, she spent every spare moment thinking about him, but he wasn't hers to love. She knew that, and she kept telling herself so, and Jono making such a declaration was making life impossible for her. She'd resolved to keep him at arm's length emotionally and this wasn't helping matters one jot. Please, God, Jono would find a way of getting Rowan sorted so he could leave her.

Not that she could really believe what was happening. Perhaps she was just deluding herself. She was a nobody and this was real life and stuff like this didn't happen to girls like her. Jono was just stringing her along. Thoughts that contradicted each other jumbled through her head as she breathed in his scent and rested against his chest.

A noise from over the MDF wall brought her back to her senses. She twisted her wrists to disengage from his grip and resumed buttoning up his jacket. He sighed but didn't resist. She threaded his cross-belt under one of his epaulettes, fastened it, and finally took his headdress out of its hat box and handed it to him.

'Perfect,' she said as he put it on.

'All nice girls love a soldier.'

'I think you'll find it is sailors that nice girls love,' corrected Gemma, desperately trying to keep her feelings from running amok.

'Whatever. And I'm sure soldiers love nice girls.'

She snorted and shushed him, feeling a glow from his kind words stoke up her emotions again. 'Now get yourself on set,' she said, trying to ignore his remark. 'I'll get the blame if you're late.'

Jono left his dressing room and went towards the ballroom. Gemma stayed behind, getting herself under control again by tidying up some bits and pieces before she followed him.

*

The ballroom was now full of the actors and extras in elegant Regency costumes, the girls flashing fans and eyes and the men swaggering about in tailcoats and uniforms. Instructions were being shouted to men up on the rigs to get the lights adjusted to the director's satisfaction. In one corner was a bank of monitors recording what the camera operators could see through their viewfinders. Gemma made her way across to this position. It was one of her jobs to make sure that there were no screaming anomalies visible on screen. The dressers had all insisted that things like wristwatches be removed, but it was possible for other items to get overlooked; spectacles, for example. And she and one of the make-up artists would also keep an eagle eye out for continuity errors, such as the girls switching fans into their other hand or taking their gloves off in one take and putting them back on for the next.

Eventually, the director called for silence and the cast was got into position for the first scene to be shot. The sound of the chamber orchestra tuning up and playing a few bars at random from their score died away, the buzz of chatter from the extras and cast was silenced and the crew stood still and concentrated on their allotted tasks. There was a tangible sense of excitement and tension as everyone waited for the shooting to start. A clapperboard was held in front of one of the cameras and then the word 'action' was said. The clapper shut with a sharp 'snick' and Jono and Rowan playing Captain Berkeley and Miss Martha Spencer strolled past a number of the cast, nodding their heads in acknowledgement at greetings being addressed to them and then they turned to each other. All very simple and short and, as far as Gemma could see, not very demanding.

'And cut,' said the director. There was a muffled discussion between the director and a couple of other members of the crew. 'And again,' said the director.

Five minutes later, some minute adjustments were made to the lighting, one of the make-up girls had darted forward and brushed powder over Rowan's forehead, the cast were back in the exact same places as before, and the clapperboard now showed that this was the second take.

The scene was run through again and to Gemma's untrained eye it looked precisely the same as it had the previous time. On this occasion, however, something was obviously better, or right, or whatever it was that ticked the director's boxes, as this one was okay and the actors wandered off the set while the lights and camera angles were adjusted for the next shot. A hubbub broke out as everyone rushed around attending to their allotted tasks, all of which seemed to take far more time than the shooting of the last scene had taken. Gemma watched in interest.

By the time they were shooting the fifth scene, Gemma's interest in the film-making process had waned dramatically and she had decided that 'tedious' was the word that seemed to sum up the whole process. But at the end of that scene, the director announced a break for lunch.

'At last,' said Gemma, stretching her aching back. The canvas seat provided for her by the monitor was far from comfortable.

She dashed off to Jono's dressing room to help him out of his costume before he went to lunch. There was no way he was going to be allowed to spill food down it. She got there first and kicked her heels until he arrived.

'How was it?' he asked when he bounced in.

Gemma smiled. 'I'm no expert but it all looked great.' She didn't think it politic to say she'd been bored to tears. She undid his cross-belt and then eased his jacket off his back and hung it up carefully.

'If you get out of the rest of your kit I'll hang it all up and make sure it's ready for the afternoon while you go and get some lunch.

'And what about *your* lunch?'

'I'll find time to grab something,' said Gemma, hoping to God she would. Breakfast had been a bit of a mission and things seemed even more frantic now then they had been then. This was apparently the way of films; hours of inactivity interspersed with short bursts of mayhem.

The front of Jono's breeches was creased so Gemma went to find the ironing board to sort them out. She had to wait her turn while Tina pressed Rowan's ball gown. She was sure Tina was taking more time than was necessary and going over and over areas that she had already pressed. How long did it take to press a dress? Ages, when Tina was doing it. Finally, looking smug, Tina relinquished the iron and even that seemed to be done in slow motion.

'Thanks,' said Gemma curtly, resisting the urge to slap her. She glanced at her watch. Lunch looked unlikely. Maybe she would be able to grab a sandwich while they were setting up shots for the afternoon. She sighed and her stomach rumbled. She decided she ought to bring in a packed lunch tomorrow, but when was she going to find the time to buy one? She left home before the shops were open and she didn't think she'd be back before they shut. On the plus side it would be good for her waistline. Feeling tired and hungry, she returned to the dressing room to hang up Jono's clothes. She knocked before she opened the door. Jono was there with a plate of delicious-looking food. Gemma tried to ignore it but the smell of lasagne wafted over to her. Her stomach rumbled again.

'You hungry?' said Jono.

Gemma stopped herself from snapping back – what do you think? Instead, she restrained herself to admitting that she was, a bit.

'Then tuck in.'

'But . . .' She didn't understand.

'I brought this for you. I've already had mine.'

'But you can't run errands for me. People will notice.'

'Let them. Now, you get yourself on the outside of that. I've got to go and find a loo.'

He disappeared out of the door and Gemma fell on the lasagne. It was amazing – and not just because she was famished. Obviously, the location catering was of the highest standard but considering the sort of people needing to be fed – people who were used to dining in the best restaurants in London, people who had their own cooks and housekeepers, people for whom money was no object – they had to produce top-grade food.

Gemma heard the door behind her open. She didn't bother to turn around but said, with her mouth half full, 'This is delicious. Thanks.'

'Well, I'm so pleased you're enjoying it, honey,' hissed Rowan, her eyes narrowed in anger.

Gemma dropped her fork with a clatter and leapt to her feet.

'And what do you think you're doing?' Rowan added.

Gemma was lost for words. 'I . . . errr . . .'

Rowan tapped her foot. 'Well, as you don't seem to have an answer for me, maybe you'll have one for David. I'm sure the production manager will want to know why you think you are too good to eat with the rest of the crew.'

'I don't. I mean . . .' But Gemma didn't know what she meant. Her heart was thudding uncomfortably and she felt sick. Whatever she said was going to make matters worse.

The door opened again.

'Hi, Rowan,' said Jono, re-entering the room. He sensed the strained atmosphere instantly. 'Something wrong?'

'I was just asking –' Rowan shook her head impatiently, unable to remember Gemma's name; instead, she said, '*her* what she thinks she's doing in here.'

Jono shrugged. 'Eating her lunch. What does it look like?'

'But this is your dressing room.'

'And I said she could.'

The pair stared at each other like two cats about to fight. Then Rowan lowered her eyes and flounced out. 'Well, I don't think it pays to get too familiar with the hired staff,' she shot back as she left.

Gemma sagged back into her chair.

'Sorry about that,' said Jono cheerfully. 'Never mind.'

Gemma pushed her plate away from her, her appetite gone. He might be able to make light of that little scene but Gemma didn't think that Rowan disliking her and thinking she was taking liberties would do her any good at all – even if Jono felt the opposite.

She helped Jono get back into his costume and returned to her place by the monitors. Sat in the corner, she was pretty much out of sight of everyone and she took the opportunity to let her eyes shut for just a second before they started filming again.

'Not interrupting your afternoon nap, I hope, Gemma?'

Gemma was propelled into wakefulness in a nano-second. David was bending over her.

'Hi,' she said weakly. 'Yes,' she added, trying to sound bright and alert.

David gave her a hard stare. 'You know, I don't ever get the impression that you're giving this job one hundred per cent.'

'But I am,' protested Gemma. 'I love it.' Why did he think that she was slacking? She'd never worked so hard in her life. Hell, she had no social life to speak of, she either seemed to be at work or in bed and there seemed to be precious little time for the latter at the moment. She was dog-tired most of the time, but she was happy. She wouldn't have believed that it was possible to devote so much time to work and not feel like a slave.

'And what's this about you eating in the artiste's dressing rooms?'

'It wasn't my idea. Mr Knighton brought me a bite because I didn't have time to go to the catering truck. Honest.' Why did she feel that this guy was gunning for her? She looked at him pleadingly. What was there not to believe? As if she'd dare to eat in the star's dressing rooms without permission.

David gave her another hard stare and told her to get over to the marquee where the extras were dressed. 'There's a problem with the paperwork for some of the hire costumes. Arabella wants you to sort it out.'

'I'll get on to it.'

'Get Tina to watch for continuity.'

'Right.'

Gemma went to find Tina. She guessed that she might be in Rowan's dressing room. The trouble was, after the incident at lunchtime, Gemma really didn't want to see Rowan again but she didn't have much choice.

Tentatively, she knocked on the door.

'Come in,' called Rowan.

Gemma eased it open a fraction and poked her head through the gap.

'Oh, it's you,' sneered Rowan. Her animosity towards Gemma was transparently obvious.

'I came to ask if Tina could go on set.'

'I need her,' said Rowan, although as she was dressed and ready to go on, Gemma couldn't think why on earth she did.

Tina smiled smugly behind Rowan's back.

Licker, thought Gemma, but she smiled sweetly and insisted, 'David wants her.'

Rowan looked less than pleased. 'You'd better run along, then, Tina. But hurry back.'

Tina slipped out past Gemma, tossing her head arrogantly as she left. She knows she's Rowan's pet, thought Gemma, and Rowan just loves the adulation. And the thought of the two of them, each feeding off the other, was unsettling.

As Gemma shut the door quietly behind her an even more unsettling thought struck her. Suppose Tina told Rowan about Jono texting her? Shit, what then? Not that there was anything she could do about it and, anyway, even if Tina told Rowan, both she and Jono could deny everything. But given the symbiotic relationship that seemed to be developing between Tina and Rowan, would she believe her own husband's denial? Probably not. Rowan wouldn't be able to prove anything and Jono might just convince her there was nothing to worry about – but maybe he wouldn't. It was a scary thought.

The rest of the week passed in a blur of activity and exhaustion. Gemma was too busy to even think about Tina confiding secrets to Rowan, and as the pace of the filming began to pick up, as the crew got used to working with each other and everyone became familiar with the location and the routine, Gemma had only just enough time to keep tabs on her own duties. She certainly didn't have any slack to worry about anything else.

On the Thursday afternoon, she brought a freshly laundered shirt to Jono's dressing room for him to wear under his uniform. He slipped off his dressing gown to put it on and she saw a hideous bruise on his chest. She raised an eyebrow but kept her thoughts to herself.

'So you're ignoring the elephant in the room.'

'What?' Gemma shook her head. What elephant? Had Jono lost the plot?

'You're ignoring the thing that's the most obvious.'

The penny dropped and Gemma shrugged. She lowered her voice, conscious of the lack of privacy from eavesdroppers. 'And what am I supposed to say? Has your wife stopped beating you?'

'Well, it seems she hasn't. You said you have some magic potion or lotion that's good for bruises.'

Gemma nodded. 'Arnica.'

'You don't happen to have any on you, do you?'

'It's not the sort of thing I keep handy. I'll bring some in tomorrow. Does it hurt much?'

'Like hell.'

'Why did Ro—?' Gemma stopped herself. It was no business of hers. But she ached for Jono. He looked so utterly miserable. Life with Rowan was no picnic, that much she had gathered, and he was suffering in every way possible. If he wasn't such an ace bloke he'd have walked out on her months, even years, earlier. But because he was basically a 'nice guy', he was sacrificing his own happiness to try to stop his bitch of a wife from completely self-destructing.

'Why did Rowan hit me? That's what you were going to say, wasn't it?' Gemma nodded. 'She was drunk, she was angry, she was feeling insecure. Christ alone knows. Probably because I was there and in the line of fire.'

'Oh, Jono, I feel so sorry for you.'

Jono smiled wryly. 'Ironic, isn't it? There am I feted, living in the lap of luxury and sharing a marital bed with a woman whom most men would give their back teeth just to be in the same building with. And then there's you, a kid working all the hours in the day for rubbish money, living in a bedsit in King's Cross, feeling sorry for me.' He shook his head sadly. 'And, somehow, I feel as though you have more going for you right now than I do. Frankly, my life is shit. My marriage is a complete sham, and I may be rich but I'm sure as hell not happy. I really envy you, Gemma. You've got it made.'

Gemma shrugged. 'I don't think so.'

'But, as I've said before, I can remember what it was like to live in grotty digs and I can also remember being where you are right now. I can remember what it was like to feel as though I'd got my foot on the first rung of a ladder that I really wanted to climb. I remember the excitement of being part of a play, of working with people who knew exactly how I felt, who had the same ambitions as I did and who thought that getting applause at the end of the evening was worth more than the pay. But now I'm in films and, sure, the pay is great, and I'm further up the ladder, but I'm not sure the view I've got of the world and my career is the one I want any more.'

'Well, why don't you go back to the theatre? If that's what you love so much.'

'You're right, of course. I should. If I'm going to be true to myself that's exactly what I ought to do.'

'So?'

'Mostly the reason I've stuck with films recently is to try and keep solidarity with Rowan, to try and keep her in the parts she needs so badly and to keep her from going off the rails completely. But she's got this deal in the States. I have made up my mind that, after we've finished on this film, when she goes off to make this series in LA, I'm going to end it and stay put. I'm fed up with looking out for her all the time, from making sure she behaves in public and apologising for the times she doesn't. I've had enough. I haven't the energy to be her minder any more. And, more importantly, I've met you.' Gemma thought that Jono looked completely exhausted and wretched, but she couldn't help feeling a thrill at his words.

'Then you must do it, if that's what you want. And get back to the stage. It's your career. You've got to be true to yourself.'

'I tell myself that, but it's tough. It's not that I'm afraid of going back to the stage or not getting the part. Maybe I will, maybe I won't, but I've got enough put by not to starve for a year or two. So, if I have you and a career back on the stage, I truly believe that I'll be happier than I've been in a long time. Except –' he paused. 'Except that I know I'm going to spend months worrying about Rowan on her own and all the things she might or might not get up to. I can't build my happiness on someone else's ruin.' He sighed and looked beaten. 'You know, I don't know I can do this.' Gemma could see what he was afraid of. That she might overdose on booze or drugs by accident – or worse, on purpose.

Gemma took Jono's hands. 'Look, she's a grown-up. She can make her own decisions. She ought to be able to look after herself. And if she can't, well, maybe she'll find someone else to take on the job of minder. Maybe you ought to walk away to make her sort herself out or find someone else who actually wants the job.'

'You think I'm right? That I should go?'

'I do.' She stared up at Jono, willing him to believe that she had no alternative agenda. That she wasn't suggesting he abandon Rowan for any reason than for his own happiness. Jono smiled back at her.

Neither of them heard the door open.

'How touching,' drawled Rowan from the door to the dressing room. 'And I didn't know you cared, Jono.'

Gemma dropped Jono's hands and spun round, feeling her heart judder with fear. She felt her blood drain down to her legs leaving her dizzy. Shit!

'You know, Tina said she thought that you and Jono had gotten close. She even said you were swapping text messages.' She snorted. 'And I didn't believe her. I mean, why?' She took a step into the room, her eyes glittering and her colour high. 'Why? Why would a guy like Jono take the least interest in *you*?' She spat the last word out. 'I mean, I can see that *you* might go after *him*. Great catch, after all's said and done.' Rowan leaned close to Gemma and lowered her voice as if she were her best friend about to confide something. 'Between you and me, honey, not wonderful in the sack, if you know what I mean, but I don't suppose you're interested in that. I expect you just fancy getting a piece of his paycheque, or a slice of the fame. Or maybe you just want a leg up in your career. Well, I suppose getting your leg over is one way to get a leg up.' She forced a laugh. 'Or maybe you get your kicks from notching up quick fucks with other people's husbands. Is that it? Is that what floats your boat?'

'Now that's enough,' Jono started, but Rowan ignored him.

She thrust her face close to Gemma's. 'But do you really want to know something, honey? I just don't care what makes you tick because that's it, as far as I'm concerned. I've had it with you to here.' She flung her hand dramatically to her forehead and if Gemma hadn't been so frightened and embarrassed she might have almost found it funny.

But this was no laughing matter. Not at all. Gemma was scared, embarrassed and shocked. And in the wrong. Jono was Rowan's husband and she mustn't forget that. Rowan had every right to be livid. Gemma wanted to crawl away.

'It's not what you think,' she stammered.

'So what is it?' sneered Rowan. 'Go on, amaze me. Because I know what it looks like and I was always taught that if it looks like a duck, walks like a duck and quacks like a duck, then it's a fucking duck. Are you telling me that I'm wrong?' She was sounding seriously dangerous now.

Jono had had enough. 'So what if there's something going on?' he snapped. Rowan went white with fury but he continued: 'You enjoy yourself, why can't I? I don't think you're in any position to make accusations.'

Gemma shut her eyes and took in a breath. Why was he making it worse? She didn't understand. She shook her head miserably. 'We're just friends,' she whispered.

'Friends? Ha!' Rowan's voice was shrill and malignant.

Gemma looked at Jono. Why wasn't he denying it? Why didn't he back her up? They'd exchanged a couple of kisses – so what? But Jono seemed to be goading Rowan with ideas that far more than that had gone on. Why? All her previous doubts came flooding back – she was nothing more than a fling, a way of striking back at his wife, and just an excuse to end his marriage. He was looking for a reason to prove how hopeless their marriage was. But it wasn't just him involved in this row. What about her? What about her job? She needed him on her side.

'It's true. Isn't it, Jono? Tell Rowan it's true,' she pleaded.

'Rowan wouldn't recognise the truth if it came gift-wrapped,' he sneered.

'Truth? Hah! Janet told me about your late-night visit.'

'But nothing happened,' protested Gemma. She looked pleadingly at Jono.

'She just came to see me. We had a meal and a drink together.'

At last, Jono was going to make Rowan see sense.

'Don't give me that,' snapped Rowan. 'I'm not buying it. That little tart has been making eyes at you from day one and you're shallow enough to be flattered.'

'So what? So what if we like each other? At least Gemma is fun and not completely screwed up.'

'Me? Screwed up? What about *you*? You think you're so goddam perfect you could walk on water.'

Gemma shook her head. If Jono thought that goading Rowan was going to make her back off, he was mad. She cowered as the two stars continued to trade insults across her.

Rowan drew breath and turned her attention back to Gemma. 'So do you know what you are going to do now?' she hissed.

Gemma shook her head miserably.

'You're going to get yourself off this lot and out of my sight. *Now!*' Rowan shouted the last word and Gemma jumped involuntarily.

'No, she isn't,' snarled back Jono. Gemma began to gather up her sewing box and other stuff. 'Wait. I'll sort this out.' But Gemma carried on. She couldn't see how anyone could save her job for her now.

'You'll do no such thing,' said Rowan.

'I'll do as I damn well please.'

'If you lift a finger to help that little tart, I'll walk off this movie.'

Jono glared at her and shook his head. 'You need this movie more than the movie needs you.'

'Wrong. And you know it. If I go, everyone here will be out of work and the millions invested will be down the john. No one is going to save a nobody like her when that much is at stake,' she hissed back. 'Gemma goes. I'm going to see David and get this little hooker sacked.'

She swept out of the room.

Weakly, Gemma sat down, her possessions clasped in her arms. She felt ill with fear. She remembered standing outside the Head's office when she had been about eleven, waiting for punishment for a misdemeanour at school and wondering if she was going to faint or throw up. She felt that same way again now – only ten times worse. Now she felt so ill, her heart was thumping so hard and irregularly, she wondered if something worse was going to happen to her. Could her body stand this sort of strain and come through it intact? And was it just fear that made her heart ache so much or was it the way Jono had acted? He'd seemed more set on getting even with his wife than defending her and Gemma felt utterly betrayed.

Jono came towards her. 'I promise. I'll make sure your job—'

'No,' said Gemma, holding up a hand to ward him off. She shouted, 'Don't you think you've done enough?' She was hurt and confused and she didn't want him comforting her or promising things she couldn't trust him to deliver. She understood her position now; she was just a convenient pawn in his plan to dump Rowan. It was the only explanation. If he felt for her the way he said he did, he would have battled for her. He knew what this job meant to her. But he'd abandoned her.

Jono backed away from her. It was what she wanted but a contrary part of Gemma was disappointed and angry. If he really cared for her, he would ignore the outburst, take her in his arms, tell her it was going to be all right, soothe her fears – not retreat and leave her alone.

She swallowed down sobs that were threatening to burst out of her and clutched her sewing box to her to stop her hands from shaking. She was hanging on to her self-control but only just. She wasn't going to give anyone the satisfaction of seeing how badly hurt she was. She shut her eyes and didn't see the hurt and confusion on Jono's face at her rejection.

A minute later, David stormed into the dressing room followed by a triumphant Rowan.

'Rowan tells me you've been behaving inappropriately with Jono,' he thundered.

Gemma, despite knowing that this was coming, was dumbstruck. She knew her mouth opened to protest but no sound came out. Besides, why was it all her fault? Except she was the one least able to fight back.

'I have also had reports that you skive off work at every opportunity. I've seen for myself that you sleep on the job. Frankly, we can do without people who aren't fully committed to this movie. There are enough people who would give every ounce to this movie, and I think the time has come when it would be easier to replace you rather than to keep on paying the wages of a lightweight.'

The tears, which Gemma had managed to hold in check, now spilled out and poured down her cheeks. This was all lies. She'd never skived off. She'd worked all the hours God had sent and then some. Who had reported her? Who hated her so much they made up lies like this about her?

'Great acting,' drawled Rowan. 'Gee, they almost look real.'

Gemma shook her head. This was all wrong. All unfair.

'I'll give you a month's pay in lieu of notice, although, frankly, you're not worth it. And I want you out of here in the next ten minutes.'

'If she goes, I go,' said Jono.

Too little too late, thought Gemma. Now David was on Rowan's side, Gemma knew she was completely out-gunned. She might have stood a chance if Jono had convinced Rowan that nothing had gone on between them but now David had waded into the fray on Rowan's side it was too late.

David shook his head at Jono. 'I don't think so,' he said. 'You want to look at your contract. Not even Max will be able to get you out of this.'

'We'll see,' said Jono angrily.

David took his mobile out of his pocket and handed it to Jono. 'Call Max. See what he says.'

While David and Jono sparred, Gemma stood up, her sewing box and other bits and pieces in her arms, and slipped out of the door. Outside the dressing room a small crowd had gathered. With the lack of sound-proofing, the row going on had been no secret and the curious had gathered to get ringside seats. In the front row was Tina.

'Shut the door quietly on your way out,' she crowed.

Gemma held her head up and walked past. The comment wasn't worth a riposte. As she was making her way back through the ballroom, followed by curious stares from those who had heard about the peremptory sacking – doesn't bad news travel fast, thought Gemma – she met Arabella.

'Gemma!'

Gemma stopped, although she didn't feel inclined to talk to anyone. She just wanted to get the hell off the set and go home to lick her wounds. But Arabella had given her her break and now she was being left in the lurch.

'So it's true.' Arabella sniffed.

'What?' she asked rudely. What did she care? She didn't care who she upset now. Nothing mattered any more. 'What? The allegations made against me or the news that I've been given the sack?' snapped Gemma, trying very hard to maintain her dignity and keep her tears under control.

'Why?'

'*Why* the untrue allegations or *why* have I been sacked?'

Arabella took Gemma by the arm and led her away to a quiet corner. 'Tell me what happened,' she said gently.

This was a side of Arabella that Gemma hadn't seen before and a lump of emotion formed once again in her throat. She swallowed and blinked and recounted the most recent events.

'And you can tell David that I've never skived. You know that. I never took time off, did I?' she finished.

Arabella nodded. 'I'll do my best, but there are people and backers on this movie who have a ton more clout than I do. I can't offer much hope. And you've been a pleasure to work with. You were an asset to the team. If ever you need a reference . . .'

A reference. Gemma supposed that was the best she could hope for out of this mess. No one was going to stick their neck out for her to keep her on the film. No, Gemma was now officially bad news and no one was going to risk their own job for hers.

She turned away and made her way off the set.

23

By the time Gemma got to King's Cross the rush hour was getting into its stride and she was encumbered by her bulky sewing box as well as her handbag. Around her people jostled and pushed as they made their way through the tunnels but Gemma was barely aware of anything. Her thoughts were entirely turned in on herself and she made her way through the Tube station on auto-pilot, barely conscious of her surroundings. Her thoughts were dominated by her shit day, her unfair treatment, her dismissal from her job, and Jono's betrayal. She was angry and upset and all she wanted to do was to get back to the flat, shut the world out, and crawl into a corner. Tears were only just below the surface and the sooner she got home the better so that she could let her emotions have full rein.

In the crowd waiting to squeeze on to the escalator from the subterranean depths, Gemma was jostled and pushed. She clutched her sewing box, hugging it against her body to prevent its corners from banging into the sides of the other commuters. Suddenly, she felt a sharp tug and a violent shove that almost knocked her off her feet. Angrily, she swung round to confront the impatient bastard who had pushed her so rudely, and saw a man clutching her handbag, its strap cut, and thrusting his way back through the crowd towards the platforms.

Her handbag! He'd taken her handbag. A wave of despair and rage rolled over her. She tried to push after him but the crowd seemed to have closed against her deliberately.

'Stop him!' she yelled. 'That's my bag.'

Others close to her in the crowd turned to watch the man melt into the mass of humanity but those at the back, intent on reaching the moving staircase and not understanding the hold up, pressed forward. Gemma, burdened with her sewing box and unable to insinuate herself through the throng, lost sight of him. She yelled, 'Stop him!' louder and with more desperation. More of the crowd began to pay attention but too late.

A couple of blokes looked at her curiously.

'Trouble, love?'

'That man – he took my bag.' Panic rose. 'He stole my bag.'

'What's he like?' the other one asked. 'The mugger.'

'Tall. Wearing a blue hoody. He's got my bag. My money, my cards, my keys.' She realised with mounting anxiety that she didn't even have a ticket. The tears that had been on the brink of falling before now spilled over. The two blokes shouldered the crowds of people aside and led Gemma to the side of the tunnel. Someone must have pressed the help button as Gemma saw two large policemen thundering down the other escalator towards her. After a brief conversation with her rescuers, one of the coppers took off in pursuit while the other led Gemma up the escalator and across the main concourse to an office. She was barely conscious of what was going on – someone else had taken charge of the situation and she had mentally shut down. This was a nightmare. This wasn't her life she was witnessing but someone else's. No one could have such a rotten day as this. No one deserved this amount of shit.

She was sitting on a hard plastic chair and brought a cup of tea while around her the bustle of a working police station continued. After a bit a female officer led her to a small office where she gave a statement and listed the contents of her bag; credit cards, cash, mobile phone, make-up, keys, address book . . . Nothing that couldn't be replaced eventually, but all things that, now they were gone, would leave a hole, would make life tricky for the next few weeks, and would cause her trouble and time to sort out. Eventually, she was free to go. As she was escorted to the front door the policewoman had tried to make the miserable incident seem less traumatic and make Gemma see that in some respects she might have got off lightly.

Gemma went through the motions of agreeing with what was said. She didn't have the energy or inclination to argue. Yes, she was grateful she wasn't hurt. Yes, it could have been worse. Yes, it would be good if she got her bag back even if it was empty. Yes, she understood that her assailant was unlikely to get caught. Yes, it was good if it meant she wouldn't have to make a court appearance.

'And you're sure you'll be all right to go home now?' asked the well-meaning policewoman.

Gemma nodded. It was only around the corner. Besides, no one was going to mug her now – she had nothing left to nick.

Finally, she was outside. She checked her watch. At

least Zoë would be home. Zoë could let her in and pour her a glass of wine while she told her about her day from hell. Zoë would sympathise. Zoë would be outraged. Gemma would be able to rant and rage.

Wearily, she made her way home and rang the bell to their flat. Nothing. She rang again. Maybe Zoë was in the loo – or taking a shower. She pressed the doorbell a third time. Where was she? She put her sewing box down on the step and reached for her phone, then leaned against the wall as she remembered it was gone. She was cold, miserable and broke and she just wanted to get indoors. Tears welled up again; tears of self-pity, anger and frustration. She slumped down on to the top step and pulled her jacket around her. This was the last fucking straw. She shut her eyes.

'Gem? Lost your key?'

Gemma jerked her head up. At last Zoë was there. Tears streamed down her face.

'Gem, what's happened?' Zoë cried, appalled. She pushed her key in the lock and ushered Gemma in ahead of her. As soon as they were inside Zoë hugged her. 'What's happened? Tell me.'

And Gemma did. Everything. Through gasping, racking sobs she told Zoë how she'd been mugged, let down and betrayed by Jono and Arabella and neither had valued her enough to fight for her, that she was jobless and worthless, that Tina hated her so much she'd lied through her teeth and she felt she wanted to die.

And Jono had lied when he'd said he cared for her.

Zoë listened in silence while she boiled the kettle and made them both mugs of strong tea.

'That bitch Tina,' whispered Zoë at the end.

'It w-w-wasn't ju-ju-just her,' Gemma juddered out,

clasping both her hands around her mug. 'It was m-m-me getting t-t-too friendly with Jo-jo-Jono, t-t-too.'

'And that cow Rowan's a bitch, too.' Zoë's eyes narrowed. 'Like she's so perfect. And as for the way she behaved on that plane!' She snorted in disgust.

Gemma blew her nose noisily on a piece of kitchen paper. 'And I w-w-was s-s-so happy in that job.'

'And Jono didn't stick up for you.'

'He did a bit,' said Gemma miserably.

'But not enough.'

Gemma shook her head. 'No.' She felt her forehead crumple as the tears began to flow again. 'I thought he really felt something for me and he let David hang me out to dry.'

'Bastard.'

Gemma nodded in agreement. 'I said, r-r-right at the s-s-start, when he began to text me, that I was the one who would get h-h-hurt.'

'And you did.' Zoë sighed and hugged Gemma again. 'Something else will turn up. You were good. You said Arabella said so. She may not be able to get you this gig back but she'll probably give you a decent reference. And you've got a month's pay.'

'But I haven't got a job.' And a fresh burst of misery assailed Gemma. The job was the thing that mattered, not the money. 'Or my mobile. Or any cash.'

'I can lend you money. And I'm sure Jean would have you back in the shop. Honest. We never found anyone to replace you. And we'll get you a new phone tomorrow.'

But both Gemma and Zoë knew that none of this was what she really wanted. What mattered most to Gemma was the loss of her job – her dream job.

And what Jono had done.

*

A week later Gemma was, as Zoë had promised, back in the shop. Only part time, but she was back doing what she was good at; demonstrating sewing machines, selling fabrics, and trying to put a brave face on things. The fact that she'd had a taste of working in films made going back to her old post even harder. But she needed the cash and the mechanics of getting up each day meant that she didn't have time to brood on what might have been. She tried to be grateful to Jean for taking her back and she tried to look cheerful for the sake of the customers, but inside she felt as if her life had been poisoned.

She looked about the shop; Zoë was trying to convince a large middle-aged woman that bonded Crimplene was no longer available or even desirable, Jean was tidying up the braids and ribbons and there were a couple of other customers perusing the books of dress patterns. But there wasn't the vibrancy or the excitement that there had been at Butterfly Films. There was no sense of urgency. No glamour. Was the rest of her life destined to be this dull monochrome of an uneventful daily routine where she worked to survive, to earn enough for her food and rent, and for no other reason?

The phone in the shop rang.

'Get that, would you, Gemma?' Jean called across the shop floor.

Gemma left off producing a complicated piece of machine embroidery and picked up the receiver. 'Hello, Sew Wonderful.'

'Gemma?'

'Yes,' she answered warily. Who knew she was working back in the shop? Apart from her very close friends and family, people whose voices she could readily identify. And the answer was no one.

'It's Arabella here.'

'Oh.' Gemma's low spirits perked up fractionally. Perhaps she was ringing to say David had relented; that Rowan had seen sense; that Tina had 'fessed up to lying . . .

'Thank goodness I've tracked you down. How are you doing?'

'All right. You know . . .' Actually, why was she even bothering to lie to Arabella? Why didn't she just say life was completely shit? She sighed.

'Look, I've heard about a job. It might interest you.'

'What is it?' Gemma knew she didn't sound gracious or grateful but she was too raw from recent events to care much about social niceties.

'A friend of mine owns a theatre, a rep in the provinces. The wardrobe mistress is going off on maternity leave. She needs someone to fill in for about nine months, maybe longer. Would you be interested?'

'How provincial?'

'Gloucestershire.'

Gemma didn't know. Did she want to move out of London? On the other hand, what was there for her here?'

'Think about it,' said Arabella. 'But don't take too long. The pregnant girl has complications and wants to leave almost instantly. They need someone pronto. They can't hang about while you dither. Oh, and my friend can let you have a room in her house till you find digs.'

'I'll let you know tomorrow.'

'No later.'

Arabella was about to ring off when Gemma stopped her. 'I need your number.'

'But you've got it.'

Briefly, Gemma explained how she'd lost her mobile.

'So that explains why I couldn't get hold of you. Sew Wonderful was my last hope. I just prayed that someone in the shop would know your whereabouts. I'm surprised you've gone back there.'

Like I had so many other offers to choose from, thought Gemma, bitterly. She wrote Arabella's number down and replaced the receiver thoughtfully.

'Who was that?' asked Jean.

'Arabella. There's a job going in Gloucestershire. She thought I might like it.'

'Oh,' said Jean, looking disappointed.

Instantly, Gemma felt a heel. 'You must think I'm just using you. Taking on this job when it suits me and not giving a thought to you.'

'Well,' said Jean and raised an eyebrow.

Gemma went over to the sewing machine and fiddled with the fabric she was stitching.

'Look, I'm sorry,' said Jean. 'I think I sound as if I'm more annoyed than I am. Honestly, I'm not. Not really. I have a couple of other people who might like to pick up some extra hours. Zoë and I cope very nicely most of the time. You mustn't lose sight of the fact that this is your career and you need to take what opportunities come your way.'

'Yeah, but Gloucestershire . . .'

'You wouldn't be able to commute, that's for sure.'

'And what about Zoë?' said Gemma. 'What about the flat?'

'What about the flat?' said Zoë, who had finally got rid of the woman intent on buying a fabric that no longer existed.

Gemma explained about her job offer.

'Coo,' said Zoë. 'Maybe Arabella isn't the snotty

cow we thought she was. So you're going to take it, right?'

'But it'll mean moving.'

'There's no problem with the flat, you know. Remember that night out we had with the girls, back when you had a job and a social life?' Gemma nodded. 'Well, when I spoke to Sian on the phone, she said she was gutted not to be able to come out with us and that she's desperate to get back to London. She said if ever you moved out she'd like your room.'

'Oh.' Gemma felt hurt. She didn't enjoy the feeling that she was so incredibly easy to replace. Part of her wanted Jean and Zoë to kick up a fuss and tell her she oughtn't to go, that they would be lost without her, but they seemed to think they would be able to cope perfectly well. 'Right.'

'It isn't as if you can't come back and visit.'

'No.'

'Great opportunity,' said Jean. 'And Arabella obviously has faith in you if she's recommending you to her friends.'

'Yes.' So why didn't she feel euphoric? Why did she feel as if she was being cast adrift? Was it knowing that the last way Jono could find her was via the flat? And if she left that, all hope that he might try to find her – however unlikely it was – would vanish. She knew she was mad holding any sort of hope that something might yet come of their short relationship but she couldn't help it. No matter how irrational it was, no matter how hurt she had felt by his actions, she still loved him and ached for what might have been.

A customer came into the shop and Gemma was left to think about her future while she finished off her piece of embroidery. Why, she asked herself angrily, was she still carrying a candle for Jono? But she knew the answer. Because it had been such a fairy tale. Wasn't it every girl's fantasy to meet some aspirational hunk, some dream date, and to think that he was interested in her? Well, grow up, she told herself. It was just a fantasy. She'd been like Icarus, lured by an impossible dream and, like him, had got well and truly burned.

Time to move on.

24

Gemma got off the bus and surveyed the town square: pretty cream-stone buildings with mossy stone roofs and muted paintwork leaned against each other with cosy familiarity; the fascia boards of the shops all advertised boutiques and businesses that had nothing to do with the chain stores she was used to and, although like London, the car park in part of the square was full of 4×4s, these ones were old, battered and caked in mud and had obviously been a lot further off the road than the grass verge outside the kids' smart city schools. In front of her was an ironmonger's that seemed to stock coal scuttles, garden tools, paraffin and mousetraps. She was riveted by the window display – an eclectic jumble of items; she wasn't aware either that people needed them in the twenty-first century or that they were still manufactured. The ironmonger's window she had passed daily on her way to Sew Wonderful had only stocked electric kettles, extension cables and gimmicky bathroom accessories, to judge by what was in theirs. Gemma realised that this was a community where being practical mattered more than style and trends. She wondered how she would fit in.

'Yoo-hoo!'

Gemma turned around. A thin blonde woman with a bizarre outfit made up of a selection of tweed, chiffon and fake fur and – ohmigod – a feather boa, was waving at her from the other side of the car park. Her thoughts about practicality, style and trends went into a nosedive. This woman didn't seem to know anything about any of those.

'Yoo-hoo. Gemma?'

Gemma waved tentatively back. This had to be Maureen Dyer, Arabella's friend and the theatre owner; who else here would know she was arriving on the bus from Swindon? But Maureen was a name Gemma had thought would belong to a sensible stout woman who wore brogues. But apparently not, if this creature was anything to go by. Maureen? Gemma gaped. Surely not.

The fashion disaster wafted across the car park towards her, both arms outstretched.

'Gemma. My life saver!' she shrieked.

Heads were turning, eyebrows were going upwards, smiles of amazed disbelief were spreading; this was clearly providing the morning's entertainment for the locals. Gemma felt herself cringing. Nine months in the company of this! This might be the worst mistake she'd made since she'd replied to Jono's text that first time.

Gemma stuck out her hand in the hope that this might ward off the full-on hug. Not a chance. Layers of varying fabrics and a fog of Devon Violets were swooshed around her as Maureen enveloped Gemma. Gemma had a fleeting memory of a film about an octopus eating a small fish. Now she understood the dreadfulness of that little sea creature's suffocating death.

'Sooo lovely to see you. Did you have a horrid journey? Is that all your luggage? How do you like Chipping

Membury? Darling, isn't it? You'll fit right in. I'm so excited to meet you. Arabella has told me all about you and how clever you are. We're frantic at the theatre. Well, you can imagine . . .'

Maureen jabbered on and Gemma felt her eyes glazing over. However, good manners demanded that she didn't actually allow them to roll up in her head as she slipped into a catatonic coma so she nodded and shook her head and smiled and kept herself conscious by wondering if this woman ran on batteries and if they would ever run down. Please, God, they would, and soon. Gemma didn't think she could cope with too much of this. Nine months. Shit!

'Let's get you into my car and I'll show you the theatre. We're so proud of it. For a little place it's just wonderful. Absolutely fabulous.'

Gemma smiled and tried to look enthusiastic. Not that it mattered, Maureen was on transmit and was oblivious to anything but the sound of her own voice.

Maureen gathered up two of the cases and left Gemma to bring the other one and a selection of carrier bags over to her car – a battered Astra that looked as if it doubled as a recycling centre for Gloucestershire; it was full of old papers, cola cans, scripts and swatches of fabric. Goodness only knew what lay beneath the surface detritus. Gemma thought it was probably safer not to know.

Her worldly possessions were dumped in the boot to keep company with a stack of old *Vogue* magazines and a moth-eaten fur coat (not faux, noted Gemma), and then Maureen swept the rubbish off the passenger seat so as to accommodate her passenger.

Gemma tried to look grateful.

'It's a bit of a drive to the theatre. The village is out in the sticks, I'm afraid, but jolly pretty. And the place is sweet. Despite the fact that it's miles from a town of any size, we get great audiences. We've built up a good reputation and people are prepared to make the journey.'

Better and better, thought Gemma. Stuck in the boondocks with a mad woman.

'And the really exciting thing is that next year we've got a touring company visiting.'

'That's nice,' said Gemma, feeling shell-shocked from the relentless battering of Maureen's gushing enthusiasm.

She let Maureen's endless, mindless chit-chat flow over and round her and instead turned her attention to the countryside passing by. The mid-summer sunshine was already turning the hayfields khaki and the crops gold. The shades of caramel, gold and camel made the fields, as they stretched into the distance, look as if they had swatches of teddy bear fur laid over them. The trees had lost the vibrancy of spring and their leaves were looking dull and dark. Some grain crops had already been harvested, leaving fields of corduroy ridges and furrows with yellow straw bales looking like great cheeses dotted over the surface. Flowers that had escaped from gardens nodded and bowed in the verges and dotted the grass with rainbow colours. Above the car the sky was deep blue with picture-book fluffy clouds sprinkled across it. It wasn't Spain, which was where she ought to have been in a week or two and to which she had looked forward to so much, but it was England at its best and so much nicer than London. Gemma thought that, despite Maureen's presence, her situation could be worse. London had been hot and stifling when she'd left Paddington and the air had smelt of diesel and soot and the sounds that had dominated had been the drone of engines and the scream of two-tones. Here, at least, the air smelt of flowers and cut grass with a note of wood smoke, and lowing cows and birdsong were all that disturbed the silence. Well, they would if Maureen gave her vocal chords a rest for a second or two.

It was about fifteen minutes after they had left Chipping Membury that they drew into a village that looked as if it was a leftover from a Hollywood movie about rural England. A stream ran along one side of the main road with a number of hump-backed bridges taking footpaths over it to a village green complete with duck pond and weeping willow. There was a post office, a pub and a shop selling knick-knacks and souvenirs. Whatever else, people didn't move to this village for the shopping opportunities. A sign over the door further along the road announced it was the outlet for a seed merchant and another proclaimed its status as a wool stapler.

How did you staple wool? wondered Gemma, who didn't have a clue what the business did. But no Woollies, no McDonald's, no Boots or Smiths – how refreshing, she thought. But where the hell did you go for a pint of milk or a loaf of bread?

'Here we are,' said Maureen. She zapped a remote she pulled from the pocket in the driver's door and a pair of impressive wrought-iron gates swung open in front of an even more impressive three-storey Cotswold-stone Georgian mansion.

Maureen drove the car across the scrunchy gravel forecourt and parked, pulling on the handbrake.

Where exactly is 'here'? thought Gemma, looking up at the fabulously proportioned façade of the mansion. Maureen had said they were calling in at the theatre first but this place didn't seem to fit the bill.

Maureen got out of the car so Gemma followed suit.

'Follow me,' said Maureen, rather unnecessarily. Gemma trotted along in her wake, across the front of the house and then down the side.

The path led through a shady shrubbery. Ahead, sunlight beckoned and then they came out into the open.

'There,' said Maureen.

There indeed. For *there* was a huge tithe barn with Bickford Theatre Company in gold on a Harrods' green background over the vast double doors that dominated one side of the building.

'Gosh,' said Gemma. She was impressed.

'Lovely, isn't it?'

Gemma nodded as Maureen pushed open a side door and led the way into the cool, dim gloom of the old building. She flicked a switch and Gemma saw they were in a small but perfectly formed theatre. The foyer that they were standing in was tiny but it had a box office and a hatch over which was the word 'Bar' in large fluorescent neon-lit letters. Maureen opened another door and there was the auditorium complete with stage, proscenium arch, stalls and a circle.

'It seats just over two hundred,' said Maureen, 'so it's quite intimate.' Gemma walked through the stalls to the front of the stage and looked back. The circle was so close above her head she felt she could almost touch it, and the distance between the stage and the rear stalls was only about fifty feet. The actors must feel as though they were almost in the audiences' laps when they were performing. *Intimate* seemed something of an understatement.

'Let me show you around,' said Maureen. She led the way up steps at the side of the stage and pushed her way through the curtains. Gemma followed. Like the rest of the place the stage was tiny.

'As you can imagine there are some limitations as to the sort of productions we can stage. *Educating Rita* is perfectly possible, but I think we might have a problem with *The Sound of Music*.'

Gemma nodded and smiled. Anyway, it suited her. Smaller productions, fewer costumes, less hassle.

Maureen led the way through the wings and into the backstage area. There were two big dressing rooms, male and female, a props store and a small rehearsal room.

'We have some outbuildings where we store scenery and make the sets. I'm afraid your empire is in the house.'

Gemma shrugged. She imagined she would be able to cope and she didn't really care where she worked as long as the light was half decent and she had a sewing machine. Maureen led her out of a door at the rear of the theatre and across a courtyard to the back of the manor.

The manor was built of pale Cotswold stone and was beautifully proportioned. Tubs of bedding plants were spaced along the wall, between several sets of French windows that opened on to the courtyard, and between the tubs were Versailles planters with a standard bay tree in each one. The courtyard was sheltered and sunny and was filled with the sound of bees buzzing and chirruping birds.

'*Voila*,' said Maureen, giving a theatrical flourish as she opened one of the French windows. She held it wide to let Gemma enter. The room was wonderful. There was a vast cutting table, shelves full of bolts of fabrics, a fantastic sewing machine which Gemma recognised as one of the most expensive that she used to sell at Sew Wonderful, an overlocker, several dressmakers' dummies dotted about – one of which was clad in a half-finished costume – and a knitting machine. It was light and airy and had a wooden floor, so it would be easy to sweep up scraps of fallen fabric and threads of cotton. On one wall was a big ornate Adam's fire place and in the grate was a large vase full of cut flowers. Being a city girl, Gemma had no idea what they were except that they were bright, colourful, welcoming and smelt delicious.

'Will this be all right for you?'

Gemma gazed about her. It was fantastic. She'd be able to produce some classy costumes with this level of equipment and all the facilities.

She nodded, her eyes bright with happiness. 'Fantastic,' she said.

'Good. Of course, through here is where we store all the past costumes.' Maureen pushed a sliding door back on its runners and revealed racks and racks of dresses, suits, capes, ball gowns, fairy dresses, knitted-string chain mail and goodness only knew what else in all shapes, sizes and colours. It was nothing short of amazing.

'A lot of your work will probably be altering or adapting something from stock, so you'll need to spend time in here familiarising yourself with what we already have.'

Gemma thought she would be able to cope with that. And she would enjoy rootling through the store to see what was there. She had a feeling there might be any number of treasures hidden in among the more mundane outfits.

'And I'll let you have a list of our next few productions so you can think about the costumes for those. Mary, the girl you're taking over from, will be in tomorrow and she'll bring you up to speed on where she is in getting everything ready for our next fabulous production.'

'Which is?'

'*Who's Afraid of Virginia Woolf.*'

At least that would probably be fairly straightforward. Nothing too taxing to start with.

'Now, I imagine you want to see your room. This way.' Once again, Gemma trotted after her employer. This time she was led into the main hall of the house, a beautifully proportioned space with a polished wood floor, a sweeping staircase leading upwards and more fabulous flowers prettily arranged in vases on side tables. The curtains at the windows that flanked the front door were beautifully made and, even at a distance, reeked of quality. The stairs were wide and shallow and Gemma felt she ought to be dressed in a more appropriate costume than her habitual jeans and skimpy top. Even so, she was probably more in keeping with the house as a whole than Maureen's mad mix of clothes. As they passed the first landing, Gemma clocked another lovely side table and the huge vase of lilies – this was a house where style and attention to detail seemed to be important, so why, she wondered, did Maureen dress like some sort of hippy leftover?

Above the first floor the stairs became a little narrower and steeper. This is where the second-best guests get to sleep, thought Gemma, although, to be fair, in this house no one was likely to have to slum it. Niches, corners and shelves still had lovely antiques or bits of pottery carefully and tastefully placed and the soft furnishings and colour scheme were delightful. On the second landing, Maureen opened a door and led the way up to the attic.

'I don't want you to think this is a garret,' she said adding a tinkly laugh, which set Gemma's teeth on edge. 'But it is a self-contained flat. I thought you'd rather be self-sufficient than have to feel you have to behave like a guest all the time. If I give you your own front door key you can come and go as you please.'

Gemma was rather taken aback by this thoughtfulness. And frankly relieved that she wouldn't have to spend hours with Maureen when she wasn't working.

The stairs behind the door were fairly precipitous but she could see from the bottom that the space at the top was light and airy. No bleak attic with rats and precious little comfort. She scampered up the stairs and was amazed at the huge space that was at their head. Two dormer windows looked out over the roof to the rest of the village. On one side was a bed and a wardrobe and on the other was a sofa and a television. Maureen opened a further door and showed her the shower room behind it and then she opened what Gemma thought was a cupboard to reveal a tiny kitchen with a sink, a two-ring gas hob, a microwave and a fridge.

'Gosh,' said Gemma. The walls were pale primrose-yellow, the bedding deep blue and white, and on the floor was a yellow carpet and some blue rugs. It was lovely and homely and Gemma regretted all the dreadful things she'd been thinking about Maureen since she'd met her.

'I'm so glad you like it,' said Maureen. 'I want you to be happy with the company – and here in the house. There's a farm shop at the end of the village that sells heaps of fresh produce and the post office sells tins and other essentials. And you must make sure you eat properly,' said Maureen, eyeing Gemma's pinched face. 'You look like you need feeding up. It can't be good for anyone to be as thin as you are.'

Irrationally, Gemma felt tears springing up. She turned away to hide them. She knew she hadn't been eating properly of late. Misery had stolen her appetite and, frankly, she hadn't cared. Why should she? What was the point? But now . . . maybe life wasn't such a bitch after all

– Maureen certainly wasn't. Gemma thought that, against the odds, she might be almost happy in this house and with this job.

'You have a good look round and then we'll get your luggage up here. Can you find your way back to the theatre?'

Considering how big the tithe barn was, Gemma thought that she had a fair chance but she didn't say so. She nodded and smiled, not trusting herself to speak in case the tears spilled.

'Right. See you in a minute. I'll be in the foyer.'

Maureen left and Gemma sat down on her new bed, wondering why she felt so emotional. Maureen, despite her prattling and her bizarre clothes, had been kindness itself, the house was delightful, her room perfect, and the theatre small but wonderful. Surely Gemma had pretty much everything a girl could wish for. Except she didn't.

She wanted the dream she had lost and no matter how good or comfortable life was going to be for the foreseeable future, she had to get used to the fact that the dream was over. The tears rolled down her cheeks.

25

Mary, the pregnant wardrobe mistress, spent a week with Gemma, showing her the ropes, introducing her to the rest of the company, and familiarising Gemma with the stored costumes, the village, the pub and the local area. She also told Gemma that Maureen had once had ambitions to be the next Zandra Rhodes but had had to face up to the fact that she didn't have the flair or the talent for fashion design. As she still wanted to be involved with dressing people up, she had directed her energies into the theatre and into designing her own outfits. At least it explained why her clothes were so weird. The house, however, belonged to Mr Dyer (first name unknown, according to Mary, who said that even Maureen invariably called him Mr Dyer), who was a retired antiques dealer, which, in turn, explained why it was so beautifully furnished. When Mary left on the Friday evening to start her maternity leave, Gemma felt a bit panicky about coping on her own but was grateful for the thorough handover. It was one thing being someone's shadow; it was something else again being in total charge.

She soon got used to the routine of the theatre. The

actors performed from Wednesday to Saturday with the rest of the week off. Rehearsals for the next production were in the afternoons so mornings were free – however, Gemma found that she was often working a few extra hours here and there to have the next batch of costumes fitted and ready on time. If she wasn't busy making or altering things then she was mending or washing the existing stock. There was never a shortage of jobs to do but she liked it like that. It stopped her brooding about what might have been back in London, back in the film industry.

She got on well with the thirty or so members of the company. Half of the backstage team seemed to have more than one job: there was Kerry, who took bookings, designed the posters and fliers, kept the website up-to-date and ran the accounts; John, who made sets by day and ran the bar by night; Una, who did the make-up and cleaned the auditorium; and Maureen, who oversaw everything and directed most of the productions. The actors mostly lived locally, and were unknown outside the area (until they got their lucky break in one of the bigger companies – which several had achieved), but the theatre's reputation was such that every now and again they were able to get some bigger names to join the regular cast, especially for the productions that ran for several weeks. Despite her time working with such big stars as Rowan and Jono, Gemma still got a thrill from chatting to people she had previously only seen on TV. She had to admit to herself that she was a total groupie.

The houses were invariably packed and the audiences appreciative, and Gemma relished being part of such a successful and close-knit team. Slowly, her heartache for the film, her old job and Jono became less acute.

Gradually, she found that Maureen's infectious good humour and optimism got to her too, and there were some days when Gemma felt almost happy. She still thought about 'what might have been' almost every day but the pain when she did grew imperceptibly less each time.

Occasionally, she wondered why Jono hadn't tried to find out where she was and had made no effort to contact her and then the stab of pain was intense. Was she so easy to forget? Obviously – a thought which also hurt; no one wanted to be expendable. So how could she have been such a little fool to have fallen for all those promises? But even those thoughts began to lose their sting. Her deep misery was eroded and after a bit she began to put on weight and to fill out, she slept without the aching dreams, and her hair regained its shine and bounce.

The productions slipped by and so did the weeks and months. Mary visited occasionally and her swelling belly went from making her looking mildly overweight to obviously and heavily pregnant. The drowsy summer days, with the air thick with the sound of birds chirping, insects buzzing and tourist cameras clicking away at the idyllic village centre, gave way suddenly to a dank autumn with not a hint of mist or mellow fruitfulness but plenty of driving rain and gales. The temperature plummeted, the tubs in the courtyard looked bedraggled and tatty and piles of leaves swirled and rustled in the corners.

Suddenly, Gemma saw that the next rehearsals scheduled were for the Christmas panto and she hadn't even thought about buying her Christmas cards, let alone writing them.

To begin with, during the summer and autumn, Gemma had tried to address the knotty problem of finding digs; there was simply nowhere in the area that she could afford to rent and without a car she couldn't look further afield. Maureen kept telling Gemma that this didn't matter in the least, but Gemma felt that the peppercorn fee she was paying for her room probably didn't even cover her gas and electricity, let alone come close to the going rate for rent in the area (Maureen had dismissed Gemma's offer to contribute more) and her sense of fairness made her uneasy about the freeloading she was indulging in. Now the tourists and holidaymakers were long gone, Gemma doubled her efforts to find rooms and used her few free days to trawl round the local estate agents trying to find a bedsit, but there was nothing within striking distance of the theatre offering anything remotely suitable. She decided to give up until after Christmas was past. Besides, Maureen and her husband seemed happy with their quiet and tidy houseguest and hadn't ever hinted that she should move out.

Gemma kept in touch with Zoë and her friends but increasingly she began to feel as though she was drifting away from them like an iceberg that had broken off the ice shelf. To be fair, Zoë did try to include her in what they planned to do socially but as their activities invariably took place on a Friday or Saturday night, Gemma could never opt to join in as she was always needed at the theatre.

'I'll never get to see you at this rate,' moaned Gemma during one call.

'Then come up on a Sunday and stay for a few days.'

'But you'll be working again on the Monday.'

'There's always the evenings. I am sure we can come up with something. Besides, it isn't as if there's nothing to do up here in the smoke.'

'I suppose.'

'Well, don't sound too enthusiastic.'

'I'm sorry. I'm just so busy here. What with the panto looming and a zillion Lost Children costumes to make. Perhaps after Christmas.'

'What are you doing for Christmas?'

'Staying here.'

Zoë was horrified. 'What! Not going home to see your folks?'

'There isn't time. We've got shows on Christmas Eve and Boxing Day and you know what it's like travelling at that time of year.'

'What does your mum have to say about this?'

'She's being very understanding,' said Gemma, a shade too defensively. 'Besides, she's got two of my sisters and their boyfriends staying for the holiday. The house is going to be bursting at the seams.'

'She'd make space for you.'

'Yeah, well . . . I'll see her after Christmas.'

'That's what you've just told me. Have you seen her since you got fired from the film?'

'No,' said Gemma quietly. 'She and Dad would have got all upset for me and I felt I couldn't cope with that. Dad would have said I ought to go to a union or something – that's his answer to almost everything – and Mum would have smothered me with kindness. It was something I wanted to deal with on my own – you know, like a wounded animal.'

'So, you're burying yourself in the country, away from your family and friends, seeing no one, cutting yourself off. What's going on, Gem?'

'Nothing. I like it here.'

'Hmm.' Zoë's scepticism was blatantly obvious. 'And what are you doing for a social life?'

'There's the pub.' Again a defensive note crept in.

Zoë snorted. 'Yeah, right. Bet that's an exciting night out.'

'Everyone's very friendly. Besides, most evenings I'm working.'

Zoë conceded that must make life difficult. 'But what about a bloke?'

'Well . . .'

'No one, right?'

'Not really.'

'Christ, Gem, you're turning into an old woman before your time. What the fuck are you doing for kicks?'

Gemma couldn't answer.

'Well, that's decided. You're coming up to London, like it or not. And the gang here will give you a night to remember. Now get your diary out and we'll fix a date now. No excuses.'

The bus and train journey up to London through the grim gloom of a wet January Sunday afternoon seemed interminable, and even before she was nearing Reading she was wondering whether the trip was going to be worth it. Yes, it was going to be fun to have a night out with Sian and Zoë, but what of tomorrow and the next day? What was she going to do in London for the next couple of days when the girls were working? She supposed she could go and take in a flick somewhere. She hadn't seen a film since she'd bolted down to Gloucestershire. And maybe there was an exhibition or something that might be worth a look. She decided to check out the listings when she got to London to see what was going on.

The train crawled into Paddington and as Gemma opened the door the familiar smell of London hit her.

Goodness, it smelled rank after months in the country. She'd forgotten how bad the sooty, grubby air in the capital was. No wonder people still referred to it as 'The Smoke'. She wheeled her case off the train, down the platform, and made her way over the concourse to the Tube. She made the journey to King's Cross without a thought, until she approached the escalator where she'd been mugged all those months back. Warily, she looked about her and clutched her possessions tighter to her as she made her way towards it. Being a Sunday, the number of passengers were less than in the rush hour when the assault had occurred but, even so, she felt her heart rate going ballistic and her palms and forehead break out in a sweat.

By the time she got to the top she felt almost dizzy with panic and stumbled out of the station, dragging her suitcase behind her, with relief. She breathed deeply to calm herself, squared her shoulders and headed for Zoë's flat.

The instant Sian opened the front door with a shriek of pleasure, Gemma saw that the flat was just the same grotty pit that it had been when she'd moved out. Sian had brought a few of her own possessions with her to try to make the place look less run down, but, like Zoë's and Gemma's before her, they didn't really help. Despite that, thought Gemma as she walked into the living room, it was good to be back. She'd had some good times here with Zoë. In fact, she almost missed the place.

Zoë came rushing out of the kitchen, yelling greetings, and thrust a large glass of white wine into her hand.

'But it's only three in the afternoon,' protested Gemma, although the thought of a large shot of booze after the trauma of retracing her steps though King's Cross was rather welcome.

'And you've missed out on months of partying,' retorted Zoë, returning to the kitchen to get two more glasses for herself and Sian.

'How do you know?'

'Oh, sorry, I forgot,' called Zoë over her shoulder. 'Bickford is the hot place to be seen. It is always getting featured in *Hello!* and *OK!*. In fact, you can barely turn a page without finding it mentioned.'

She gave Sian her wine and the three of them chinked glasses.

Gemma took a slug of her wine. 'Glad to know you've spotted that. I must say I'm sick of being papped.'

'Bickford,' said Sian with her heavy Welsh accent, 'Bickford? Where in God's name is that?'

'I rest my case, m'lud,' said Zoë. 'Now drink up. You can unpack later. We're going uptown and you're going to have a *good time*.'

Gemma swigged back her glass of wine and kicked her suitcase to the side of the small sitting room. This was going to be a great few days. She was going to have fun and laughs with her mates. Being in Bickford for the last few months was like convalescing after a nasty illness. Well, she was better now, fully recovered, and it was time to get back into the swing of things. Going out on the lash with a couple of chums had definitely been missing from her life for too long. Now she was going to have some fun. She'd forgotten that life was for living. Time to start remembering!

The next morning, *live now pay later* was a phrase that thudded around Gemma's head, along with a monumental headache, when Zoë shook her awake on the sofa bed with a cup of tea.

'I left you as long as I could, but I've got to go to work now. How are you feeling?'

Gemma groaned.

'That answers my question, then. Serves you right.'

'I can't have drunk that much,' said Gemma, wincing as Zoë opened the curtains.

'Actually, you probably didn't. God, but you're a lightweight. Time was when you could shift Chardonnay by the pint. Now? Rubbish, frankly.'

Gemma groaned again. 'I'm just not in training any more. I don't get out much these days.'

'Well, I've got to get out to work. You've got the whole day to recover, so plenty of time to sort yourself out before we see if your capacity for drink has been improved at all since last night. I've arranged to meet Sian in the wine bar around the corner from her office. I said we'd pitch up around seven thirty.'

'Sian's office? Where's that?'

'She told you last night – you can't have been drunk at that point, can you?'

Gemma shrugged. How the hell would she know? Most of the previous evening was a complete blank.

Zoë told her where the office was and how to find the wine bar and Gemma closed her eyes. Even the mention of wine made her feel queasy, let alone the prospect of drinking it ever again.

By lunchtime she felt well enough to eat some toast and then she left the flat to reacquaint herself with London. Unsurprisingly, after her previous day's flashback, the Tube didn't appeal, so she walked along the Euston Road to Tottenham Court Road, and from there to the shops of Oxford Street. She'd forgotten the extent of the choice

London offered and there were even a couple of sales still on. Feeling better and with the prospect of some further therapy being offered through a bit of shopping, she dived into Marks and Spencer and then Miss Selfridge. Oh, the bliss. The countryside had its good points – less pollution, less noise, kind people, cosy pubs, but you didn't move there to keep abreast of the fashion scene, that was for sure; wellies, waxed jackets, cords and thick sweaters were the only fashion that the residents of Bickford seemed to need – Maureen and her mad wardrobe excepted.

Gemma drifted around the shops buying a few odds and ends and enjoying the buzz of London. She stopped at a newsstand to pick up an *Evening Standard* and then went to a smoothie bar to rest her feet and make a plan of action for the following day. She ordered a drink, winced at the price she was asked to pay – shit, she'd forgotten how expensive London was! – and found a table. She flicked through the cinema and theatre pages to see if there was anything that appealed enough for her to spend good money to go and see.

A headline caught her eye. JONO AND ROWAN TO ATTEND MOVIE PREMIERE. In a whoosh all her past feelings for Jono resurfaced. During all those months in the country she'd finally managed to suppress them. She'd battened down the hatches over those heady weeks when she'd believed that he'd really cared for her. She'd pushed the memories away, got on with her life, and she thought she'd succeeded. But just seeing his name again in the paper was enough to resurrect it all.

She began to read the story. Jono and Rowan had flown from the States, where Rowan was filming for an American TV series, for tonight's premiere of the film she'd been working on. It seemed Jono had put his career on hold to accompany her out to LA. Gemma snorted in disgust. So much for his decision to let Rowan go off on her own so he could return to the West End. Huh! He'd lied about that just like he'd lied when he'd said he was mad about her. And yet the realisation that he'd lied to her still hurt. When would she get over him? Gemma put the paper down on the counter in front of her as her hands were shaking so much the print was blurring.

She couldn't understand why this story was upsetting her so much. She'd known which way the wind blew when she'd been thrown off the film and Jono had hardly lifted a finger to defend her. It hadn't come as a huge shock to discover that, when he was forced into making a choice, he'd chosen his wife. After all, he'd known her for ages longer than he'd known Gemma, he had worked with her, lived with her, and was probably financially tied to her to boot. But the fact that it now seemed that everything he'd said ever said to her had been lies and fabrication was what hurt. Why had he pretended to confide in her? What was the point? Had she been a part of some sick prank? Did he get off on making young, impressionable women think that he was interested in their advice as well as getting them into bed? She'd been had, conned, tricked and cheated – that was the truth. He'd thrown her a line and reeled her in as easily as if she'd been a fish.

She put her hands in her lap to try to control the tremor. Tears of self-pity, anger and hurt pride threatened to spill down her face. She felt such a fool. How could she have ever believed that heel, that utter shit? She should have gone along with her first instincts – that he was an actor. He acted all the time. Nothing he said or did could be believed because it was all an act. Why, she asked herself, bitterly, when she had known that, had she let him talk her round?

She stared at his picture in the paper. But now he ought to know that she'd sussed him out, that she now knew he was a complete bastard, that she had his measure. She looked at her watch. Six o'clock. She slurped back the last couple of gulps of her smoothie and gathered her bags and handbag up from under her seat. She'd show him. If she got the chance, she'd give him a right old piece of her mind.

The crowds at Leicester Square were bigger than she imagined. The place was packed outside the cinema where the premiere was taking place. Somewhere among the throng was the red carpet that Jono and Rowan would process along for the benefit of their adoring fans and the paparazzi. Well, maybe the fans wouldn't be quite so adoring, and maybe the paparazzi would get a better story, if they all knew that Rowan was a lush prone to fits of violence and that Jono was a lying, cheating womaniser – if their fans knew this, perhaps the couple wouldn't be quite so popular after all.

Gemma began to work her way to the front of the crowd. She wanted to look Jono in the eye and tell him to his face she thought he was a shit. Would he have any remorse? she wondered. In fact, she wondered if he would even remember her. He'd probably pulled a whole string of girls since her. Perhaps those girls hadn't had her principles about not dating married men. That was probably her attraction, she thought, as she pushed and shoved her way past dozens of over-excited and underdressed teenaged kids. It was the very fact that she hadn't swooned and thrown herself at him that had kept his interest in her for weeks rather than hours. If she had responded from the outset, he'd have just got his leg over before dumping her. Well, she'd show him.

But she knew she was lying to herself. She hadn't come here to do anything of the sort. She'd come to get a glimpse of him. She knew it was a terrible idea but she couldn't help herself. She still loved him. Even if he hadn't been honest with her, she owed it to herself to own up to the truth.

Breathless, and ignoring the snide comments from the fans about her whom she'd pushed past to get to the front, Gemma emerged at the edge of the red carpet. Around her searchlights were sending beams up into the grim January night to bounce off the lowering cloud base. Reporters with mics in hand and cameramen shadowing them were prowling along the carpet, stalking the minor actors and celebs who were arriving early to try to get maximum exposure before entering the cinema. The fans around her were screaming out names and thrusting scraps of paper and pencils at anyone on the carpet in the hope of grabbing an autograph. And away to Gemma's left a line of limos were depositing their occupants in a well-choreographed operation.

She suspected the drivers and the passengers had all been through this process countless times. Once out of their cars the celebrities stood still and posed for pictures, then moved smoothly off, as if on a belt, to allow the next carload of passengers space to exit their vehicle. They then worked their way along the carpet, shaking hands, posing for pics, signing autographs and doing interviews without getting in anyone else's way or stealing another's limelight. All very tidy, thought Gemma as she watched the process.

A louder shriek from the teens made her pay closer attention but it was the arrival of the latest pop phenomenon that had caused this outburst and not the stars of the movie. However, from the way the snappers and the hacks were gathering at the top end of the carpet, it was obvious that the arrival of the megastars was going to happen soon. Even the searchlights seemed to be sweeping the skies with more urgency.

And there he was.

And Gemma's heart raced.

She might have tried to kid herself she was over the worst of her feelings for him but she knew for an absolute certainty now that she wasn't and even at a distance of some fifty yards he was affecting her. Her head knew he was a liar and a charlatan and she ought to hate him, but her body and her heart weren't in agreement. It was torture to be near him again. It was physically hurting her. She had to get away, but the crowd behind was pressing her against the temporary crush barriers and she couldn't even turn around let alone flee.

Although inside she was wretched with heartache, she was mesmerised. She watched him and Rowan progress along the carpet – he was working one side of the crowd, she the other. A pair of reporters took first Jono and then Rowan aside for brief interviews. Gemma could see them smile and nod and look gracious. She wondered what Jono was saying. She wanted to shout out to him, tell him how much he'd hurt her by his lies, but her throat had closed up and her breathing was irregular. The reporters swapped interviewees and then Jono and Rowan continued along the carpet, but this time working the opposite sides. Gemma realised that she was on the wrong side for Jono to see her.

Disappointment drenched her. He wouldn't see her. He was almost opposite her now and talking to some fans on the other side of the carpet. A few more feet and he'd be at the entrance to the cinema. Gemma felt her whole body, from her shoulders down, sag.

A barrage of flashlights fired just beside her and Jono turned around. Their eyes met. He stared straight at her then began to walk across the carpet. Rowan, shaking hands with fans and scribbling on bits of paper, smiled at Jono, thinking he was going to join her. Then she saw he was looking fixedly at something in the crowd and followed his gaze. Her eyes narrowed and her colour rose when she saw Jono's target.

Gemma couldn't face another confrontation with Rowan. Not in public. Not a second time. Panic gripped her and she dived back into the crowd. Pushing, shoving, driven by a blind desire to get away from Jono and Rowan, she didn't care what the fans around her were saying, what mayhem she was causing, the toes she trod on, the people she upset. Then, panting and dishevelled, she was at the edge of the crowd. A bench was nearby. Slowly, Gemma made her way over to it and sat down and sobbed.

26

'Headache still bad, Gem?' asked Zoë when she plonked herself on a chair in the wine bar. She shoved a large glass of white on to the table and leaned forward to study her friend.

'Hmm,' said Gemma, not really listening, hoping the redness of her eyes had subsided.

'I said ... Oh never mind.' Zoë narrowed her eyes, realising that Gemma looked miserable rather than ill. 'What's the matter? You look really down.'

'Nothing,' replied Gemma dully.

'Nothing, my arse. Come on, tell your Aunty Zo.'

'It's nothing,' insisted Gemma.

Zoë took a swig of her wine and stared at her friend. 'So the fact that Jono Knighton was in town today is irrelevant?'

'How did—'

'For fuck's sake, Gem, I read the papers too. Did you see him?'

Gemma nodded.

'You went to Leicester Square, right?'

Gemma nodded again.

'Well, I hope you were close enough to knee him in the balls after what he did to you.'

Gemma shook her head.

'Damn,' said Zoë. 'I suppose it was because they were too small a target. Better luck next time then. Did I tell you he came sniffing round the flat after you'd legged it to Bickford?'

Gemma looked up. 'No!'

'I wasn't in, but Sian dealt with him. Told him you never wanted to see him again and to fuck off in no uncertain terms.'

'She didn't!' Zoë missed the anguish in Gemma's voice completely.

'She certainly did. You would have been proud of her. He wanted to know where you were. Of course, it helped matters that Sian didn't actually know your address, so all she could say was that you had left for the country. According to Sian he wasn't too pleased.'

'He came looking for me?' Gemma was incredulous.

'Yeah. Sian reckons he wanted to gloat. I said I didn't think he was that mean, but you never know. After all, he was a complete shit to you when David sacked you. He could have put in a good word for you. Hell, he might have used his clout to prevent it. So . . . once a bastard, always a bastard.'

But Gemma wasn't really listening. Jono had come looking for her!

But what good would it do while Rowan was on the scene?

'Good time in London?' asked Kerry, the theatre's administrator and general office manager, on the Wednesday. She studied the dark shadows under Gemma's eyes as Gemma sat at a sewing machine in her workroom in the big house. 'Blimey, did you get any sleep at all or did you spend all three days out on the tiles?'

Gemma shook her head. 'It wasn't that wild a time. Honest.'

'No? And I'm Dolly Parton.' Considering Kerry was flat-chested, brown-haired and tone deaf (judging by her performance at a karaoke evening at the village pub), Gemma couldn't help grinning.

'London's a noisy place compared to here. I didn't sleep well.'

'Didn't sleep at all, I should think. I've seen pandas with smaller circles. Anyway, I'm not here to talk about your social life but to tell you that, finally, I've got a space in my diary to update the website.' Gemma looked puzzled. 'No, not the one for the upcoming productions, but the site about the theatre itself. That has been ignored for months now. In fact, it still has Mary on it as the wardrobe mistress. It's about time I put the record straight. So . . .' Kerry produced a slim digital camera from her jeans' pocket. 'If you would like to go and glam yourself up a bit, I'll take a snap of you for the site.'

'Must you?'

'Yes, I must. And I have freed up today to do it so I won't take "no" for an answer. Now get upstairs and shove some slap on. And do something about those shadows,' she called after Gemma, who was going out the door, 'or you'll frighten the punters away.'

Gemma was back in ten minutes, make-up on, hair combed, and looking marginally better. While Kerry was snapping away, trying to get a shot of Gemma that made her look 'more human than junkie', Gemma asked why she suddenly had time to get on with the task of updating the website.

'Because, if you haven't noticed, in a month a touring company is bringing their own production of *The Importance of Being Ernest* and it's due to run for three weeks. Now smile and turn you head slightly,' said Kerry, looking at the image on the back of her camera before pressing the button once again.

'Of course I've noticed. And I'm looking forward to it. For once it means that apart from making sure the costumes are clean and pressed, I don't have to do anything.'

'Precisely.' Kerry squinted at the last image she'd captured and sighed. 'Let's try it with you sitting at your machine looking as if you're working.'

Gemma sat down. 'And . . . ?' Then the penny dropped. 'You mean the touring company is updating *our* website about *their* production for us, so *you* don't have to do it?'

'Yup. One very big job less for me to do. Smile please.' She clicked the camera. 'It's the same for everyone here. They're bringing almost all their own scenery, props, costumes – everything – which means the heat is off the rest of us. And they sent me all the stuff for the Internet, so I just have to drop it in; no pics to take, no copy to write, no biogs of the actors to produce. Try looking at me. And smile . . .' Click. 'So I've got time to get on with this. And, God, do I need every second of it, if everyone is going to be as tricky to photograph as you are.' She looked at the last shot she'd taken. 'I think that'll do. At least I've got one of you that doesn't either make you look like a member of the Addams Family or like a police "wanted" poster.'

'Thanks,' said Gemma.

'Just being honest,' said Kerry with a grin. 'Take a look.'

Even Gemma had to admit that the picture Kerry had got was incredibly flattering. She smiled. 'Cor, thanks.'

'Who says the camera never lies?' Kerry shot out of the room and slammed the door behind her before Gemma could retaliate.

The Importance of Being Ernest, which ran over the Easter period, was a huge hit. Sell-out audiences raised the roof every night with their applause and the local papers gave it rave reviews. Maureen was ecstatic.

'Darlings, what a triumph,' she said at the end of the first week. 'A credit to you all.'

Gemma was at a loss to understand why, as the touring company had brought almost everything they'd required with them. Sure, John and the rest of the stage hands had shifted the scenery each night and their lighting engineer had helped the touring company's one. Gemma had helped the artistes dress and Una had helped with the make-up, but the wigs and the clothes had come with the company and they hadn't had to design or organise them. The production had been a doddle for all of them. So it was a bit rich of Maureen to suggest that the Bickford Theatre Company ought to take any of the credit except for providing a lovely theatre for them to perform in. Still, it was fun to be involved with something that was moving on to a theatre in London and the cast, while not stellar, were all quite well known and had a list of credits, between them, that were pretty impressive.

In the middle of the second week, the touring director approached Gemma in her workroom. She was busy preparing costumes for the next Bickford production, which was to be *The Cherry Orchard*. Luckily, most of the costumes she could adapt from stuff in stock and all she had to do was a few alterations. It was a lovely warm April day, the hyacinths that crowded the tubs either side of the French doors into the garden filled Gemma's room with their scent, and she was humming along to music on the radio as she worked.

'Sweetie,' said the director, as he came in from the garden.

'Ben. What can I do for you?'

He perched on the edge of her work table and fingered the fabric of the costume she was working on. 'Ooh, wool challis. Lovely.'

'Maureen says that cheap fabrics don't last and look tawdry on stage. Not my budget, so I don't mind. I do as I'm told.'

'Would you like your own budget?'

'It's a scary prospect. I'm not sure.'

'Did you have anything to do with the budget at Butterfly?'

Gemma was surprised that he knew about her past. She certainly hadn't told him, and none of the others in the company knew . . . except Maureen.

'Did Maureen tell you about that?' She wasn't sure whether she was flattered or annoyed that Ben and Maureen had been talking about her.

'She told me a friend of hers thought very highly of you. Arabella Minton.'

'Yeah, well.' But not highly enough to defend her when David was busy sacking her. But perhaps it wouldn't be politic to mention it. It might sound bitter and negative – which was exactly how she felt, but better not let the whole world know.

'So you've worked on a big project.'

Gemma nodded. 'I was only an assistant.'

'How would you like to be in charge?'

'I am.'

'Of something rather bigger than this. I mean the theatre here is great, fabby, but there are other, bigger theatres.'

Gemma stared at Ben. 'Just what are you offering me?'

'I've been asked to direct a production of Shaw's *Joan of Arc*. In London. I want it modern and different. I have lots of ideas and I need someone who is willing to experiment and go out on a limb with me. I think you're the person.'

'But I specialise in historical costumes.'

'I had a look at some of the pictures of the stuff you've done here. Kerry showed me. It's great. I think you've got talent and vision. No wonder Arabella thought so much of you. So what do you say?'

'I can't. I owe Maureen. I can't walk out on her.'

'And what happens when Mary comes back?'

Shit, Ben *had* done his research. He knew an awful lot about her situation here. 'I don't know. I haven't thought.'

'Then you should. You're only covering for her temporarily. When is that due to end?'

'Soon, I suppose.'

'Exactly. Have you asked Maureen about your future?'

Gemma shook her head.

'Then you should. If I know Maureen, she's embarrassed about facing the fact that she's going to have to let you go in a few weeks. I hear your predecessor had her baby a couple of months ago and is due back to work any day now. Then what?'

Then what indeed? Gemma had been half hoping that Mary would decide that motherhood was better than working and opt not to come back to the theatre after all, but it was a long shot. Her mother lived in the next village and childcare wasn't going to be a problem. Gemma knew she'd been behaving like an ostrich over this but she was happy and settled and she really didn't want to be moving on again after less than a year in Bickford. Yes, it had always been the deal, but part of her had hoped that if she ignored the problem it would just go away.

'Can I think about it?'

'I'll give you to the end of the week.'

And it was already Wednesday. Great.

27

'Zo? Can I sleep on your sofa for a week or so?' There was silence down the phone which was worrying. 'Zo?'

'Well, it isn't terribly convenient.'

This wasn't what Gemma had expected. She hadn't imagined Zoë would welcome her back like the proverbial prodigal offspring, but she had thought that a bit more enthusiasm than she was showing right now would be forthcoming. Perhaps if she explained, Zoë would be more open to the idea. 'I've got a job offer in London. A West End play . . .'

'Oooh, well done, Gem. That's brill. You must be thrilled.'

That was a better response. Gemma's spirits rose a degree or two. 'Yes, I am, but I've got nowhere to stay and I need digs.'

Again the worrying silence. Then, 'Trouble is, Gem, it's a bit cosy here right now.'

'Oh.' Gemma had expected there to be no problem with staying at Zoë's while she hunted for a room some-where. A big spanner was clattering around in her proverbial works.

'Sian's boyfriend has moved in and it was enough of a squash with just the two of us. Now with three it's positively claustrophobic and, to be brutal, I can't face four.'

She had a point. Four? No way in that tiny flat. 'Bugger,' swore Gemma quietly. A bed at Zoë's while she looked for her own affordable place had definitely been part of her plan. Without that, could she really afford to take herself back up to London and pay through the nose for B&B accommodation while she trawled around looking for a bedsit?

She finished her conversation with Zoë and took herself off to Kerry's office. Kerry was doing the accounts and had piles of coins and bar receipts all over her desk.

'Can I have a go on the Internet?' asked Gemma.

'Be my guest.'

She Googled 'accommodation + London' and got a selection of sites on the screen.

'Moving?' asked Kerry, glancing over to see what Gemma was doing as she tipped a handful of pound coins into a bank bag and deftly made it secure.

'Keep it under your hat, because I haven't told Maureen yet, but Ben's offered me a job for when Mary comes back here.'

'In London?'

Gemma nodded.

'Wow. Good luck with finding somewhere to live.'

She carried on cashing up and sorting out the accounts. Gemma clicked and scrolled and sighed and snorted and got more restless.

'Problems?' asked Kerry.

'I don't know. I mean, I know I'm really lucky to get this break, but I'm not sure I can afford to move back. Just look at this.' She clicked on one site and read the details out. 'And when all is said and done it's one poky room and £250 a week. I mean, who the hell can afford that?'

'Yes, but even I can see it's a nice part of London and pretty central. What about further out?'

'If I move out it'll cost me a fortune on the Tube each day.' Gemma explained to Kerry about her knock back by Zoë; how she wasn't going to be mollified easily and didn't want to look for positives. She sighed angrily. 'It would be just my luck to have to turn this down because I can't afford a frigging flat. There's nothing there that I can even think about renting. Nothing. Zip. Zilch.' She stamped around the office.

'Well, do you know anyone else in London who might be able to put you up?' Kerry asked reasonably.

Gemma shook her head. She probably did, but she was so put out she wasn't really prepared to admit there might be another solution.

Kerry calmly carried on putting coins into bags and noting amounts down on her calculator. 'I'm sure something will come up,' she said blandly.

'Huh.' Gemma wasn't convinced.

'When do you have to decide?'

'Ben wants the answer on Friday.'

'Yeah, but if you say yes, how long do you have before you need digs?'

'A month.'

'That's ages. Take a risk. Go out on a limb. Have faith that it'll pan out right.'

Gemma wavered. Kerry could have a point. Maybe she should try flying by the seat of her pants. After all, what did she have to lose?

*

But a week later she was starting to panic. She was trawling the Internet again when her mobile rang.

'Gemma?'

'Yes.' She recognised the voice but she couldn't place it.

'It's Jean.'

'Jean?'

'Sew Wonderful.'

Gemma felt embarrassed. 'Jean! Sorry. You caught me out there. What can I do for you?'

'*Au contraire*, sweetie, *au contraire*.'

Gemma didn't have a clue what Jean was on about so she decided just to sound non-committal. 'Really?'

'Zoë tells me you need digs for a while.'

'Yes.' Gemma held her breath. Jean wouldn't be phoning to gloat. This had to be something positive.

'Since my son went on his gap year I've got a room free. It's nothing special and it's in dire need of redecoration, but you're welcome to use it for a few weeks. Till you find a place of your own.'

Gemma kept schtum about her similar deal with Maureen – made the previous year and which had never quite panned out. 'That's great. What sort of rent do you want?'

'Shall we call it £100 a week including gas and electricity? You can use my kitchen to cook and do your washing. I imagine once the production gets going we'll be working different ends of the day, so we won't be under each other's feet very much. Deal?'

Gemma thought that sounded pretty fair, considering what Jean might have commanded on the open market; her Internet search had left her an expert on London rents. 'Done,' she said with enthusiasm.

'You haven't seen it yet,' said Jean. 'The walls are deep purple.'

'I don't care,' said Gemma.

She put the phone down.

'Sorted, then,' said Kerry, happy for her colleague.

'Yup.' She felt as if life was really picking up again. A job in the West End, digs, and friends who cared. Yes, things could be a lot worse.

Gemma's sadness at leaving Maureen's theatre was tempered by her excitement at moving back to London. John, the barman-cum-set designer, drove her and all her possessions up to the city in his battered van and helped her unload her cases and carrier bags into Jean's hall.

'It's like having my son back,' said Jean ruefully. 'Clutter everywhere.'

'But I promise I'll tidy it away today,' said Gemma.

'That's more than he ever did. Tom always assumed the housekeeping fairy would wave her magic wand. Let me show you your room.'

Jean led the way upstairs and down the landing. 'Here.'

The room was very purple. Gemma took a breath. Jean had warned her, and the rent was low. But even so . . .

'Can you bear to live in this?' asked Jean.

Gemma slapped on a smile. 'Of course. It's fine,' she said bravely. 'I shan't be here much,' she added, trying not to sound too hopeful.

'Right, well, I'll leave you to get settled.'

Jono was in Max's office, looking out the window at Soho Square.

'We're going to have to let the press know. Do you want me to issue a statement?' Max looked at Jono's back view, trying to gauge his mood.

'Well, you can bet your bottom dollar that Rowan is doing exactly that in LA.'

'So what are we going to call it – a trial separation?'

Jono turned round. 'To quote Rowan at her most eloquent, "if it looks like a duck and walks like a duck and quacks like a duck then it's a fucking duck",' he said calmly. 'No, Max, we're going to say that I'm filing for divorce.'

'If you say so, Jono. Rowan isn't going to like that.'

Jono ran his hands through his hair. 'Do you know, I'm not that bothered any more what Rowan likes or doesn't like. This is the last straw. It was a miracle the press didn't get wind of that bender she went on in Spain.'

'Well, a studio like Butterfly is good at keeping that sort of thing quiet.'

'Yeah, but Magnum Opus heard, didn't they?' Jono sighed. If Magnum Opus hadn't got wind and threatened to cancel her contract unless she went TT, he would have been free of her months back. As it was, he'd succumbed to her crying and sobbing that she wouldn't be able to cope without him; that she needed him to keep off the sauce; that without him she'd lose that job. She'd said she relied on him, that she loved him, that she'd do anything for him – even give up the booze for ever. And he'd been suckered. God, what a fool he'd been. Maybe, if he'd found Gemma, he might have been more resolute, but losing her made his life seem directionless and pointless. Right then, going to LA with Rowan was no worse an option than anything else.

Rowan's naked cavortings snapped by the paparazzi hadn't come as a shock, if he was to be completely honest. He'd suspected for a while that 'fidelity' wasn't a word in her lexicon and that business on the 747, and now this, just confirmed it. She might try to deny it, yet again, but this one would be a tough one to wriggle out of. There was the evidence, in a surprisingly clear black-and-white photo of Rowan and Pete Montgomery standing at the window of some hotel in LA, both stark naked (although the paper had thoughtfully blurred the lower half of the two bodies), both laughing, and both drinking champagne, to judge by the shape of the glasses they held. With a statement from a chamber maid to say she'd seen them in bed together, the *Sun* was unlikely to retract the allegations this time. HAS JONO HAD HIS DAY? asked the headline. Jono threw the paper back on the desk.

'Yeah, well . . . I should have gone before. I know I'll be better off out of it.'

'Maybe. But she'll try and flay you all the same.'

'She can have it. The whole lot. I don't care.'

Max's eyebrows shot up.

'I'm serious. It's only money and possessions. I was saying a while back—' With a jolt, he remembered to whom he had said it. He stopped. It was the day Gemma had been sacked. 'I remember saying a while back that I miss the old days; when I had everything to look forward to, when everything was exciting, when I still got a kick about acting and being on stage. And, to be honest, I find the thought of starting again rather liberating.'

'Sure, you miss the grotty rooms and not knowing if you were going to get another part and waiting tables to pay the rent.'

'Look, I'm not saying it was all a bed of roses, but I want out of films.'

What he wasn't admitting to Max – what he was only just admitting to himself – was that he wanted to be based in London so he could spend his free time trying to find

Gemma. The last few months had been hell. After she'd been sacked he'd rung her number constantly to tell her what he'd tried to do to get her back on the film – which had been everything in his power – but her phone was always switched off. He supposed it was her way of screening calls. Eventually, he'd wangled enough time out of the shooting schedule to go round to her flat only to be met by a strange Welsh girl who told him that Gemma had left the country and that she never wanted to see him again. He would have looked for her then but shooting moved to Spain and as soon as they'd got back from that, Rowan, once she'd dried out sufficiently, had started filming in the States. In that small window of time he'd had in the UK he'd tried every avenue he could think of to find Gemma but she'd sunk without trace. He had thought about asking Arabella if she knew where her colleague had got to but had stopped when he remembered Gemma telling him about her snooping round Gemma's texts. If there was no love lost between the two then there was no point.

He knew now it had been a big mistake to go to LA with Rowan, but then, he'd reasoned, if he couldn't have Gemma he would bury himself in his work, and in Hollywood he was in a better place to get more deals – deals that would keep him busy and stop him thinking about her.

With both of them busy on different projects in LA, life was almost tolerable.

And then Rowan's series bombed.

That was it – the final straw. In an instant she'd gone back to her boozy, bitchy old ways and Jono had had enough. His acting work wasn't compensating for the misery of living with an increasingly unstable and psychotic wife. He'd phoned Max, asked him to see what opportunities there were on the stage in London, then packed and left; fled back to the house in Kingston. And Rowan, judging by the pictures in the paper, had found consolation in an instant.

'Max?' he asked, trying to sound casual. 'If you wanted to find someone, how would you do it?'

'Hire a private detective. Why, do you want to get hold of Montgomery?'

'No.'

'Who then?'

'A girl.'

Max jerked a thumb at the window. 'For fuck's sake, Jono. This is Soho. You want a girl you don't have to pay for a gumshoe to find one.'

'Not that sort of girl.'

'Then what sort?'

'Gemma.'

'Gemma? I'm not with you. I don't know any Gemma.'

'She was the costume assistant at Butterfly.'

Max still looked bemused. 'Don't remember her. Was she a looker?'

'I thought so.'

'So is she still in costumes?'

Jono shrugged. 'Rowan had her thrown off the picture.'

Max narrowed his eyes. 'What did Gemma do? Stick a pin in Rowan's ass?'

'Nothing so satisfactory. Rowan thought there was something between Gemma and I.'

'Was there?'

'Not like Rowan thought. Gemma had rather higher standards than my soon-to-be-ex-wife. She wouldn't date me because I was married.'

Max looked stunned. 'You're losing your touch, old

man,' he said. 'Time was you could have pulled any woman you wanted and the last thing they would have cared about was your marriage.'

Jono shrugged. He didn't care now. There was only one woman he wanted and it seemed she didn't want him. 'But I still want to find her,' he said.

Max didn't understand his client. Why make life difficult when there were any number of women ready to throw themselves at his feet? He sighed. 'Remind me of the broad's name.'

'Gemma. Gemma Brown.'

Max looked up at him. 'Have you any idea how many girls are going to be out there with that name?'

'I know, I know, but can you try for me? Please, Max.'

'**H**ow are the designs coming on, Gemma?' asked Ben over the phone.

'I'm quite pleased. I've got a couple of ideas for the main characters and I've come up with some overall idea for a complete look for the production. Do you want me to show them to you now, or do you want to wait until I've got some more done?'

'I'm going to set up a production meeting for next week. Bring them over then so we can have a look in conjunction with the set designs. You and William need to collaborate on this if it's going to look like a seamless whole. Both of you have got my brief but—'

Gemma laughed. 'Yeah, but you want to be sure that William and I aren't interpreting your ideas completely differently.'

'Precisely, ducky, precisely.'

Gemma switched her mobile off and returned to her sketchpad. The ideas were beginning to bubble. It was a process she found quite exciting. In the past, her costume designs had been based on reality: the cavalry in this period wore jackets in such-and-such a style; the fashion for ladies was so-and-so. It was all documented and catalogued and there were original examples in the Victoria and Albert Museum or in the Costume Museum in Bath to copy or to draw inspiration from. But this was new ground for Gemma and she was having a ball letting her imagination rip. The only problem was, she was having to work from her room in Jean's house. Her plan that she would be escaping from the purple paint on a daily basis wasn't going to come about until the company moved from production offices and rehearsal rooms into the theatre and that wasn't going to happen for another three weeks. In the meantime, she was busy with her designs, sourcing possible fabrics, organising makers to transform her ideas into reality, and hoping that Ben liked what she had come up with.

Outwardly, she looked content, even happy. She had cheap and comfortable digs, a good job, and a network of friends. But deep inside she was still torn apart by thoughts of what might have been. At night her sleep was disturbed by dreams of Jono, Rowan and Tina. She kept wondering if she had handled the whole situation better whether she'd still be in films. She tried to tell herself it was just tough, spilt milk, water under the bridge, and all those other clichés. But she knew she was kidding herself.

She got on with her sketches and tried to work out what the best fabrics would be to get the right look on a huge stage. She knew that what she'd done at Maureen's little theatre would look the same from almost any seat there, but from the front of the stalls to the top of the gods, in the big London theatre Ben's production was going into, was a huge distance. She had to be careful to get this right so the detail that could be seen from the back wasn't overpowering from the front and stuff that looked right from a distance of a few yards wasn't completely lost from view for those at the back.

She dragged herself back to her easel and her designs. She needed to get on with this if she was to have everything ready for the next production meeting. The whole thing was going to be in black, white and red and in the style of chess pieces; the costumes, the set, the props, the lot. It was Will's idea and Gemma wasn't entirely sure that it was going to work but she was going to give it her best shot. It certainly was a departure from anything she'd done before and it was also liberating. And it wouldn't do her portfolio any harm to have something more avant-garde in it, either.

She worked on until lunch and then a loud rumble from her stomach made her realise that she hadn't eaten since the night before. Breakfast wasn't her favourite meal and she often skipped it, but she usually made up for that omission mid-morning with a couple of biscuits and a cup of tea. But not today. She pottered down the stairs to Jean's cheerful kitchen and opened the fridge door. On her shelf was a packet of ham, a lump of cheddar and a couple of tomatoes. But nothing else.

Damn, she forgot she'd eaten the last slice of bread the day before. Never mind. There was a shop a couple of streets away that sold everything. She'd take a stroll in the spring sunshine and get some bits and pieces. She'd do a proper shop later in the week. She grabbed her jacket off the hook in the hall and sauntered out of the house. On her way to the corner shop she thought about all sorts of trivia, considered a couple of ideas for designs that she'd had, enjoyed the nice weather, and savoured the prospect of a toasted cheese and ham sandwich for lunch. Maybe she'd splash out and buy a jar of Branston too. Feeling reasonably happy she almost skipped into the little shop, grabbed a wire basket, and began trawling the crowded shelves for bits and pieces.

At the checkout there were a couple of locals queuing ahead of her, which gave her the chance to peruse the headlines of the papers and magazines in the stand by the till. She realised that she hadn't read a paper for days, maybe even a week. She didn't have a clue what was going on in the world. On impulse, she picked one up at random and chucked it in on top of everything else.

A few minutes later she was letting herself in through Jean's front door. She shrugged out of her jacket, flicked the grill on, and unpacked her shopping in a couple of economical movements and then, once she'd got the bread under the grill, scanned the front page of the paper. Gloom, doom and destruction, she thought sadly. But this wasn't a day for getting depressed so she shuffled through the pages until she got to the more trivial sections; arts, entertainment and the like. She glanced at the stories on the page.

'I'M A ONE WOMAN MAN,' SAYS JONO KNIGHTON, a small headline said. Gemma picked up the paper to read the story:

Jono Knighton, whose divorce from the actress Rowan Day was announced today, has said he only ever truly loved one woman. He said he wants time on his own to come to terms with the fact that the one woman he really adores doesn't want him and has disappeared out of his life for ever.

How could he? She'd seen the pictures of Rowan and Pete a couple of weeks ago. The whole world had. How could he still love her after all that? Gemma shook her head, unable to understand his reaction. Maybe that was the problem, maybe she'd never really understood him and that was why she'd ended up hurt. Well, it was his turn now. She knew how unrequited love felt, how much it screwed up your emotions, how raw it made everything. He'd have to get over it, just like she was.

The smell of burning toast brought Gemma back to north London and away from the tribulations of the two Hollywood stars. Dragging the grill pan from under the flame, she stared at the charring bits of bread before chucking them in the bin. Face it, she said to herself, your dreams of Jono are like your lunch. Toast. He only ever wanted Rowan. It was never you. Get over it.

'I just love this, sweetie,' said Ben, as he eyed her designs, spread out as much as they could be in the space that Gemma had been allocated in the production offices. Her room – until they moved into the theatre – was dominated by a big table on which was placed her sewing machine; around the edges were racks of clothes, a couple of dress-maker's dummies and an ironing board, which explained why the room smelt of hot fabric. What little you could see of the walls had cork boards nailed up with swatches of fabric and earlier sketches pinned to them. The final designs Gemma had drawn out with extreme care and were now being shown to the director and the set designer.

Will, the set designer, squashed into what space was left, looked over his shoulder. 'Wow,' he said. 'It's like you could read my mind. Just the look I was after.' He turned round and hugged Gemma.

She blushed and lowered her eyes. 'I just did what you suggested. It was almost all your idea.'

'It's fab,' said Ben. 'Wait till the cast get a load of them. They'll be thrilled.'

'Have we got a final cast list?' asked Gemma.

'Yes, all done and dusted. We're getting their measurements sent in as we speak. I imagine you want to get the maker to measure the principals.' Ben reached into his briefcase and pulled out a sheet of paper. 'Here you go, sweetie. This is who we've got lined up.'

Gemma ran her eye down the list. 'Gosh,' she said. 'Leo Findlay is going to play the Dauphin. And Jenny Mills as Joan. She's got a hard act to follow. Didn't Sybil Thorndike get the role once? And Dame Judy?'

'Jenny's a pro. She'll be fine,' said Ben. Gemma thought she detected a note of panic in his voice. 'And she's young. Joan was incredibly young, you have to remember. Only about twenty-four when she died.'

Still, thought Gemma, Ben was going out on a limb casting such a youthful actress in the title role. On the bright side, the kid would be easy to dress as she had the gamin figure required to make her transformation into a soldier pretty easy. No big boobs to get in the way.

The next few weeks passed in a whirl. The maker delivered the toiles and Gemma did the fittings, the rehearsals moved to the theatre itself, as did Gemma. At last she had a proper wardrobe department with enough space for her to work efficiently, fixing, altering, mending and making sure the costumes were going to be ready for the final stages of rehearsal and then the opening night. The set began to take shape on the massive West End Stage. The lights were rigged, the props delivered, the lines became more polished, the publicity machine began to grind out stories and press releases, and the ticket sales got off the ground.

The tension in the theatre began to mount, tempers frayed, the actors became demanding, Ben became impossible and Gemma considered walking out. If working for Butterfly had been bad this was a nightmare. And yet, bizarrely, she loved it. This was hands on. There could be no retakes for the actors when they went out in front of an audience. If they fluffed, the audience would know. If the audience hated it, the actors would know. The critics' reactions might make or break the play and the reputations of all involved. Everyone was working as a terrific team in order to make the production as perfect as possible. One weak link and the whole thing might flop and Gemma was as determined as everyone else that she wasn't going to be that link.

'So how's it going?' asked Zoë when she and Gemma met for a drink only a few days before the opening night.

'Mad,' said Gemma. 'Mad. Ben has decided that the lighting for the bit when Joan gets barbecued is all wrong and he's having a terrible spat with the lighting director. The ASM was having an affair with the props girl and has taken this moment to split with her, so the atmosphere in the wings is poisonous. Half the actors seem to have forgotten their lines and one of the cast has put on so much weight I'm having to make her a new costume. Apart from that, it's just peachy.'

'And you?'

'Surviving,' said Gemma with a lop-sided grin. 'Surviving.'

'And your love life?'

'Fuck, Zoë. I see poor old Joan getting the Spanish Inquisition treatment every day. I don't need you taking a leaf out of their book too.'

'Just asking. I imagine that means no.'

'Well, you know how it is. I'm so busy right now I don't have time to go dating.'

'You mean you're not even looking. Isn't that it?'

Gemma took a slug out of her wine. 'Not right now. Maybe when this production settles down into a proper run, assuming we last longer than a week, that is, I'll have heaps of time to look.'

'But there must be loads of single men involved in the production. Look at all those hunky actors. And what about Ben. He isn't married, is he?'

'He's gay, Zo,' explained Gemma patiently, wondering if Zoë was having her on. She'd already met him . . . surely, her gay-dar would have spotted it.

'You're jok—' Zoë looked at the expression on Gemma's face. 'You're not, are you? A babe like that. Wasted.'

'His boyfriend doesn't think so.'

'Bugger.'

'Not a phrase I'd use unless you intend the pun.'

They both laughed. 'Well, at least you can see the funny side of life again, Gem. That's something. Finally got Jono out of your system.'

Gemma didn't think she ever would, but admitting such a thing to Zoë was only going to cause trouble. She changed the subject. 'All excited about coming to the first night, then?'

'I can't tell you!' Zoë's face lit up. 'I've never been to an opening before. What's the dress code?'

Gemma shrugged. 'It'll be all arty types there. Anything, I should think.'

'And will you introduce me to Leo? Please!'

'If I can. I don't know him that well myself. He's stellar, I'm just backstage.'

'I can't wait. Only three days to go.'

'I know,' said Gemma, frowning and thinking just how much had to be crammed into that time.

On opening night it didn't help Gemma that the stars' dressing rooms were so full of flowers that there was hardly space for their occupants to get dressed.

'And do try not to get lily pollen on your costume,' she implored Leo. 'It stains terribly.'

'Worry not,' said Leo, with a theatrical flourish that had the sleeve of his robe just a millimetre from the flowers.

Gemma considered taking all the flowers and piling them on Joan's pyre and setting light to them personally. Bloody things had been a menace ever since the florists' vans had started arriving that day.

'Right,' she said from down by his knees where she was making a last-minute alteration to the length of his sweeping cloak. 'Done. And if I've left a pin in, I'm sorry, but I have to dash.' She grabbed her sewing box and headed for the door. 'Break a leg,' she said as she began to leave.

'Thank you, darling,' said Leo who, she noticed, was beginning to look ill with nerves.

On impulse, she turned back and gave him a peck on the cheek. 'It's going to be wonderful. Honest.'

Leo smiled. 'I think so too. I just hate first nights so

much. Sometimes I get in such a state I'm sick before I go on.'

Gemma left, wondering why actors punished themselves so much. Maybe they couldn't help it. Maybe not acting was worse than the ghastly nerves. Poor loves, she thought. What a way to earn a living. Not so bad for the ones in film; they didn't have to face their audiences in quite the same way.

She passed one of the front-of-house staff with another armful of blooms.

'What's the house like?' Gemma asked.

'Packed. A sell out. Fingers crossed they like it.'

So much rode on it being a success for all of them, thought Gemma. The nerves were beginning to get to her, too. Supposing they booed the set and her costumes. Supposing the critics panned it. Supposing it all went wrong. Suppose they closed before the week was out. It had happened to other productions, it could happen again.

On her way to Jenny Mills's dressing room, she met another member of the company with a bouquet. 'Here,' said Jacqui. 'These came for you.'

'Me?'

'Your name was Gemma last time we met. Anything changed?'

Gemma grinned with pleasure. She really hadn't been expecting flowers, considering herself to be far too lowly in the pecking order. Besides, who would splash out on her? She looped the handle of her sewing box over her arm and took them. She'd look at the label when she got to Jenny's dressing room. She wondered who on earth might send them to her.

She knocked on the star's dressing-room door and went in. Jenny, who was about the same age as Gemma, was dressed in a startling red costume that alluded to a pawn on a chessboard. Her make-up emphasised her huge eyes as did her cropped hair. She looked beautiful and vulnerable and utterly scared.

'Costume okay?' asked Gemma.

Jenny nodded. 'Those for me?'

'Um, no. Sorry. Someone sent them to me. Can you believe?'

Jenny seemed relieved to be able to talk to take her mind off her impending ordeal. 'How nice. A friend?'

'I imagine so. I haven't had a chance to look.' Gemma put the sewing box down on the floor – the only flat space available, the other surfaces being covered with make-up, flowers and good luck cards. She twisted the card, which was attached to the stems, around so that she could read the inscription. '*Your best friend*,' she read. 'Aw. That's my mate Zoë.'

'Is she here?'

'I hope so. I wangled a ticket for her.'

'You'll have to tell me what she thinks about it.'

'She'll love it,' said Gemma firmly.

Jenny looked at her. 'But it's not her that counts, is it? It's the critics.'

'But if the public love it, won't they still come despite what a few hacks say?'

'Not necessarily,' said Jenny. 'And we'll know in just a few hours.' She fiddled with a tube of pan-stick. 'Are you coming to the first-night party?'

'Wouldn't miss it for the world.'

'I don't know whether to or not. I can't stand it when we all wait around for the early editions. If the reviews are good it's one thing. But if they're bad . . .'

'They'll be fine,' said Gemma confidently. But the look

on Jenny's face said, 'And what do you know?' as clearly as if it had been written on her forehead in felt tip.

The tannoy ping-ponged and a voice told them they only had five minutes before curtain up. Jenny went even whiter.

'Oh my God,' she whispered.

Gemma leaned forwards and gave her a peck, too. 'Off you go. Break a leg.'

Jenny took a deep breath, pushed her shoulders back, and went to find out what fate had in store. Gemma made sure that Jenny's next change of costume was ready, grabbed her sewing kit and flowers and followed. She wanted to hear the audience's reaction to the set when the curtain went up.

She tiptoed into the wings. Behind the curtains the lights were burning with a bruising intensity. On the stage the actors playing Robert de Baudricourt and his steward were in position. Jenny was waiting for her cue to go on. The set, a modern, minimalist design in red, black and white, looked stunning, and the tension was palpable.

And then the curtain rose. A black void slowly appeared through which cut the spotlights from the rigs in the auditorium ceiling. And the applause thundered.

It was a full minute before Robert could shout, 'No eggs! No eggs!' and the play got underway.

Gemma longed to stay where she was in the wings and to watch it from the sidelines, but she had too much to do. She legged it to her department and shoved her flowers in a jug of water then raced along to the dressing rooms to make sure all was ready for the next set of changes; that the actors yet to make their appearance were happy; that no one had pulled off a button or caught a heel in a hem.

When the curtain came down for the interval, tension

had been replaced by elation and excitement. The theatre was buzzing and fizzing with positive vibes and good feelings, but Gemma didn't have time to enjoy it as she had to race around making sure that the principals were ready for the next half of the production. Towards the end, Gemma crept back into the wings to see the final few scenes of the play.

The actors making their exits and entrances still seemed to be brimming with positive feelings. Gemma picked up on this and found herself jittering with excitement. And then it was the final scene and curtain.

It was over.

Gemma clung to the edge of the wings as the cast swept past her, to be in place for their curtain call, and for a few seconds she thought the thundering she could hear was the sound of running feet. The realisation dawned that it was the sound of the audience stamping and hollering to add to the cacophony of their applause, which was muffled by the thick fabric of the curtains.

Then the curtain rose and the wall of sound that hit the stage was unbelievable. The roar of the ovation made Gemma's insides judder with the level of the volume. It was amazing and exciting and wonderful.

It took seven curtain calls before the audience finally let the cast go. Looking simultaneously drained, shocked, thrilled and elated, the company trooped off the stage, some chattering with excitement at the reception, some silent as if they were trying to hold the moment.

Gemma rushed downstairs to help Jenny out of her costume and then take it away to check it for marks or smears of make-up that would need sorting before the next performance. She hoped Leo's dresser would insist he got out of his costume quickly so she could do the same with his. It had been a long day and she wanted to get it all squared away quickly so as she could make a swift appearance at the party and then slope off to bed. She was knackered. It wasn't just her work and the length of the day that had exhausted her but all the excitement and emotion as well. What a roller coaster!

She took Jenny's costume back to her department and hung it on the rail with the others. She began to examine it. It was going to need a press before the next performance. Perhaps she'd get that done while she was waiting for some of the other costumes to come back to her. She plugged in the iron and stood by the board waiting for it to warm up.

'Gemma?'

It was Jacqui, the girl who had delivered the bouquet to her. 'The friend who sent the flowers is here to see you,' she said.

'Oh, Zoë! Send her down, Jacqui.'

'Zoë?' said Jacqui, frowning. 'I didn't get a good look, but it's not Zoë. Not unless Zoë's a bloke.'

It was Gemma's turn to frown. 'A bloke?'

'Look, I'll tell your friend where to find you.' Like Gemma, Jacqui also wanted to finish all her jobs and get to the party. She darted off before Gemma had a chance to quiz her further.

Gemma returned to her ironing. The steam hissed out as she carefully pressed the fabric back into shape.

'You got the flowers then,' said a voice behind her.

Gemma froze. She knew that voice. Despite her racing heart, she carefully replaced the iron on its stand before she turned round.

'Jono.'

'Yes.'

She stared at him for a second or two, completely bewildered. 'Why? Why the flowers?'

'A peace offering. For letting you go. For losing you. For not realising how much I love you.'

Gemma felt even more at sea. 'But you love Rowan.'

'*Rowan?*' It was Jono's turn to be bewildered.

'I read it in the paper. When you announced your divorce. You said you'd only ever loved one woman and that you were having to come to terms with the fact that she had disappeared out of your life.'

'But I wasn't talking about Rowan. I only went with her to the States because' – he shrugged – 'well, I lost you and there didn't seem much point in staying here. I couldn't bear to be in London without you, but life in LA with Rowan was hell. I suppose it was only what I deserved. I should have called Butterfly's bluff over my contract with the film and walked off the project with you. Losing you was my punishment.'

Gemma still didn't understand. 'So who . . . ?'

'It was you I was talking about,' he said quietly. 'You are the only woman I've ever loved.'

'Me?' Gemma shook her head. 'But this doesn't make sense.'

'I tried and tried to ring you after you got fired from Butterfly and I got no reply. I felt so guilty about what had happened and I needed to explain to you, to make it up to you. And I couldn't. You never answered. So I went round to your flat and a strange Welsh girl told me you'd left the country and then told me to fuck off. Of course you hated me and I could only think that you wanted to put as many miles between the two of us as possible. I don't blame you. I should have backed you up on the set more than I did but I was so taken aback by what happened, by Rowan, by the accusations, that I completely mishandled the whole situation.'

'I got hung out to dry, Jono. In front of all those people.' The humiliation of walking through her colleagues who had all overheard the row and accusations still stung.

'I know.' Jono looked shamefaced. 'I behaved like a shit. I was more concerned with having a go at Rowan than I was about you and that was so wrong. I know that now. You have every right to hate me. I hate me.' He looked so contrite, Gemma almost felt sorry for him. 'But I did everything I could to try and get you back on set but Rowan was impossible. She threw such a tantrum at one point we lost a day's shooting. David went spare, the backers went ballistic and I was told that if I forced the issue they'd pull out. That would have put a couple of hundred people out of work. I decided I'd find you, make a grovelling apology and try to make it up to you. Great plan, except I couldn't find you.'

'I didn't blank your calls, you know. I got mugged on the way home from the shoot – the day they fired me. Talk about a shit day,' she said, shaking her head at the hideous memory. 'I lost everything, including my mobile. The phone company blocked the number of my phone automatically. That's why my phone was never answered.'

'Mugged! My poor Gemma. I don't believe it.' Jono moved towards her.

Gemma held her hand up. She didn't trust him enough yet to let him get close to her. 'It's taken me a year, Jono. A whole year to get over you. It's been tough.'

'If I said that I must have thought about you every day in that time – would you believe me? When I saw you at the premiere, I couldn't believe it. And then you were gone. Vanished. But I knew you were back in the country.

At least I knew that. It gave me hope that perhaps we might get back together. That I might find you.'

Gemma was so busy trying to come to terms with what Jono was saying that she didn't bother with wondering about why he thought she'd left the country. That was the least of her concerns. 'I don't know that I can believe you when you say you thought about me. There are still too many unanswered questions. You could have found me if you'd *really* wanted to. I wasn't in hiding. My friends knew where I was. Hell's bells, even Arabella knew where I was. If you'd asked her she'd have told you. How long did shooting last? You must have seen her every day. Why didn't you ask her about me?'

'Arabella? But you hated each other.'

'No, we didn't. What gave you that idea? She was difficult, could be quite tricky on occasion, but she wasn't nasty. She liked my work and I respected her. Not like Tina.'

'But you said she'd snooped through your handbag. That time we went out for a pizza, you said your colleague was spying on you.'

'But it wasn't Arabella I was talking about. She is far too proper to do something like that. It was Toxic Tina. Arabella got me another job – with a theatre company. In the country, deepest Gloucestershire.'

Jono stared at her, assessing this last load of information. 'So when your mate told me you'd left the country, what she really said was that you'd left *for* the country. Shit.' Gemma's lip began to twitch. Talk about a comedy of errors. Jono saw the beginnings of her smile and shook his head. 'I probably needn't have got a private detective on your case after all.'

'You did what!' Gemma's eyes narrowed and she looked extremely dangerous.

'I was desperate to find you. What was I supposed to do?'

'You mean I've had someone on my tail, following me?'

It was Jono's turn to laugh. 'Not a bit of it. In fact, after I'd paid him his retainer, I felt a complete jerk. He put your name into Google, found some theatre website with your picture on it, made about three phone calls, and discovered you were working on this production. Even I might have managed that.'

This time, Gemma really did laugh. 'You dumb-ass. How much did that cost you?'

'Enough.'

There was a flurry at the door and Gemma looked past Jono to see Zoë skidding to a halt in the entrance. Her eyes darted around the room.

'Oh,' she said. 'You know he's here then.'

'If you're talking about Jono, yes, I think you can say I am aware he's in the building.'

'I saw him in the interval but have only just been able to come and warn you. Sorry, I'm too late.' She eyed Jono sternly. 'Hi, Jono, have you come to wreck Gemma's life again?'

'No, I haven't!' said Jono.

But Zoë's look of sheer disbelief spoke volumes. She'd make damn sure he didn't or he'd have her to answer to. Zoë turned her attention back to Gemma. 'Fantastic costumes, by the way. The punters in the bar in the interval were saying as much, too. They all think the whole thing is fab.'

Gemma gawped. 'Really? Is that what they said? Fantastic? They loved them! Oh my.' She jigged on the spot and turned red.

'And why not?' asked Jono. 'It was stunning. A triumph visually. Honest.'

'And what would you know?' said Zoë, still hell-bent on protecting her friend.

Gemma burst out laughing. 'I think Jono knows as much about the theatre as I do. I should think he can judge.'

'Pah.'

There was more movement at the door to Gemma's department as Leo's dresser arrived with his costumes. She noticed the rather odd atmosphere and Zoë's belligerent stance, hung the clothes up and fled.

'Come on,' said Jono. 'Switch that damn iron off and let's get out of here.'

'I promised I'd take Zoë to the party.'

'We can all go to the party,' said Jono.

Gemma wasn't sure she wanted to go to a party with Jono. She needed time to work out quite what was going on. She thought she'd got over him. She'd come to terms with the thought he hadn't loved her, that he'd just abandoned her, and now it seemed as if most of her assumptions were wrong.

'You and Zo go. I'll finish up here.'

Zoë looked at Gemma. 'Can't this wait till tomorrow?'

Of course it could but Gemma was desperate for a bit of breathing space. 'I won't be long – promise.'

'But . . . I mean, will they let me in without you?' asked Zoë.

'I should think Jono here will probably be the equivalent of a golden ticket,' said Gemma.

Zoë sniffed. 'Just because he's famous doesn't mean they'll want him there.'

'True. But these acting types may be quite flattered to have a big Hollywood star show up. Some of them are dreadfully shallow.'

'Don't I know it,' said Zoë, giving Jono a long,

meaningful look. 'Come on, then. We'd better leave Gem in peace. The quicker she finishes here the quicker she can join us.' She dragged him out of the room.

The silence after they had gone was total. The theatre seemed to be deserted. After the noise and clamour of the first night, it was now hollow and echoing.

Gemma sat on a chair and tried to get her head around everything. Maybe he did have feelings for her after all. He *had* come looking for her. He *had* tried to find her after she'd been sacked. If her friends hadn't been quite so protective, if she hadn't been mugged . . . So many ifs. So many maybes. She went over and over events, trying to work out where she'd misinterpreted things, what she might have done differently, trying to assess if Jono's reappearance in her life was what she wanted or if she needed to keep him at arm's length for ever. Around her the old building creaked and ticked as it settled down for the night and Gemma suddenly realised that she was getting cold. She pulled her jersey around her shoulders and looked around for her handbag.

'Penny for them.'

Gemma jumped. She hadn't heard anyone approach. 'Jono. What are you doing back here? What about Zoë?'

'Zoë is fine. I left her making sheep's eyes at your set designer guy.'

'William?'

'That's him.'

'I came to find you. I seem to spend a lot of my life trying to find you.'

Gemma nodded. 'I haven't been hiding.'

'Don't make me hunt for you again, Gem.'

'I don't know. I'm not sure.'

'I've always told you the truth, Gemma. About you,

about me, about Rowan.'

Gemma picked up her handbag and held it protectively in front of her. 'Come on. We'd better leave before we get locked in for the night.'

'You're avoiding the issue.'

'Yes. I can't bear the thought of going through these past few months again.'

'And neither can I. I need you, Gemma. I've missed you more than I could have thought it possible.' He looked at her and reached forward to stroke her cheek. This time Gemma didn't back off. 'You've missed me too, haven't you?'

Gemma nodded, not trusting herself to speak.

'Come here.' Jono wrapped his arms around her and pulled her against him.

The slight chill that Gemma had been feeling disappeared as the warmth of his body enveloped her. She gave a little sigh.

'What do you say, Miss Brown? Will you date me now, if I ask you?'

'It's only married men I don't date, Mr Knighton. I thought you knew that.'

little
black
dress

brings you
fantastic new books like these
every month - find out more at
www.littleblackdressbooks.com

And why not sign up for our
email newsletter to keep
you in the know about
Little Black Dress news!

Pick up a *little black dress* – it's a girl thing.

IT MUST BE LOVE
Rachel Gibson
PB £4.99

Gabriel Breedlove is the sexiest suspect that undercover cop Joe Shanahan has ever had the pleasure of tailing. But when he's assigned to pose as her boyfriend things start to get complicated.

She thinks he's stalking her. He thinks she's a crook. Surely, it must be love?

978 0 7553 3746 0

ONE NIGHT STAND
Julie Cohen
PB £4.99

When popular novelist Estelle Connor finds herself pregnant after an uncharacteristic one-night stand, she enlists the help of sexy neighbour Hugh to help look for the father. But will she find what she really needs?

One of the freshest and funniest voices in romantic fiction

978 0 7553 3483 4

Pick up a *little black dress* – it's a girl thing.

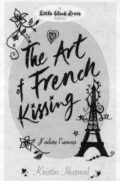

978 0 7553 3828 3

THE ART OF FRENCH KISSING
Kristin Harmel
PB £4.99

When Emma lands her dream job in Paris, she starts to master the art of French kissing: one date, one kiss and onto the next delectable Frenchman. But what happens if you meet someone you want to kiss more than once . . .

A très chic tale of Paris, paparazzi and the pursuit of the perfect kiss

THE CHALET GIRL
Kate Lace
PB £4.99

Being a chalet girl is definitely not all snowy pistes, sexy ski-instructors and a sensational après-ski nightlife, as Millie Braythorpe knows only too well. Then handsome troublemaker Luke comes to stay at her chalet and love rages, but can he be trusted or will her Alpine romance end in wipeout?

978 0 7553 3831 3

You can buy any of these other **Little Black Dress** titles from your bookshop or *direct from the publisher*.

FREE P&P AND UK DELIVERY
(Overseas and Ireland £3.50 per book)

TO ORDER SIMPLY CALL THIS NUMBER

01235 400 414

or visit our website: www.headline.co.uk

Prices and availability subject to change without notice.